MR. NOTTING HILL

LOUISE BAY

Published by Louise Bay 2022

ISBN – 978-1-910747-841

BOOKS BY LOUISE BAY

The Doctors Series

Dr. Off Limits

Dr. Perfect

The Mister Series

Mr. Mayfair

Mr. Knightsbridge

Mr. Smithfield

Mr. Park Lane

Mr. Bloomsbury

Mr. Notting Hill

The Christmas Collection

The 14 Days of Christmas

The Player Series

International Player

Private Player

Dr. Off Limits

Standalones

Hollywood Scandal

Love Unexpected

Hopeful

The Empire State Series

<u>**Gentleman Series**</u>

The Wrong Gentleman

The Ruthless Gentleman

<u>**The Royals Series**</u>

The Earl of London

The British Knight

Duke of Manhattan

Park Avenue Prince

King of Wall Street

<u>**The Nights Series**</u>

Indigo Nights

Promised Nights

Parisian Nights

Faithful

Sign up to the Louise Bay mailing list at
www.louisebay/mailinglist

Read more at www.louisebay.com

ONE

Parker

Only two things in life were better than chocolate-covered raisins: Dressing up in high heels to go with your beautiful —but rented—pillar-box red evening gown, and raising money for a charity that helped sick children and their families. Combining all three was pure bliss. As I shook more chocolate-covered raisins into my palm and surveyed the cavernous ballroom before me, I allowed myself to bask in exactly three seconds of bone-deep contentment. After all, I needed to go through the auction lots one more time to make sure everything was in order. Then I'd check on the kitchen, and finally, when everything was ready, I'd change.

One of the large ballroom doors creaked as it opened and my best friend, Sutton, who I'd roped into helping, slid inside. "It's huge in here."

"More people means more money."

"This is the auction table?" she asked. I'd put her in charge of showing off the lots as guests arrived and encouraging people to bid.

"Yes. If the items are really expensive or they can't be put on the table because it's a holiday or something, there's a picture. But full details are in the auction catalogue. There's one on every seat and a back-up pile under that table." I pointed to a side table draped in a floor-length cloth and topped with a slightly over-the-top floral arrangement. When I'd been put in charge of the gala, I'd tried to think of everything, including where to hide necessary administrative materials. For an event this critical to our success, the details mattered.

"I'll put some out here so people can grab them." She pulled out a handful and put them on the corner.

I was aiming to raise fifty thousand from the auction tonight, plus another fifty from ticket sales. My stomach churned at the thought of how much was on the line. The blissful contentment I'd basked in just a minute ago was shunted aside to make room for a pit of dread in my stomach.

"How did I let you talk me into this?" I asked Sutton, regretting the fact that I was going to be one of the auction lots—up on stage like a spa gift basket.

"I was being entirely practical. You're beautiful. Every man at this charity will want to bid on you and take you to dinner. That means more money for the kids."

I took a breath. She was wrong and she was right. I had no doubt people would bid on the chance to take me on a date, but not because of their desire to spend an evening in my company. No, people would bid to please my father. As head of one of the biggest investment banks in the world, my dad had been a titan of the financial world for decades and wielded a kind of power that never really made sense. To me he was just my dad. Sutton was right—we were about raising money tonight and it shouldn't matter why people bid on the lots. It was just important that they did.

"When are you getting changed?" Sutton asked, glancing at me from head to toe.

"What do you mean? You don't like my dress?" My hair and makeup were done, but I was wearing my lemon Zara shirt dress. I grinned at her. "There's no way I'm getting into my dress until the last possible moment. Not until I've done everything I need to do. I'm bound to throw something over myself. Speaking of, I'm going to check on the kitchen." I glanced at the clock. Any minute now people would start to arrive.

"Go," Sutton said. I was already across the room when she added, "And good luck!"

I took the stairs at the side of the stage and slipped behind the curtain. It was chaos. People carrying stuff from left to right and right to left, someone up a ladder doing something with electrical wires. Another person testing microphones that let out intermittent high-pitched squeals. I stepped back as someone with a radio mike on rushed toward me and then past me as if I wasn't even there.

I caught the eye of the hotel events coordinator across the room and she gave me a sharp nod and a thumbs-up. It could only mean this pandemonium was all part of her plan. If she'd needed to deliver devastatingly bad news, like the band was stuck in traffic or the chef had walked out, I'd given her the opportunity and she hadn't taken it. I called that a win. Next stop, the kitchen.

I navigated my way through the hustle and bustle and out to the corridor. As I opened the kitchen door someone screamed, "Get out!" The chef was a little temperamental, to put it mildly, but his food was amazing. I sidled up to the maître d', Metual. "Is everything going as it should?"

"We're just out of space. And the desserts are melting because it's so hot in here. We're having to move them over to the empty conference room." Waiters holding metal trays whizzed past me.

"Let me take a tray. I'm going to get changed and it's on my way."

"Thank you," Metual said, handing me a tray.

The desserts looked impossibly delicious. All pastry and cream and hazelnuts. Would anyone notice if one went missing?

He held the door open and I followed the snake of waiters heading toward the conference room.

"Parker," Paddy, one of my team said, as he approached me from the opposite direction. "Do you want music on as people arrive?"

"Yes, the big band stuff we talked about."

Paddy thrust his hands into his hair like I'd just asked him to conjure up a marching band of giraffes and scurried off.

The parade of waiters carrying the rest of the trays had disappeared down a corridor that, for all I knew, led deeper into the bowels of the hotel. I decided to take a short cut through the hotel lobby with my tray. I needed to focus or we'd be halfway through dinner before I sat down. I picked up my pace and headed for the conference room.

I didn't want to greet anyone before I was dressed so I kept my gaze trained on the tray, avoiding eye contact with anyone in the lobby in case they were guests of the gala.

Then *slam*, I walked into a wall.

The tray tipped up and hit me in the chest, narrowly missing my face—thank goodness. I didn't have the time that it would take to reapply my makeup and fix my hair.

When the tray fell to the floor, I was left with every dessert I'd been carrying stuck to me as if I was a Christmas tree decorated with choux pastry and cream. "And that is why I don't get changed until the last minute."

I glanced up to find it wasn't a wall I'd walked into but a very tall man. A very tall man who *felt* like a wall.

"Are you okay?" he asked, peering down at me with sparkly blue eyes that looked full of mischief. "Sorry, I didn't see you down there."

Down there? Okay, I was only five foot two, but he was talking like I was Lilliputian.

"It's fine," I said, peeling a pastry bun from my boob. It was squashed but it still looked delicious. No one else would eat it now, right? And there was no bad time for a snack. I mean, it might help settle my nerves. I held the dessert to my mouth and took a bite.

"Mmm." It was heavenly. I swallowed and offered the man in front of me a bite. "You want to taste?"

He chuckled, and I got the urge to smear the crinkled skin at the corner of his mischievous eyes with cream and then lick it off. "As much as I want to say yes, I'm going to pass."

Made sense that he wouldn't eat dessert. No one got a body like his eating pastry and cream. It was tall, hard muscle I'd hit.

"Hey," he said. "Eyes up here." He pointed to his eyes with two splayed fingers.

I laughed. I suppose I had been trying to engage my x-ray vision to see exactly what that chest looked like through his dinner jacket. "No more short jokes. I'm looking right in front of me."

A couple of hotel workers swarmed around us to clear

up the pastry and cream explosion. "I'm so sorry," I said. In the corner of my vision, I spotted my father coming through the entrance of the hotel. That meant I was late.

"Gotta go!" I turned and sped out of the lobby, leaving a trail of destruction and a very hot man in my wake.

TWO

Tristan

I wasn't what you'd call a 'party person'. I liked my work, my friends, and women. Not necessarily in that order. Swapping anecdotes with people I'd never see again was not at the top of my list, but there wasn't much I wouldn't do for Arthur Frazer. Without him, I wouldn't have a career in cyber security. I'd still be hacking MI6 for kicks. If it wasn't for Arthur, I wouldn't be wearing my barely-worn dinner jacket, standing in a hotel lobby about to attend a charity dinner. I certainly wouldn't have just been mown down by a cream-puff-loving pixie. A beautiful pixie with bright red, completely kissable lips. If only she hadn't rushed off like a cream-covered Cinderella. I'd been stuck in front of my screens all week and had only the faintest whiff of fresh air when I'd cracked open a window. I certainly hadn't had an opportunity to engage my flirting muscles. I'd keep a look out for her. Maybe she was a guest at this dinner. Or a waitress. That might keep my mind in the room this evening.

I headed to my table, found it right at the front, and

spotted my name card next to my mentor. I was well aware that it was an honor to be seated next to Arthur. Everyone in the room would be wondering what I'd done to deserve it. But it also meant I would have to resist checking my phone all evening. There'd be no escaping the spotlight, and I didn't want to appear rude. With my job, where calamity could be created in an instant, unplugging for even a couple of hours made me itchy.

I wouldn't know anyone here tonight other than Arthur. But that didn't matter. I just needed to eat, make a generous donation, and go home.

I glanced around the ballroom as it gradually filled with people. Vertical banners stood at intervals around the perimeter, each showing a different picture of infants and children in hospital beds. The young patients smiled, seeming unbothered by the tubes and machines surrounding them. The name of the charity was embla-zoned at the bottom of each banner: *Sunrise Foundation for Children with Congenital Heart Defects*. My stomach twisted. Shit. Why hadn't I checked what tonight was all about? I'd seen an invitation from Arthur and accepted without giving it much thought. If I'd known . . .

Not that raising money for children with congenital heart defects wasn't a good cause—it was. I knew as much firsthand. I just didn't relish the idea of spending the evening submerged in memories of my baby sister. I would have made up an excuse, sent a big check, and avoided this room and its pictures of happy, healing children.

Arthur arrived, followed by a trail of people wanting a few seconds of his time and attention. He greeted me with a handshake and thanked me for coming. We didn't get any further. Interruption was followed by interruption as people came up to him to introduce themselves, tell him they'd sent him an invitation or email, ask if they could discuss this business opportunity, invite him to that lunch. It was like getting seated next to the Pope or something. Everyone wanted his blessing or advice.

When the food came out, the interruptions slowed but didn't stop.

"So, Tristan, how are things with you?" Arthur asked during a rare quiet moment.

"Good. Busy but good."

"I appreciate you making the time to come tonight. My daughter organized it. She's very passionate about the cause." His sigh hid something he wasn't saying.

"It's an excellent cause. I'm grateful you invited me."

"Whatever Parker's involved in is always an excellent cause. She tends to throw herself in headfirst." He took a sip of his wine. "She's very kindhearted. And generous. Her lovely nature can lead to some people taking advantage."

Before I could ask him anything more, we were interrupted by a familiar-looking man—a member of the cabinet, if I wasn't mistaken.

My phone buzzed in my pocket. It was a three-buzz buzz, which meant it was important.

I headed out unnoticed by Arthur or the minister. As I made my way to the back of the room, I scanned the tables for a certain cream-covered pixie. She was nowhere in sight.

The three buzzes turned out to be a false alarm, but now I was in the lobby, I scrolled through my notifications just to check everything else was in control.

As I headed back into the ballroom, proceedings had heated up. There was an emcee on the stage with a small woman who looked rather familiar.

The red-lipped pixie.

Now she was *sans* cream puffs, she looked even more

delicious. She wore a fire-engine-red dress that cinched in at her tiny waist and matched her lips perfectly. Her sleek black bob and diminutive height weren't my normal type, but there was no doubt she was beautiful. She had one hand on her hip and was forcing a smile.

"Fifteen hundred," the emcee said. "Do I hear sixteen hundred?"

Several auction paddles were thrust in the air and I couldn't help but notice that most of them weren't looking at the stage or the auctioneer. They were looking at Arthur. Was it his lot or something?

He must find it uncomfortable having eyes on him all the time. I was well known by name in some circles—after all, I was the best at what I did when it came to protecting the online presence of the biggest companies and ultra-high-net-worth individuals. But people didn't know my face. And thank God.

"Are you bidding, sir?" a woman behind a trestle table by the door asked.

"What's for sale?" I asked.

"A date with the beautiful woman on the stage," she replied.

I narrowed my eyes. Cream Puff was an auction item? "Can I get a paddle?"

She handed me what looked like a table tennis bat, and I strode toward the stage as the bid for a date with Cream Puff went up in one-hundred-pound increments. Bids were starting to slow as the auctioneer asked for two thousand pounds.

"Twenty-five thousand," I bellowed, raising my paddle.

Gasps echoed around the room and I felt a thousand pairs of eyes swing from Arthur to me. Cream Puff squinted, trying to see who she was going to have to go to dinner with, but the lights of the stage were shining right at her—she wouldn't have been able to tell that it was the man she was ogling earlier in the evening.

I slid back into my seat and gave my name to the woman with the clipboard who'd come over to take my details.

"Interesting," Arthur said from next to me. "If you'd wanted to date my daughter, you could have done it for free."

My heart sank to my knees. Cream Puff was Arthur's daughter? "I had no idea she was your daughter, Arthur. My apologies. Of course, I won't take her out. This is a wonderful cause and the point was to make a donation, not win a date." That explained why everyone's attention was on Arthur during the bidding. Everyone wanted to impress him.

"I hope you're not going to back out. It's about time Parker did something that was about enjoying her life rather than trying to fix the world. It will be good for her." He turned to me and patted me on the shoulder. "For you too, I think. And better you than some of the old men in this room. Make sure you both have fun."

"I'll treat her like glass, Arthur. You have my word."

Dinner with Arthur's daughter wouldn't be so bad. It just would be better if I wasn't so attracted to her. I'd just have to keep my flirting in check and make sure things ended when dinner did. No problem . . .

As long as she didn't cover herself in cream and tempt me to lick it from her.

THREE

Parker

Twenty-five thousand pounds? For a date with me? I was a little dumbstruck at the figure and frustrated I hadn't been able to make out who had placed the bid. The lights had been so glaring that I'd not seen anything.

Sutton rushed up to me as I was helping to pack up backstage. "Trust you to have the hottest guy in the room bid on you."

"I did? Did you recognize him?" It was kinda nice that someone handsome had bid. It might be fun to go on a date under these circumstances—where it was nothing to do with attraction or the possibility of a relationship. Instead, this was all about Sunrise.

"I recognized that I'd like to climb him like a tree, does that count?"

I elbowed her in the side. "Maybe you should go out on a date with him."

"Speaking of." She elbowed me back and nodded to the door where the hard hunk of muscle I'd crashed into earlier stood. I glanced back at Sutton. "*That*'s the guy?" Maybe covering myself in cream just before one of the most important nights of my life hadn't been for nothing.

We locked eyes as he strode toward me, the sexy crinkles at his temples sending my stomach into a spin. That's when my father bellowed, "Parker! I want to introduce you to your dinner date. Meet my very good friend, Tristan Dubrow."

My heart, which to that point had felt like it was attached to a hundred helium balloons, landed with a thump. Of course. The hunk knew my father and was no doubt trying to impress him with a high bid.

I plastered on a smile. "Good to be introduced."

"Very good to meet you." He took my hand in his. I was acutely aware of how small mine was in his giant hand. He could crush my bones into flour if he squeezed too hard. "I'm Tristan, and I'm looking forward to our dinner very much."

I sighed. He'd won the bid. He'd impressed my father. He could stop. There was no way this was going any further. There was a reason I'd been single for three years; I'd had enough of guys who were interested in dating the daughter of Arthur Frazer and all that entailed. "Oh, there's really no need to actually go through with it. They have your bank details, right?"

"There is every reason," my father replied. "This man paid twenty-five thousand pounds for the privilege of a night with you. You better make it worth his while."

Tristan cleared his throat.

"Dad," I said, in the *you're embarrassing me* voice I hadn't used since I was a teenager. "You're making me sound like a hooker. The auction catalogue didn't say anything about me providing my date with a good time."

"Good grief, Parker. I didn't mean it like that. But Tristan here is on strict instructions to take you out and show you some fun."

I rolled my eyes. My father was the worst. "Okay, Dad."

Thank goodness, someone interrupted before he could say anything even more inappropriate. He allowed himself to be guided back toward the ballroom with a silent wave.

"So," I said, tipping my head back to meet Tristan's gaze. "Dinner it is. Somewhere we can sit down so I don't get a sore neck."

He chuckled. "Do your dates often take you to restaurants without seating?"

"I've been strictly food markets until now."

"I think we can do a little better than that. Give me your phone."

I handed it to him and he punched in some numbers. As he was typing, a notification went off on my phone. "Gillian wants to know if you're going to Pilates tomorrow," he said.

"Hey, don't read my messages."

He laughed. "Don't hand strangers your phone."

"You asked for it!" Who was this guy?

"Oh, and what's this?" he said, sweeping his thumb down my screen. "Oblix Holdings just debited sixty-seven pounds from your account."

I groaned. "Not again." I snatched the phone back from him. "Sixty-seven? That's worse than last time." I opened up the message and sure enough, the charity account had another debit from a company I'd never heard of.

"You okay?" he asked. "You look like you have to go on a date with a stranger for money."

One side of his mouth was curled up in a half smile and his almost-irresistible laugh lines were back.

"I'll figure it out. I just keep getting these debits from my account and I don't know why."

"They're unauthorized?" He snatched the phone back from me. "Have you spoken to your bank?"

"Yes!" I tried to wrestle my phone back but he just held it up higher than I could reach.

"How many times has it happened?" His voice had taken on a dark, serious note. I tried to ignore the buzz it sent between my legs.

"None of your concern. Give me my phone back, please. This is my problem. Not yours."

He tossed me my phone and I caught it. "You could make it my problem," he said. "It's what I do, after all."

What was it with guys who thought they knew better than me?

"Thanks. But I've got it covered." I didn't have it covered. I didn't have much faith that my bank had it covered, but better to do nothing than have a perfect stranger asking questions I didn't want to answer.

"Give me a call if you want me to help. Otherwise, text me your address and I'll pick you up on Saturday at seven." He turned and headed out.

"Wait," I called after him. "I'm taking you to dinner, not the other way around. I can't do Saturday."

"Sure you can," he said as he kept walking without turning around. "I saw your calendar. You're not busy on a single Saturday night between now and Christmas."

How could one man be so thoroughly annoying, and at the same time, send lust circling between my thighs?

I turned to find Sutton at my side. "Can you believe that guy?" My outrage was completely fake. Not many men spoke to me like Tristan had. Having a man like Arthur Frazer as a father took care of that. Every man I'd ever dated had either taken me out because I was his daughter or found out shortly after we'd started dating and had *continued* to take me out because I was his daughter. Either way, it meant I had dictated the terms of every romantic relationship I'd ever had. My boyfriends had never contradicted or denied me.

My dad might not have a crown, but he was a king and I was treated like a princess. Great in theory, but not so good when it came to figuring out whether or not my boyfriends liked me for me or for the advantageous connection to my father our relationship would provide. History told me my father's wealth and power coaxed the worst kind of men out of the woodwork, like ants following the scent of sugar.

Despite Tristan clearly bidding on me to impress my father, he didn't seem exactly like the others. No doubt he'd prove me wrong.

"He's totally hot. And you get to spend the evening with him. Plus, he donated twenty-five grand to this charity. You could have been a little nicer to him."

Sutton was right. I should have been nicer to him—he was a major donor tonight. Which reminded me, I'd need to check we got his money. I didn't want him changing his mind and backing out. "I suppose. But if he's taking me out because of who my dad is—which he obviously is—I'm not sure nosing into my business is the best way to go about it."

"Maybe he's just being himself instead of the suck-ups and grifters you've dated in the past. Maybe he's different. Maybe *he's* the guy you end up marrying."

Urgh. I wish Sutton would stop going on about her half-baked idea to marry me off. "Don't be ridiculous. I've told you I'm not getting married just to get access to my trust fund." There was a time when I thought marrying the man of my dreams would be part of my twenties—not to get my hands on my trust, but because I loved the man who'd asked me. But that ship had sailed.

"Stop being so stubborn. Getting married would be an easy way to raise the money for the parents and care givers program you want to establish."

I sighed. The twenty-five thousand pounds Tristan had donated was a lot of money, but it wasn't enough. Tonight, Sunrise, the charity I'd worked so hard for over the last three years, would bring in an additional hundred thousand pounds. It was a huge amount of money but it was nothing compared to the twenty-five million I'd be able to donate if I got my hands on my trust fund. "Better to convince my dad to change the rules of the trust than to marry someone. I'm not giving up my last name for anyone." I'd learned my lesson. I wasn't going to make that mistake again.

"You don't have to give up your last name just because you get married. This isn't the nineteen fifties. But that's not the issue at hand. You want that twenty-five million and you've been trying to convince your dad to change the rules of your trust for the last three years. If he was going to do it, he'd have done it by now. You're going to have to face up to the fact that if you want access to your trust, you're going to have to get married. There's no other way."

"So what, you think I should just marry someone I meet in the street?"

She shrugged like it was an actual possibility that I was going to march to the altar with a complete stranger. "You'd need to get a prenup obviously."

"Sutton!"

"It's a win-win. If, like you say, Hottie McGorgeous is trying to impress your dad—what better way than to marry his daughter? The only problem is . . ."

A knot of regret pinched in my stomach that there

might be a serious obstacle to her hair-brained scheme. Not that I was actually considering marriage to Tristan as a possibility. "What?"

"You're going to look a little funny together. He's a foot and a half taller than you."

"Stop exaggerating. He's six two, max. That's a foot."

It shouldn't have, but the thought made me shiver. I'd bet he could pick me up in one huge hand. I wasn't sure I'd object if he tried.

FOUR

Parker

It had been a long month. The hours I'd been working to prepare for the Sunrise gala had been brutal, and now it was all over. We'd far exceeded our one-hundred-thousand-pound target—by twenty grand. I was going to make the most of having a Friday evening off.

I padded through my flat, wearing my favorite cow print pajamas with a freshly applied facemask that promised a dewy, youthful glow. I bet Tristan had plenty of dewy, youthful girls at his beck and call—no face mask required. I wasn't competing, yet at the same time, I didn't want tomorrow night to be a pity date. He might have bid on me to impress my father, but I was going to trick him—not into marriage as Sutton suggested—but at least into a good time. He'd see that I was date-worthy, regardless of who my father was.

I'd just poured out my specially prepared ginger and turmeric tea that promised me the immune system of a floor-licking toddler. All I needed now was a couple of episodes of *Cheer* on Netflix, and life would shift gears into the sublime. The chocolate-covered raisins I had poured into a bowl and balanced precariously on the sofa arm might have to be consumed for me to reach true nirvana.

Just as I picked up the remote control, there was a bang on my door. No one just turned up to my flat, not unless it was an emergency. I raced to my door and flung it open to find none other than Tristan towering over me.

He prodded at my face. "I preferred the cream."

I pushed his poky finger away. "What are you doing here?" How did he get by the security at the front desk?

"The security in this building is horrible," he said. "I got in using a key fob I bought on Amazon. That's how bad it is."

Why was he here at all? I hoped he wasn't trying to move our date up. He wasn't supposed to see me in novelty nightwear and a face mask.

"Thank you for the feedback." I went to close the door but he caught it with his hand. The big, strong hands that had the ability to crush my bones into a fine powder. Later, I could think about why that was so appealing.

"Hey, I have some questions about that unauthorized payment you said left your account."

"Just wait a minute. First you need to tell me how you found out where I live. Then you need to explain what in the hell you're doing here. And then you need to leave. In that order."

"I told you. It's about the payments made to the charity. I think I might have remembered the name incorrectly. It's not bringing up anything when I do a search."

Had my building started spiking the cold tap with

vodka? Was I passed out drunk on my sofa and this was all a bad dream? There had to be an explanation for the twilight-zone conversation I was having right now.

"What are you searching for and why?"

"The fraudulent payments from your account, and because it's my job," he said. "Sort of."

Things were starting to make sense. Tristan was my dad's stooge. Dad must have arranged to have Tristan bid on me at the auction, then hired him as some kind of security guard. "My dad sent you?"

He looked at me like I'd just said I liked to ride an elephant down Regent's Street to work.

"Your dad? What does he have to do with anything? I dropped by because of the payment that flashed up on your phone. I didn't want to call or message when we don't know what we're dealing with. If I remembered its name correctly, the company that took the payment out of your account has hidden their tracks well. I don't want them to know we're onto them."

"Okay," I said slowly, though a lot of what Tristan had just said sounded decidedly not okay. "So . . . you're trying to help me?"

He widened his eyes and nodded like I'd just come from planet Stupider.

"How did you find out my address?"

"I'm an expert in cyber security. If I couldn't find out your address given your electronic footprint—which is everywhere by the way—then I wouldn't be able to call myself an expert."

"So when you said getting involved in my bank issue is what you do, you mean it's *literally* what you do."

"Of course. What did you think I meant?"

I chose not to answer that. "I'm feeling a little freaked out," I said instead. The guy hadn't tried to cross the threshold of my apartment, but it wasn't normal for a near-stranger to show up unannounced and tell you he found your address online.

"You might have reason to be. People who make these fraudulent claims from bank accounts can be tied to Russian mafia and even ISIS."

"I mean *you*, Tristan. *You're* freaking me out."

"You're a fine one to talk, given . . ." He looked me up and down. "Your face. And the cows."

"But I didn't show up at your door, having neither been invited nor given your address."

"Oh, I see what you mean. I'm doing you a favor. I don't normally get involved with shit like this. Call your father. He'll vouch for me."

I grabbed my phone from the console table just inside my door and called my dad. Tristan waited patiently, his head buried in his phone while I told my dad about Tristan wanting to help with the mysterious payments. After he assured me he'd trust Tristan with my life—and when that didn't satisfy me, all his money—I was reassured.

"You'd better come in."

"Agreed," he said.

"Give me a minute to change and wash my face."

"Don't bother. I've only got a couple of questions and then I have to leave." He stepped across the threshold but didn't follow me as I headed toward the lounge. I turned and waited for him to look up from his phone.

Right then, I was just going to have to stand across from the uber-hot guy while I wore cow pajamas and a face mask. Now I knew he wasn't a weirdo stalker, I would have liked to impress him on our date tomorrow. But that ship had sailed. That cow had mooed.

"Can I see the account so I can make sure I got the name right?" he asked. Dutifully, I opened the banking app on my phone and showed him the payments. "And how many have gone through?"

"It started about a month ago. Just a pound here and there. The amounts are getting larger every couple of days."

Tristan nodded, a little crease appearing on the bridge of his nose. What was it with this man and his wrinkles that gave me that wobbly feeling in my stomach? "This company is well protected. Most fraudulent payments come from organizations that are shut down within a week. You can get in and find out who they are like they left a rolled-out welcome mat in front of an open door. Whoever's taking from you looks a little more sophisticated."

"Can you stop them?"

He nodded. "Sure."

"So great. Stop it and the problem's solved."

"Yeah, I can install some software on your account to block this company from taking any more payments. The bank has this software, so I'm not quite sure why they haven't activated it. But I'll do it."

"Thanks. That's really nice of you. I appreciate it."

"Of course. You're Arthur's daughter."

I tried to hide my irritation. "Well, Arthur's daughter thanks you."

He pulled his eyebrows together in a look of confusion but didn't ask for clarification. "Right, that's done. But keep an eye out for payments you don't recognize to someone else. If they're targeting you specifically, they'll be back." He looked up and we locked eyes, and I did an internal groan because I was wearing a face mask that made me look like a serial killer's science experiment. "I'll see you tomorrow night." He turned and opened the front door. Big hands and a nice bum. Our date might be fun.

"Okay then," I said, but he was almost at the lifts and couldn't hear me. Obviously, there was no need for him to ask for my address. What else did he know about me that I hadn't told him? I'd have to wait until tomorrow to find out.

FIVE

Parker

Having a date on a Saturday night was unusual. Having a date with a hot man who created a flutter between my legs when we locked eyes—face mask or no face mask—was unheard of. Not many people had the capacity to shock me, and it was intoxicating. I told Tristan I had to work and would go to our date right from the office. That way, I didn't have to see him in the doorway to my apartment again. Without the lust-killing pajamas and face mask, I might just pull him inside and jump on him.

I was a little surprised when he texted me the address to a restaurant about three hundred meters from where I lived. Men who were trying to impress me because of whose daughter I was usually picked a fancy restaurant in the middle of town. One had even flown me to Paris on his plane. Apparently, Tristan Dubrow had more down-to-earth tastes. And that meant going to my favorite Italian restaurant.

I knew what I'd order before I sat down.

It also meant I didn't need to dress up. My favorite jeans and a red blouse with a ruffly collar said that I was making some effort but not too much. My concession to making an effort was strapping on some heels. I was determined to bridge the height gap between Tristan and me even if we were sitting down.

I caught sight of Tristan through the sticker-covered glass of the restaurant door. He looked enormous sat at the tiny table for two in the corner in front of the kitchen. Enormous, and undeniably handsome. He wore a blue shirt that pulled slightly across his arms and his messy hair had streaks of dirty-blond on the ends like it was hanging on to a memorable summer. His jaw was grazed with stubble, and for a second, I wanted to know how it felt against my thighs. If this was a real date, I'd be looking forward to this evening.

I pushed the door open and his gaze shot to mine.

I waved at Antonio behind the till and slid into my seat opposite my handsome date.

"Interesting choice of restaurant," I said.

"You look beautiful." His comment came from the back of the throat—raw and guttural, an animal response.

I grinned. "I like your shirt."

He looked at me like he hadn't heard me and I looked away, a little unsettled at the intensity of his stare.

"Shall we get a menu?" I suggested.

Tristan cleared his throat as if he had to deliberately knock himself back into the moment. "I've ordered already."

I frowned like a toddler who'd just had her ball yanked away from her. I liked the crab ravioli and the chicken parmigiana. I'd been looking forward to it.

"You want some wine?" he asked.

"You're asking?" I replied. "That makes a change." I'd never been particularly good at hiding what I was thinking.

"Trust me." He gestured for one of the waitresses to come over and ordered a bottle of Franciacorta.

"Not a prosecco fan?" I asked, wondering if he was trying to impress me.

"Hate the stuff. I drink beer mainly. But dinner with a beautiful woman deserves something more. And I'd rather drink cows' urine than prosecco."

"Something we have in common."

He nodded as if I hadn't told him anything he didn't know already. "I figured."

"You know this isn't a date though, don't you? I mean, you don't have to impress me."

"I paid twenty-five grand for tonight. If it's not a real date then I want my money back." The way his mouth curled up slightly told me he didn't want his money back at all.

"So why this place? You live around here?"

"I live in Notting Hill, but I figured this place was local to you and it has a great reputation. I guessed you'd been here before and enjoyed it. Am I wrong?"

I shook my head. I couldn't argue with that logic. "I love this place." Truth be told, the kind of thought Tristan had put into choosing this place was way more impressive than taking a private plane to Paris. Anyone could get their assistant to make table reservations and charter a plane. Tristan had genuinely thought about what I might like.

But I wasn't running down that rabbit hole. Like all the rest, Tristan was trying to impress my father, not me. He was either interested in furthering their business relationship or getting his hands on some of Dad's money. Better to find out now which one.

"Tell me how you know my dad."

He shrugged like there wasn't much to tell. "He gave

me my first break. Spotted potential in me, I suppose. I started doing cyber security for his bank and . . .Long story short, he gave me my career."

It sounded like he owed my dad a lot. Although I couldn't ignore the pinch in my heart that told me I'd prefer it if he hadn't known my father at all, I admired the lack of ego he displayed. Most men wouldn't fully credit someone else for their success. They might acknowledge they'd had a leg up. Maybe. But to say my father *gave* him his career? There was something sexy about a man who could recognize the shoulders he stood on.

Our starters arrived and a plate of crab ravioli was placed in front of each of us.

I looked up at him. As if he could read my thoughts, he said, "Antonio told me this was your favorite. Looks great." He picked up his fork but waited as I tentatively reached for mine. I couldn't decide if Tristan finding out my preferences was creepy or incredibly thoughtful. All I knew was I was sitting in my favorite restaurant, eating my favorite thing on the menu. Like Sutton said, I needed to just go with it.

"That's delicious. Must be the lemon," he said after his first bite.

The way he'd said *delicious* echoed in my brain and made me shiver like it was me he was eating, not the ravioli.

"I'm surprised you like this kind of place," I said.

"What? Great food, great wine, great company? Yeah, why would I like that?"

I smiled and he looked up at me from under his eyelashes. He took another mouthful of ravioli and for a split second I wondered how his lips would feel on my neck. How his hands would feel circling and pressing against my body. I needed to keep my imagination in check. Remember why we were here.

"I thought with the whole twenty-five grand bid, you might be a bit flash."

He chuckled. "I'm wiped out now. Nothing left in my bank account. You should be grateful we didn't end up on a park bench eating takeaway fish and chips."

"I like fish and chips."

"Me too."

Unable to gauge his seriousness, I felt bad. "Are you being serious? Has your donation left you—"

He chuckled like I was Ricky Gervais. "Don't worry. I'm still liquid. I'm just not—" He paused as he seemed to try to find the right words. "I like flash in the right circumstances, but not every day. Anyway, you're Arthur's daughter. You've seen flash before and it's not like it's going to impress you. I wanted to do something you'd enjoy. Was I wrong?"

I couldn't think of anything more right than this evening. If I'd been looking for a date, this one might be as perfect as it got.

Once our starters were cleared away, I shouldn't have been surprised when the waiter placed a plate of chicken parm in its place. Tristan had the same. "Antonio told you?" I asked, glancing down at my plate.

Tristan nodded. "Looks great."

"What does a cyber security specialist do? Make sure people are changing their passwords and stuff?"

Tristan chuckled, popped a forkful of chicken in his mouth, and nodded. He swallowed before he said, "That's exactly it. I make sure all my clients are regularly changing their passwords."

He was very clearly being sarcastic, but I was genuinely

hoping he'd elaborate. "So who are your clients? Companies? Or people like my dad?"

"Both. Anyone who understands the importance of cyber security."

Why wasn't he like some normal guy, boastful about how important and successful he was? "Cyber security being...?"

"I keep data safe."

"Data on computers?" I asked.

"Yes."

"Data on phones?"

"Yes. These days most data is stored electronically. So basically *all* data."

"This is a lot of talk about data," I said on a sigh.

His eyes did that mischievous sparkly thing as he smiled. "You started it."

"I'm trying to get to know you," I said. As soon as I said it, I wished I hadn't. I *was* trying to get to know him, but why? We just had to pass the time until dinner was over and we could go back to our respective lives, but Tristan interested me. Too much.

"You're trying to understand what I do. That's not who I am."

"I can't remember the film, but in it there's a scene where a woman says to her boyfriend or ex or something that it doesn't matter who you are in your head, it's what you do that counts."

"Rachel says it to Bruce in *Batman Begins*: 'It's not who you are underneath. It's what you do that defines you.' Best of the three Nolan Batmans in my opinion. People loved *The Dark Knight* but I thought it was overrated."

I wasn't going to tell him, but I kind of loved *Batman Begins* and I kinda loved that he could quote from it. "Okay,

Gotham geek, you've just contradicted yourself. You said *what you do* defines you, did you not?"

"But Rachel isn't talking about Bruce's job. She's talking about his actions. Also we're pre-supposing that Rachel's right and only actions matter. I never said I agreed with her."

I couldn't help but smile. He was right. He was cute. And he was smart, but not in a showy way. He exuded confidence without cockiness. It was a welcome change.

"*Do* you agree with her?"

He winced. "Yes and no. Yes in the context of Bruce seemingly being an indulgent playboy with the heart of that *same great kid he used to be*. But more generally I think some actions we take can be a mistake. No one wants to be judged on their worst day. So in that sense, what we do isn't always representative of who we are."

I liked that he was listening to me. And that he was interesting to listen to. If I took Tristan at his actions, he had donated generously to Sunrise, and he'd been thoughtful in picking this restaurant and in ordering for me. Should I therefore believe he was a generous, thoughtful man? Was it all for show, or were his actions a genuine reflection of his personality?

"So tell me why you ended up bidding so much for this dinner. What is it that you need from my father?"

He narrowed his eyes. "Need? You think I'm after something?"

"Most people are."

He nodded slowly. "I suppose so." He paused and seemed in no rush to continue. Eventually, he said, "There's nothing I wouldn't do for Arthur. I didn't know you were his daughter when I bid. I'd stepped out to take a call and when I came back, the beautiful woman who'd bumped into me earlier that day was on stage. Sans pastry cream, wearing a stunning gown."

Heat swept over my body like I was stepping off a plane in Dubai. He hadn't known who I was? A fizzle of excitement spun in my stomach. The hot man opposite had just wanted a date with me without knowing my last name, or the reputation for wealth attached to it?

"You think everyone else who bid was trying to impress your father?" he asked.

"Impress him. Use me. Pick your poison."

"Wow," Tristan said, a grin unfurling on his face. "How did you get so . . . cynical?"

"I'm a realist. I don't expect people to be anything but human and therefore, focused on their own best interests."

He shook his head. "I don't believe that of the human race, and I don't believe *you* believe that, either."

"You're really going to sit there and tell me what I believe? It's true. We're hard wired to be selfish and fulfil our own needs."

"Yes, I'm going to sit here and tell you that you don't believe that. You work for a charity that raises money to help people. *Other* people. And you're not the only one— you have colleagues, donors, supporters. If your theory was true, charities wouldn't exist. People wouldn't volunteer. I'm not saying people won't try to fulfil their basic needs. Of course they will. But some of them try to do more than that. Some of us don't have an agenda other than wanting to donate to a good cause and spend the evening with a beautiful woman."

He couldn't be right *and* charming. That was a step too far.

"There will always be exceptions to every rule." It was the best response I had. I'd run out of road and his smile was getting to me. Especially when he was pointing out how wrong I was. A little voice inside my head started telling me that maybe *he* was an exception to the rule. I needed to find the mute button for that voice. There was a good reason I hadn't had a date since I'd broken off my engagement. Exceptions were rare. And I wasn't going to fall for another man who pretended to be someone he wasn't.

A waitress I'd not seen before cleared our plates and reset the table for pudding. Tristan waited for her to leave before he answered.

"Maybe, but I think it would have been an exceptional man in that ballroom who wouldn't want to be sitting opposite you here tonight. Lucky for me, I get that privilege."

"So you're saying you have no interest in impressing my father?" If that was the case, Sutton's idea of getting Tristan to marry me fell apart—there was no motivation.

"If I was trying to impress Arthur, dating his daughter wouldn't be the first thing I'd try."

"So you'd have no interest in marrying me then?"

"You're proposing? On a first date? I must have impressed you a little at least."

He was way too cute—I could hear the danger sirens already.

I shrugged as if I'd just told him I'd been planning to split the bill. "Yeah. I mean, if you'd been wanting to impress my father, it would have been a win-win solution to all our problems. But given you don't, I guess that's put pay to my idea."

He chuckled and the sound reverberated across every goosebump that peppered my skin.

"I don't tend to say yes to marriage proposals on the first date. But like you said, there are exceptions to every rule."

SIX

Tristan

Parker was better company that I'd expected. Not that I'd been expecting tonight to be bad. I just never had expectations when it came to a date. All too often, I'd thought a date would go well and been sorely disappointed—either we didn't have anything in common or I found myself making all the conversation. I'd kind of given up. I had my fair share of hookups, but dating had taken a back seat to most things in my life. After tonight, I might be reassessing my priorities.

Parker was more beautiful than I remembered. The sassy almost-black bob and her ruby red lips were far from my usual type, but there was something about her that I couldn't look away from. She was sexy—not just because of how she looked, but because of how she was.

"I'm intrigued," I said. "Tell me how marrying you would be the solution to all our problems."

"If you were my father's son-in-law, you'd get anything you needed from him."

"Except I don't need anything from him."

"Right, but I didn't know that until just now."

"Okay, and why would it work for you? Don't tell me you just want me for my body."

She grinned and the flush in her cheeks told me she didn't mind my body one bit. "My charity always needs money and I'd like to donate my trust fund to supporting not just the children who have heart defects, but their families too. The strain this kind of illness puts on a family is unimaginable."

It wasn't unimaginable to me.

"I want to provide support for the entire family—accommodation close to the hospital if they need it, counselling for parents and siblings, academic support if it's needed. That kind of thing."

I nodded, trying to push down the memories of my family before my sister died. Looking back, it was no wonder my parents split up. With constant relays to the hospital, they rarely both stayed under one roof. The pressure of having to make life-and-death decisions on a regular basis, the limbo we all lived in—it was an impossible situation. I'd buried myself in my computer, grieving the loss of my family way before my sister died and my parents divorced.

"I could do all that if I had access to my trust fund. But stupid rules say I have to be twenty-five and married."

I frowned. She didn't look old, but she looked over twenty-five. "How old are you?"

"Twenty-eight, so no problem there. My issue is I'm single—and happily so. I was never that girl dreaming about her wedding day. My work is my life. I don't have time for anything else. It's just I wouldn't mind the twenty-five million I'd get if I walk down the aisle."

"That's a lot of money. And a lot of incentive to get married."

"It is. I don't want it for me. I just know I could do so much good if I could get my hands on it." She shrugged. "Anyway, I wasn't really serious about getting married. My friend suggested I should ask whoever won the date, because if you were trying to impress my dad, you might be willing to do it."

We were interrupted by Antonio coming over with our pudding.

"I hope it's what you were expecting," Antonio said, glancing at me. His nose wrinkled in disgust at the bespoke dessert I'd ordered.

"Thank you," I said. "It's appreciated."

"Cream puffs?" Parker said, her eyes twinkling in surprise.

"Could it be anything else?" If it hadn't been for cream puffs, I would never have bid on her. We wouldn't be sitting opposite each other right now—a possibility that became more distasteful to me with every passing minute. Thank God for cream puffs.

"Wait, are these chocolate-covered raisins? How did you know these are my favorite?" She looked up at me, wonder in her sea green eyes as if I'd just pulled a bunny from a hat.

"I pay attention," I said.

"Do you have cameras in my place? Was that the reason you came to my flat yesterday?" She was smiling but I could tell she wanted an answer.

"Like I said, I pay attention. Last night you were obviously having some *me* time, what with the pajamas and the mask—"

She groaned. "Don't remind me."

"You had a bowl of chocolate-covered raisins set up next to the sofa, so I figured you liked them. And I know you like cream puffs. They look good on you."

She smiled so wide, I felt it deep in my gut. "You want me to stick one on my shirt?"

I chuckled. "As long as I get to watch you eat one, I'm good." The way she'd just casually taken a bite out of the puff when the tray landed on her had been adorably sexy, but apparently adorably sexy was her default mode—cream puff or no cream puff.

"So, you pay attention, huh?"

"More than most people, I think. Observation often provides more information—and certainly more accurate information—than asking questions."

She nodded slowly as if she was a little unsure what else she might have given away.

She raised the cream puff to her lips and took a large bite. Inadvertently she daubed a dollop of cream on her nose. I was more than a little disappointed when she wiped it off with the back of her hand. I might have liked to see her try to get at it with her tongue.

"We both know I don't need to impress your father, but just for kicks, tell me more about the marriage of convenience you were going to propose."

I liked watching her talk, and what she said told me so much about who she was. She laid it all out there like a red carpet, enticing me to step inside and learn more.

"For kicks?"

"Like I said, I owe your father my career. I'm not about to trick him out of twenty-five million pounds."

"It's not his money," she snapped.

It might not be Arthur's money, but I wasn't about to lie to him about wanting to marry his daughter. No way.

"Humor me," I said, wanting to hear her vision for what she thought this game would look like. "Tell me what you were thinking."

She held my gaze while she stuffed a mouthful of cream puff between her lips, chewed and swallowed.

Sexy. In everything she did.

"The rules of the trust say I need to be married for ninety days before the funds are released—hence I can't just marry someone for the weekend. I have to satisfy my dad and the other trustee that it's a real marriage. That's my plan."

"Prenups in place?"

"Postnups, otherwise they're not enforceable in the UK. We'd negotiate them before, sign them after."

I nodded. "Right. So you need to find someone you can trust, or they could not sign the papers after you're married and claim half of your trust fund."

She sighed. "Right. I'm hoping if they're trying to impress my dad, they'll play by the rules."

"Except they might not need to impress him with half your trust fund in their back pocket." There were some very unscrupulous people around that would say anything Parker wanted to hear if it meant they got their hands on that kind of money.

Her shoulders sank. "Yeah. You're right. I need someone I can trust."

"Okay, and what else? You'll have a big wedding? Buy a house together? A dog?" I asked, genuinely intrigued about her plan.

"We'd have to have a wedding. It's got to look legit for at least ninety days. But there's no point in buying a house for three months. Maybe he could move in with me?" She shook her head. "Not that it matters. I've not got anyone in mind now I know you're not interested."

I wasn't interested. Not that I had a problem marrying someone who needed access to their trust fund. It wasn't like I believed in the sanctity of marriage or anything like that. I just liked and respected Arthur too much to lie to him.

"What about sex?" I asked. I leaned back in my chair and enjoyed the blush that swept up her cheeks.

"No sex required."

"And here I was just thinking I might be changing my mind."

She picked out a chocolate-covered raisin and launched it at me. "No you weren't."

I chuckled. "No, I wasn't. You wouldn't tell anyone it's all fake?"

She winced. "I wouldn't be able to. I couldn't risk my father finding out." She paused. "You'd know. And my best friend. But apart from that, I'd keep it a secret."

I liked the idea of us having a secret.

"I guess that means there's no second date," I said. "Given I've turned down your marriage proposal."

She laughed. "I guess not. Unless I get a ring at the end of a first date, I never say yes to a second."

That was a shame. Parker was the first woman in a long time who had genuinely intrigued me. Maybe it was the cow-print pajamas; maybe it was the marriage proposal. Maybe it was her sea-green eyes and semi-permanent half-scowl. Whatever it was, I would have liked to see her again. And if she hadn't been Arthur's daughter, I might just have married her.

SEVEN

Tristan

There was rarely a need for me to go to my clients' offices. I got more done when I was working at home, and I liked the anonymity I got from doing things across email and telephone. I tried to avoid video calls as much as possible for the same reason.

I could admit to myself that my presence at Arthur's offices had more to do with Saturday night than Arthur's bank's security. Though she hadn't done it deliberately, Parker had put me in a difficult position. Now she had told me of her plan to get her hands on her trust fund, I was keeping something from Arthur. And if I told Arthur, I'd be betraying Parker's confidence. Rock. Hard place. And the sound of my bones being crushed as I got caught between the two.

I was shown into Arthur's office by his assistant. Arthur had a desktop computer that was joined to the bank's network, and an entirely separate, independent laptop. Today was as good a time as any to do my regular checks to make sure everything was in order. Checks I ordinarily did remotely and automatically.

Today, I'd decided to do them manually and in person.

I slipped into Arthur's chair and switched on his laptop. A silver photo frame by the side of his desk caught my eye. Parker smiled back at me. She looked like she was on holiday, glowing in the sunshine, her bob slightly less sleek than I'd seen it before. Beautiful.

"Tristan! Maureen told me you were here." Arthur strode into his office.

I shot up from his seat. "I thought you were in meetings, Arthur. I was just passing and thought I'd drop in and do your regular checks in person. A site check is sometimes helpful."

He indicated that I should sit back down as he slipped into one of the chairs opposite his own desk. "You carry on. My meeting went unexpectedly short, which doesn't happen very often."

"You're going to watch me work?"

"No, you're going to work while I ask you questions about your date with my daughter."

Internally, I sighed. We were edging toward dangerous territory. But that was why I was here, wasn't it? I'd wanted a way to tell him without telling him what Parker was planning to do to get her hands on her trust fund.

"We had a lovely evening. She's very charming," I said, my fingers working on the keyboard, wanting to get these checks done so at least that didn't turn out to be a lie.

"So you'll see each other again? It's been a while since Parker had a boyfriend. She needs something or somebody to distract her from working every minute of every day for that charity."

Boyfriend?

"You must be very proud that she's so passionate about something that's so . . . important."

Arthur exhaled and gripped the arms of the chair. "Of course, I'm proud. So many offspring of my peers spend their entire lives hopping from party to party, spending their trust funds on meaningless designer clothes. Parker has never been like that. I just wish . . . I wish she was better at balance. She needs to have more fun."

I paused and glanced across at Arthur, wondering if he wanted me to tell him what I thought or whether he just wanted me to listen. Arthur wasn't easy to read. "No doubt your parents felt the same way about you. No one becomes successful without being single-minded and driven."

Arthur nodded. "Agreed. But somewhere along the way I managed to find an amazing woman to marry and we had a family. I want that for Parker too."

From our conversations on Saturday, a real marriage and a family weren't even on Parker's radar. It was one of the reasons I liked her idea of a sham marriage. If her father had been anyone but Arthur, I might have said yes. It wasn't like she seemed to put any value on being married.

"Maybe she doesn't want that for herself."

"If she just didn't want to get married, that would be fine. I don't have a problem with that. But the issue is she's given up. Stopped trusting people." There was a sadness in his eyes I'd not seen before. "When it came to putting in place her trust fund, I wanted to make sure the idea of someone to share her life with was still a possibility. Getting married is one of the requirements for accessing her trust." He glanced up at me.

I couldn't pretend I didn't know. "She mentioned that."

Arthur held my gaze. "Mentioned it how?"

I was walking a tightrope. I'd known Arthur longer,

owed him more than anyone could possibly imagine or repay, but Parker had done nothing to deserve my betrayal. "She said being married was one of the requirements of getting her trust fund."

I'd half expected Arthur to be angry, but it was mirth I saw on his face. "That's a funny subject to come up on a first date . . . unless—" He chuckled. "Did she propose?"

I sucked in a breath. Faced with a straightforward question, I wasn't going to lie. "She said something about it."

"That kid. She's smart." He shook his head. "She wants that money for Sunrise. Am I wrong?"

I didn't respond, but that was an answer in itself.

"I hope you said yes," Arthur continued, which threw me a little. He was clearly missing something. Or I was.

"Don't worry. I'm not about to fake marry your daughter and lie to you about it."

He paused before finally saying, "It wouldn't be fake. If it were, she wouldn't fulfil the criteria. And you're not lying to me about it because now I know."

I pushed the chair away from his desk. "You're suggesting I marry Parker so she can get access to her trust fund?"

"Why not?" he asked. It was hardly the reaction I'd been expecting. I'd assumed he'd be furious that Parker was going to try to trick him. "Even a fake wedding would require Parker to put her trust in you to a certain extent. You're a good guy. You could show her that not all men are —" He stopped himself from going further and changed tack. "She'd be forced to see life from a slightly different perspective. You and she would have to spend time together —to come to our place for Sunday dinner. And of course you'd have to live together after you're married. Maybe even after you're engaged. In fact, the more I think about it, the more I think it's an excellent idea. Might do you good too, Tristan. I've been thinking for some years that maybe you need some balance in your life. You work too hard."

"I have plenty of balance, but I appreciate you looking out for me."

Arthur continued like he hadn't heard me. "At least I'd know she was with someone who could be trusted. There are some scoundrels about. And not just in banking."

That was true. "Maybe you could have a word with her. I'm unlikely to be the last person she asks. It's a lot of money and like you say, she's passionate about what she does. It's unlikely she's going to give up finding a fake husband because I said no."

He nodded but wasn't listening. "Think about it, Tristan. You'd have my blessing," he said. "In fact, you'd be doing me a favor."

My aversion to deceiving Arthur had been my primary objection to a fake marriage. But if he was fully aware of what was going on and was fine with it, what was my problem? I would be helping out Parker, Arthur, and a very worthy cause. Wasn't I an arsehole if I said no?

"The only thing I ask," Arthur said, "is that you don't tell Parker I know. If she finds out I'm okay with her sham marriage, she won't put any effort in and the entire reason for that requirement in the trust will have been for nothing."

So now he wanted me to lie to Parker? It didn't sit well with me but at the same time, his motives weren't bad. I'd always said I'd do anything for Arthur. Now I was going to have to figure out if that was true. Was I prepared to marry his daughter?

EIGHT

Parker

I couldn't deny myself my cow pajamas, but I was drawing a line at putting on another face mask. I wasn't expecting company, but then again, I'd not been expecting company when Tristan had dropped around the other day. I'd been caught off-guard. Once bitten . . .

I poured some chocolate-covered raisins into a bowl, scooped up my tea, and padded into the living room. I hadn't even had time for a single sip of my drink before someone knocked on my door. Even though some part of me had been anticipating the interruption, I still shot up ten feet in the air. Why would he be here again? I glanced down at my attire. Did I have time to change? Fuck it. He'd seen them before.

And it probably wasn't him, anyway, right?

I swung the door open to find a towering Tristan Dubrow standing over me. Even with his head bowed, scrolling through his phone, he still looked gorgeous. Why couldn't I get a guy like that to marry me? Sutton was right,

I needed my trust fund money. If getting it required some subterfuge, so be it. I was going to marry someone this year if it was the last thing I did.

"Someone's taking your money again." He looked up from his phone and right at me. It was as if I'd been shoved, his stare was so intense. I took an involuntary step back.

"Come in," I said to cover the visceral reaction my body had had to a simple look from him.

Again, he slipped inside and stayed in the hallway.

"How do you know?" I asked. "Did you break into my bank account?"

He pulled his eyebrows together. "Yes. How do you think I blocked the first company creaming off payments?"

I shouldn't have asked. "I like the way you're perfectly comfortable hacking into my bank account but God forbid you marry me so a charity can be up twenty-five million." I sounded pissed off and I had no right to. He didn't have any obligation to me. We'd spent a sum total of three hours together. Why would he agree to marry me? We needed to start again. "You want some ginger tea?" I asked.

"Sure."

I hadn't expected him to say yes. I headed into the kitchen and set about making him a drink. "How much have they taken?" I asked.

"Seems to be following the same pattern as last time— just small amounts each day. It was three seventy-five today." He pursed his lips together like he was in the middle of today's Wordle.

"Three hundred and seventy-five?"

He shook his head. "Three pounds seventy-five."

"Can you block them?"

"Done." He slid his phone into his back pocket and took the mug I offered.

"This place is small," he said, glancing around my apartment.

"Thanks." I headed back out into the hallway and slid onto the sofa, next to my bowl of raisins.

Tristan followed me. "I'm not saying it's bad. I just expected you to . . ."

"Be more flash?" I finished his sentence for him. "I run a charity. There's not much room in my salary for flash."

"I guess I thought Arthur would—"

"I stand on my own two feet." I took a raisin and popped it into my mouth. "I've always worked. I've always supported myself. Arthur is Arthur. I'm me."

He held my gaze two seconds too long. "You're trying to prove something." It wasn't a question but almost like he was thinking aloud.

"I'm trying to eat my raisins and drink my tea in peace. But a certain someone keeps interrupting my 'me' time."

The corners of his lips curled up. "Who would want to skim money off a charity?"

"Thieves?"

He raised his eyebrows at me. "But why are they targeting Sunrise? They know they've been caught, yet they've come back for more."

"Isn't it just like . . . some bot that does it?"

"Exactly my point. It usually is. And if the bot gets blocked, they don't try that account again. Not for a while at least. It gets put to the bottom of the list."

"Maybe they know we know that, so they're banking on us assuming the account is off their radar. You said yourself that they seemed sophisticated."

"My gut tells me it's personal. It's Sunrise they're interested in. Have you made any enemies?"

Enemies? Me? "We're not a front for the CIA. We're a charity for sick children."

"It's just weird. Have a think about it. And make sure you're keeping your doors locked."

My stomach somersaulted. "What makes you say that?"

"Just a precaution until I figure out what's going on." He squinted at me. "What's the matter?" he asked. "You look like I just told you you can't ever eat chocolate-covered raisins again."

I played over me coming back to my flat this evening. "It's just that when I came home from work today, the second lock on the door wasn't on. And I'm pretty fastidious about making sure my flat is locked up when I leave. I was a little weirded out by it, but then I came inside, everything was fine, and I forgot about it. Maybe I missed it but . . . You think I'm being paranoid?"

Tristan's eyes went dark and he stood. "Let's go. Pack up some things and let's leave. I don't believe in being paranoid."

"What? I'm in my pajamas. I'm not going anywhere."

He tucked his hand under my elbow and pulled me up and off the sofa. "Come and pack a bag or I'll do it for you."

I shrugged him off me. "You're being paranoid. I probably just forgot to lock it."

"If you believed that, you wouldn't have mentioned it to me. You wouldn't have even thought twice about it."

He sounded like my father. He was always trying to convince me to take more security precautions. More than once, he'd encouraged me to use a chauffeur to get around town, or employ a bodyguard whenever I left the apartment. It was nonsensical, and I'd never agreed to any of it.

"You're not in charge of me," I said. "You can't make me pack a suitcase."

"No," he said, "I can't. But if you don't, I will. And if I do that, I'll probably put the wrong day-of-the-week underwear in or forget your . . . sheep pajamas. Pack a case and we can discuss it on the way."

Day-of-the-week underwear? Did I really look like a woman who wore day-of-the-week underwear? I glanced down to see the faces of a dozen happy cows looking up at me. "On the way where?"

Before I knew it, we were in my bedroom. Without asking, he'd pulled my suitcase from the top of my wardrobe and was buried deep in his phone while I filled it. I needed to change. I grabbed some jeans and my favorite Snoopy sweatshirt and slipped into the bathroom.

Tristan looked at me and chuckled. "Love is a warm puppy? Really? You asked a complete stranger to marry you on Saturday night so you could get your hands on money. You can't tell me you're all warm puppies and chocolate-covered raisins inside."

"I love Snoopy. He's all I need."

"Wrong. You also need a wedding band on your finger so you can get your hands on your trust fund." Without waiting for a reply, he flipped over my suitcase, zipped it shut, and lifted it from the bed like it didn't have half my possessions in it. He strode to the door and I scampered after him.

"I'm not ready. I have to turn the TV off, and make sure the oven's off. I have to water my plants and—"

"You don't have plants."

"I'm being metaphorical. You can't just bundle me out of the door. It feels like a kidnapping."

"Well, go water your metaphorical plants and let's get out of here."

I quickly switched the TV off, picked up my phone,

tablet, and bag and scanned my flat. I'd be back tomorrow. Wouldn't I?

We rode the lift down to the lobby side by side in silence. I wanted to question him. If someone wanted to take something from my flat, they had the opportunity while I was out all day. If they wanted *me*, they would have waited until I was home. Why was he so sure I was in danger?

"Just trust me," Tristan said.

"I didn't say anything."

He looked down at me and smirked. "You don't have to. The way you pull your hair behind your left ear tells me you have things on your mind." My hand dropped to my side. "If I'm being paranoid, great. You get a sleepover at mine and you go home when I've figured out what's going on. If I'm not being paranoid. Well, great—you were safe at mine."

"A sleepover? At your place? I'll just go to a hotel."

We stepped out of the lifts and headed outside.

"Nope. I want you where I can see you."

This guy was exasperating. At the same time, there was something comforting about the feeling of having someone care. If his intentions were genuine. "I hope you have choco-late-covered raisins at your place."

Tristan had parked outside. He opened the car door for me. "It can be arranged."

I slid into the passenger seat and waited while Tristan put my case in the boot and got into the drivers' seat, ready to take me to a deliciously hot, almost-perfect-stranger's house to stay the night.

BEING in Tristan's house made me feel like a teenager who didn't have her shit together. Whereas my flat was a hodge-podge of knickknacks, Christmas presents, and holiday souvenirs, Tristan's place looked like it belonged to a grown-up. It was all dark grey, petrol blue, and forest green paints; wood-paneled rooms; carefully curated mid-century modern furniture; and art that looked particularly chosen for the space.

"Nice place." I pulled open a kitchen drawer and peered inside. His cutlery was all beautifully arranged in an oak tray. I pulled open another one to find carefully pressed tea towels.

Everything was just perfect.

I looked up to find him watching me. "Like what you see?" he asked.

Heat flushed up my body because looking at him—yes. Yes, I did like what I saw. So much it was a little embarrassing. The dirty blond hair that looked perfectly disheveled. The shoulders that were nearly as broad as I was tall. Even the crinkles by his eyes were sexy somehow. Men shouldn't be as attractive as Tristan. It wasn't fair.

"I guess," I replied, trying to be deliberately vague.

"You're used to nice places," he replied. "You just don't live in one."

"Hey. I live in Maida Vale."

"Maida Vale is nice. But your flat . . . It's like you're deliberately trying to make it not nice."

"Not all of us have the money for fancy Victorian villas in Notting Hill."

"No. But you do. I have no doubt that if you wanted to live in a nicer place, Arthur would make it happen. I think you like to torture yourself. I just haven't worked out why yet."

I had no desire to torture myself, but I didn't need a fancy house to prove it. Like Tristan said, I'd lived in a fancy house growing up. It didn't define who I was.

"People forget that it's my dad who has money, not me."

He shrugged as if it didn't matter what I said, he was going to form his own opinion.

"How old are you?" I asked.

"Thirty-four," he said.

"You have quite the setup. Cyber security must have been good to you." Houses like this in Notting Hill didn't come cheap. He definitely paid north of five million for this place. But a nice house in a good area didn't always mean someone was rich. It just meant their debts were bigger.

"I have no complaints."

"Your place is nothing like I expected."

"There seems to be a theme developing where I'm not what you expect. Did you envision tiger skins and gold lamé, or maybe you thought we'd be sitting on upturned milk crates and using torches to read comic books in my sleeping bag at night?"

"It's like you can read my mind." I was joking but at the same time, I wasn't. There were moments where it seemed like Tristan had crawled inside my head and set up camp. I hadn't known him long enough for him to get me like he did.

A bang on the door interrupted and I jumped.

"Chocolate-covered raisins," he said in explanation.

"You had someone go and get them?"

"If Uber Eats counts."

Oh. Of course.

"And ginger tea," he said, coming back into the living room with a carrier bag.

"That's very sweet of you." He was right—he paid attention. To me.

He looked away as if he were embarrassed. "You want a cup now?"

I shook my head. "I wouldn't mind putting on my PJs though."

He nodded and picked up my suitcase. "Follow me." He took the stairs two at a time before stopping at the second door on the galleried landing. "There's a gold lamé bodysuit in the wardrobe." A grin spread across his face. "I'd probably pay another twenty-five grand to see that."

"Get out of here."

"You don't need help at all? In changing?"

I play pushed him out of the door. "Go make me some tea."

He left and I slumped onto a bed made up with soft white linen sheets. Antique furniture with a modern twist surrounded me—an old mahogany bedroom chair displaying a bottle green and orange cushion. A glass and copper light fitting. It was modern but in keeping with the house. There was something about seeing inside Tristan's world that made him quadruple in attractiveness, if that was even possible. No wonder he wouldn't marry me. Someone like this deserved a real wife, not a fake arrangement exclusively for the purpose of gaining access to my trust.

When I'd managed to tear myself from the comfort of the bed, I changed and padded downstairs.

"Your tea is on the side," he said, looking up from his phone from where he was sitting on one of the two vintage benches that flanked his matching dining table. "Thought you might have gotten lost up there."

"Your house is . . . It's beautiful. But it's also comfortable."

He nodded. "Good. Just don't mention to anyone where you are." He continued to watch me as I slid onto the bench opposite him. "Not until we figure out what's going on."

"I'll need to let work know, obviously . . ."

Before I finished my sentence, he was shaking his head. "No one. Please. Just until I get more clarity." He stayed silent, tapping away on his phone for a few minutes. He winced and those sexy little lines by his eyes appeared again. "I just want to figure out who's taking money from your account and whether anyone broke into your building yesterday. Not that it would take a lot if an Amazon key fob can get me in."

I shivered at the thought.

"You okay?" he asked.

"I'm fine. You just do a good job at freaking me out. I probably just left the door unlocked."

"But you know you didn't."

I wasn't one hundred percent sure.

I looked away and my eyes landed on the fruit bowl in the middle of the table. "Can I have a banana?" Stress eating was always the solution.

"Sure." He moved a bowl of raisins in front of me too.

"You're a great housemate," I said. "And a great date. Such a shame you don't want to marry me."

He chuckled and looked up from his phone at me.

I alternated mouthfuls of banana and chocolate-covered raisins while Tristan tapped away on his phone. It was weird being in a near-stranger's house, about to stay the night. But my dad said I could trust Tristan. If he was asking me to stay, I should listen to him.

"I need a favor from you," Tristan said as I was on my last mouthful of banana.

"Okay," I replied.

"Can you skip work tomorrow, or at least work from here?"

"Come on. You're being over the top."

"One day is all I'm asking. It will just buy me some time. I've got a lot on at the moment and I need to figure out what's going on."

One day wasn't a big deal. I was half thinking about working from home tomorrow anyway. I wanted to go through our donor list from the dinner and auction. "On one condition. I get to cook us dinner in this fan-fucking-tastic kitchen."

"Double win for me."

NINE

Tristan

I'd arranged to meet Dexter a little earlier than the rest of the guys. And I'd told him to bring some engagement rings with him. He arrived with a little panic in his eyes. Then he closed the door to the private room that we always used and took a seat, looking at me like I was an exhibit in a museum.

"If people were going to practice dark arts, this would be a perfect spot," I said.

Dexter was always teased for choosing this place—its deep red walls and golden sun ceiling. It was quirky and a little dark, and it suited Dexter perfectly.

"Is everything okay?" Dexter asked.

"Sure."

He pulled out a velvet box from his pocket and laid it on the table. "I brought what you asked me to."

I sucked in a breath. "Thanks." If I was going to marry Parker, I needed a ring, right? Fake marriage or not, people were going to expect an engagement ring.

"You want to tell me what's going on?"

"Well," I said, sliding my hands down my jeans. "I'm thinking about proposing."

"Fuck, Tristan. To who? I've not even heard you talk about anyone, and out of nowhere you're marrying her?"

Before I could answer, Joshua poked his head around the door. "You two are early. I thought I'd be here on my own." His eyes darted to the velvet box on the table. "What's going on?"

"Tristan's proposing," Dexter said as Joshua sat.

I sighed. I hadn't decided anything yet. And now I was going to have the Witches of Eastwick chipping in to tell me what they thought. I wanted to make my own decision on this. However much I loved them, my friends wouldn't understand.

"Right," Joshua said, clearly not believing a word of what Dexter was saying.

"I'm thinking about it. I thought seeing a ring would . . ." I'd thought I could keep this just between me and Dexter. That if I saw some rings, I'd either freak the fuck out and realize there was no way I could go through with Parker's scheme, or it would be no big deal and I could do this because it would help Parker, please Arthur, and make a real difference in people's lives.

"You thought seeing the rings would make up your mind?" Joshua asked. "Jesus, I think it should be about how you feel, not what the ring looks like."

"These are great rings, but I agree with Joshua. You shouldn't be deciding whether you propose by looking at rings."

I wish I'd brought my headphones. Or not come. It was like being pecked to death by a couple of overinvested star- lings. I pushed the box back toward Dexter. "Let's skip this. Forget I even asked. I wanted to meet you early so I didn't get into this with the whole bunch of you." I shot Joshua a look.

"I'll go and grab some wine for all of us. You two talk." Joshua pushed out his chair and stood. "Then I'll come back and you can repeat it. How about that?"

"Make sure you get the good stuff, you cheap bastard," Dexter said as Joshua headed out. He turned back to me. "Sorry if I said something I shouldn't have."

"They were all going to find out soon enough anyway." I'd invite them all to the ceremony, even if it wasn't for real.

"So who is this woman you're picking out rings for?"

I reached over for the velvet box and opened it. There must have been twenty rings staring back at me, but I was drawn to one immediately. A small emerald ring the same color as Parker's eyes.

"This is pretty, right?" I looked up.

"Yes. It's not traditional, but I love emeralds. And it's about as good quality as you can get. The diamonds either side are the same. Not the most expensive of the rings here —not by a long shot—but really nice, just the same."

"She wouldn't want flash," I replied. I picked out the ring from the box and looked at it more closely. It was small and a little quirky but pretty as hell. A lot like Parker.

"You want to tell me who *she* is?"

"It's not what you think. I'm considering doing a friend a favor."

Joshua poked his head around the door again.

"Come in. You might as well hear this from the horse's mouth. You can be the second person to tell me I'm being an idiot."

As Joshua poured out our wine, I began to tell them all about the auction, the date, and Parker's proposition.

"But do you like her? Or at least want to bang her?" Joshua asked. "It could get complicated."

If she wasn't Arthur's daughter, my answer would be a definite yes. But I couldn't unlink her from the man to whom I owed so much.

"It won't get complicated. Arthur means too much to me."

"And he's fine with it?" Dexter asked.

"More than fine. He's positively encouraging me to do it."

"And it's just ninety days?"

"Yeah, we can split after then, although I think a divorce takes a year—We can't get an annulment or the whole thing doesn't work."

"Are you okay with that?" Joshua asked.

"I'm trying to think of a reason why I wouldn't be. You all will know. Arthur knows. I'd have to figure out something with my parents, but it's doable. It doesn't have to be a big deal if we don't let it be a big deal. Right?"

"I guess," Dexter said. "I just know that marrying Hollie felt . . . special."

"But it doesn't have to, right?" I asked. Just because it was one way for Dexter didn't mean that it had to be that way for me.

"Nothing in the rule book says you have to marry for love," Joshua said.

"Exactly, and it's not like it's forever. Worst-case scenario, it will be over in a year. We won't have to live together after ninety days."

"You have to live with each other?"

"The rules of the trust state that it has to be a proper marriage. If we don't live together, how is that a marriage? Anyway, as long as I keep her in bananas and chocolate-covered raisins, I think she'll be fine." I grinned at her borderline obsession with the snack. I could think of worse obsessions.

"Chocolate-covered what now?"

"It doesn't matter. Point is, she won't be hard work to live with. She's been staying with me the last couple days and she—"

"She's staying with you? Why? Are you shagging?" Dexter asked.

"No. Definitely no shagging. She needed a place and— it's not a big deal."

Dexter and Joshua exchanged a look. It was clear they weren't entirely approving. I got it. They were both with women they wanted to spend the rest of their lives with. My relationship with Parker wasn't going to be that kind of marriage. I was doing her a favor. A favor that had the potential to keep together families that would otherwise fall apart. Love may be a good reason to get married, but I'd never heard of better reasons than the ones Parker and I would be marrying for.

All twenty-five million of them.

TEN

Tristan

I couldn't wipe the grin from my face as I turned the key in the lock and opened my front door. "Hi honey, I'm home," I called.

It was Parker's third night at my place, and I planned to tell her tonight that I agreed to her marriage scheme. I wasn't quite sure how exactly. Obviously, I'd never fake-proposed to anyone in my life. It wasn't usually difficult for me to ask for what I wanted—and I definitely did want to marry Parker. It was just that, even though our marriage would be fake, I liked her. I found her attractive. If she wasn't Arthur's daughter, I'd certainly have tried to seduce her by now. And that complicated things. Slightly.

"Hey, I'm in the kitchen." Of course she was. She loved my kitchen. When the time came for her to move out, I wasn't sure I'd be able to drag her away.

"I hope my dinner's on the table."

I set down my messenger bag and headed to the kitchen,

following the smell of home-cooked food. Marrying Parker just for her cooking ability wouldn't be a terrible idea.

She bounced up and down on her tiptoes as I came in, her hands behind her back, grinning at me like it was my birthday. "I cooked again. This kitchen is my spiritual home. I may never leave."

I glanced up. The lights were dimmed and the table was set for two.

"This looks cozy."

"Doesn't it though?" she said. "Did you even know you had candles in your uber-tidy drawers?"

"I didn't," I confessed, selecting a bottle from the wine fridge. "But they look good." I pulled two glasses from the cabinet and uncorked the wine. And then I caught sight of what Parker was wearing.

A shorter-than-short red skirt, matching lipstick, and what looked suspiciously like one of my white business shirts.

Whatever she was heating up on the hob, she looked like a mighty fine main course. I wanted to stalk over to her, circle my hands around her waist, and bury my face in her neck. I wanted to knee her legs wide and reach up under her skirt and rip off her underwear.

I needed to muster a little self-control. I wasn't a horny teenager. Typically, I loved to charm and flatter women. A good bit of flirting made a woman feel sexy, and that confidence was my catnip. It felt unnatural for me to hold back with Parker, but I'd resisted so far. Still, there was something about her that just drew me in, made me want to listen to what she had to say, and watch as she tucked her hair around her ear, enjoy the blush that crept up her cheeks when I made the most innocent of remarks.

I'd always seen flirting as a way of creating a connection, but maybe all this time, I'd been putting up a barrier. Although I couldn't understand why I would want to.

"I like your outfit," I said, skirting dangerously close to being flirtatious.

She spun around from where she was facing the hob and grinned at me. "You don't mind?" She tugged on the collar of my shirt that she was wearing. "It was hanging in my wardrobe."

I could see a corner of her white lace bra, where she hadn't done the buttons up high enough. My cock twitched.

Shit. Arthur's daughter, you creep.

"You don't have to pretend you haven't snooped," I teased. I knew she hadn't. I had a security system in my house that told me when each room of the house had been accessed.

"What are you talking about? Of course I haven't snooped. Granted, only because I assume the place is full of hidden cameras. You're so paranoid, Tristan."

I chuckled. "Maybe. Better to be safe than sorry. Speaking of, I noticed you haven't had any more unauthorized payments leave your account for the last couple of days."

"Nope. Maybe whoever they are have gone to bother someone else. Does that mean I can go back to my flat?"

I hadn't managed to find details on either of the companies that had been filtering funds from the charity bank account, but neither had I found anything concrete that I could point to and say, "See, that makes me uncomfortable." There were just a few things that lay like sludge in my gut and told me that I should say no. I should say anything that would keep her here. Safe with me.

"Let's talk about it over dinner." Hopefully she'd get

distracted by the emerald I had burning in my pocket and she wouldn't mention it again. "What are you making?"

"Man food," she said brightly. "Beef bourguignon."

My stomach rumbled. "Smells good. You're a great cook." I was terrible unless I set aside the entire day, and even then I had to carefully follow a recipe. Cooking for myself at the end of the day was just time out of my working day that I resented. It was why I ate out a lot.

"Thanks. I enjoy it."

"It isn't a real strength of mine."

"Why is it that when you say it like that, I can't help but think of what isn't a strength of mine? Like . . . I'm really not into home organization."

"Really? I never would have guessed." Her flat was stuffed full of things like it was some hoarder museum. "At least you're small so you don't need much room among your junk."

"Hey. That junk is *my* junk." She grinned at me. "It's all sentimental stuff." She glanced around. "Can you hand me some dishes?"

I handed her the white bowls my interior designer had picked out for me.

"Your china is really nice," she said as she ladled in the stew.

"I can't take any credit," I said. "The woman who designed the interior picked them."

She turned to me. "I guess it makes sense you didn't pick everything out. You're busy and I'm sure it's not top of your priority list, but it's all so *you*. It fits you perfectly."

"I'll take that as a compliment." *So me?* I liked that it was important to her that things people surrounded themselves with reflected who they were. I hoped she thought the same thing about the ring I'd picked out. It was how I saw her: simply beautiful. I hoped it was how she saw herself.

We finished dishing up dinner and took our now almost-familiar positions opposite each other around my dining table.

"This feels . . . nice," she said. "Unless you want me to turn the light up?"

The candlelight was romantic. Perfect for a proposal, even if it was a fake one.

"I've been thinking about what you said the other day about your trust fund," I said. "And how you want access so you can use the money for your charities."

Her eyes brightened and it was like sunshine through stained glass. It lit her up. "You have an idea? I've spoken to lawyers but they always tell me the same thing—the rules can't be changed."

"I think we should get married."

Her fork was midway between her bowl and her mouth and she froze, staring at me as if she wasn't quite sure she'd heard me right.

"You know," I said. "So you can get access to your trust." In my head, I knew that she knew this wasn't a real proposal. But I just wanted to make doubly sure.

She was knocked out of her suspended animation like a stuck record that had been freed, and she grinned. "Really? Tristan? You'll marry me for ninety days?"

Warmth burrowed into my stomach at seeing her so happy.

"Sure. No big deal, right?"

"What about you not wanting to upset Arthur?"

I shrugged. "Like you said, I'm going to be his son-in-law. How will that upset him?" To distract her from any potential pitfalls, I pulled out the ring box from my pocket and slid it onto the table between us. "I figured you're going to need a ring if we're going to pull this off."

"You got a ring?" Her eyes grew large. She seemed momentarily hypnotized by the box. "I could have gotten a ring."

"I think that's normally the groom's job."

She pulled in a big breath and shook her head. "I can't believe it. All that money—just think of all the things we're going to be able to do, Tristan. It's going to be amazing for all those families."

She hadn't asked to see the ring and I had a twinge of regret that it wasn't important to her. But of course she was focused on her charity. After all, that was the reason we were getting married.

"I hope so," I said.

"I guarantee it. There's going to be so much good I can do." She glanced at the box. "I know it's not real and everything, but can I see the ring?"

A tightness in my chest loosened. "Of course. I bought it for you."

She smiled and I opened the box for her to see.

She flattened her palm against her cheek and sighed. "It's beautiful, Tristan. Really beautiful. And . . ." She glanced at me. "If I was going to pick out an engagement ring, this would be the exact ring that I would choose. It's . . . it's perfect. It's completely believable that this is something I'd wear."

I bloody knew it.

"Try it on," I said.

"I suppose I could. To see if it fits at least."

Tentatively, she reached for the ring and slid it on. This was a fake proposal—she knew it and I knew it—but there was an unexpected gravity to the moment that took me by surprise. Whether or not we were in love, the woman opposite was going to be my wife.

"It looks beautiful on you," I said.

A sweep of red tinged her cheeks. "I suppose we should start to discuss logistics," she said as she slipped the ring off her finger and put it back in the box.

I frowned. "You should keep it on. We're engaged now."

The corners of her mouth twitched like she wasn't sure whether I was joking, but she put the ring back on. "As far as I'm concerned, the sooner we can sign those papers, the better."

"You're thinking we should elope?" I asked, turning my attention back to the stew.

She sighed. "I wish. But we can't. My mother and father eloped and it caused shockwaves in the family. My grandmother didn't speak to my mother for years after their wedding. My mother made me promise that I'd never do anything like that again."

"Okay. No elopement. But we can say we don't want a big wedding, right? Your parents don't get to choose that."

"Absolutely. And I agree that the fewer people we lie to, the better."

"I'm going to have to figure out what to do with my parents. I don't think they would be understanding about our ruse, which means I'm going to have to lie to them. I don't feel great about it but I don't see another way."

"Okay," she said. "That makes sense. The fewer people who know, the better. The key people we need to convince are my parents and the trustees. But it needs to look like a real wedding."

"It's going to be a real wedding," I said. "Which means you're going to have to move in here. Seeing as you're here already, and we're going to get married as soon as possible, you might as well stay."

Her back straightened and she pulled her eyebrows together. "Why would you assume we're going to move into your place? Maybe I want us both to live—"

I fixed her with a look. "You don't need me to tell you why we're going to live at my place. It's ten times the size, and doesn't look like it's a museum of holiday mementos. If you think I'm going to squeeze myself into your flat, I'll have that ring back."

She rolled her eyes and I fought my grin at her faux indignation. There was no way she imagined I'd agree to move into her place. "I suppose. It's going to be weird being a lodger in someone else's house for months on end. I'm going to get far too used to this kitchen." She looked over at my kitchen wistfully. "We might have to agree on visitation rights when all this is over."

"Visitation rights for my kitchen?" I chuckled.

"It's a great kitchen."

I couldn't argue with that. And if she could produce meals like this in here, she was welcome any time she wanted.

ELEVEN

Parker

Most women would be ecstatic at the thought of marrying Tristan Dubrow. I thought *I'd* be ecstatic at the idea that I was finally going to get my hands on my trust fund. It was just that when Sutton and I had brainstormed the idea of me getting fake married, I hadn't thought through how many people I'd have to pretend to.

"You okay?" Tristan asked. He locked the car and turned to me as I stared up at my parents' house.

"I hope they believe us."

He scooped up my hand in his and guided me to the door. "Only one way to find out."

I stared at our joined hands and up at Tristan. A little over a week ago, I'd never met this man, and now here I was, about to announce to my parents that we were getting married. It didn't help that he seemed so relaxed about it. Tristan seemed to take everything in his stride. He didn't seem to mind the fact that I'd completely taken over in the kitchen. I'd rearranged his cupboards so everything I needed for cooking was instinctively where it should be. I'd made a space on the hallway table where I put his unopened mail. I'd bought fresh flowers for the dining table.

He hadn't raised a single complaint.

"You know you're a great fake fiancé," I said.

He squeezed my hand and I felt oddly comforted as he lifted the giant door knocker on my parents' front door. I'd called them, Tristan by my side, the evening after he proposed. They'd insisted we come to dinner the following evening. So here we were.

"Not so bad yourself."

"I wish we'd just eloped," I said. "You think we can pull this off?"

"Absolutely." He sounded so sure. Then again, Tristan always sounded sure about everything.

My mother flung open the door. "Parker. My baby." Was she getting emotional? "I never thought I'd see this day." She pulled me into a tight hug and then practically threw me to the side when she spotted Tristan.

"You must be my future son-in-law."

Tristan extended his hand but she completely ignored him and pulled him into a hug. "I'm so pleased you're joining the family."

An hour and a half after her hug had become awkwardly long, she finally released him and pulled him inside. "Come through to the garden. We can have drinks before dinner and I can show you a few things."

"Sounds great," Tristan said and grabbed my hand. Thank God he seemed more adept at acting like a newly engaged couple than me.

My heart sunk to my knees as we made our way through the house to the back and the garden came into view. Several tables were arranged around the garden, each covered in different flower arrangements. What had my mother been doing?

"I thought we'd kill two birds with one stone," she said, pre-empting me asking what the holy hell was happening. She turned to us and grinned. "I've got Lauren here to help." I did my best not to roll my eyes.

Lauren was my mum's best friend and a party planner extraordinaire among London's wealthy. Lauren had never heard of the phrase "less is more" and thought a party wasn't a party unless there were at least two hundred and fifty guests, Ed Sheeran performing, and lobster served at a sit-down dinner.

Lauren being here was a disaster.

"Parker!" Lauren said as she held my face in her hands. "I never thought I'd see the day when I'd be planning your wedding. We're going to pull out all the stops, aren't we, Michele? Let me tell you, after all these years, your wedding is going to be the event of the decade. We're talking world-wide infamy." She gestured at the sky as if it were God she was trying to convince. "But we're going to start with the engagement party. Just an intimate thing. Depending on Tristan's guest list we thought—Tristan!" Lauren shrieked, when she finally realized she'd not even acknowledged my fiancé. "Tristan, my darling." She grabbed his face and kissed him on the cheek.

Tristan just wasn't ready for the women in my family. Lauren might not be a blood relation but she was always there at every important family occasion—Sunday lunches, Friday dinners, weddings, funerals, graduations, and Christmas. And she'd organized most of them.

"So," Lauren continued. "As I was saying, Michele and I have been talking and started to put together a guest list for the engagement party. Depending on the size of your list, Tristan, we were thinking five hundred, maybe the ballroom at the Dorchester or—"

"Lauren, I'm delighted to meet you," Tristan interrupted. "When you say five hundred, are you talking about number of guests?"

"Yes, my love. About the same at the wedding."

"No," I said. "Tristan and I want a small wedding. Very small. Minute in fact."

"I had to talk her out of eloping," he said.

My mother and Lauren gasped.

"You're not eloping, Parker," my mother said, in the same tone she used when I was sixteen and wanted to go to Ibiza. "We're going to have an engagement party. And then you're going to have a proper wedding like I've always dreamed for you."

A big fairy-tale wedding may have always been my mother's dream for me, but it had never been my dream. I wasn't wealthy and my wedding should reflect that.

"Mummy, Tristan and I just want something small. Perhaps we could do something out here," I said, hoping that the idea of throwing the wedding in the back garden would distract her from the idea of five hundred guests in a ballroom on Park Lane.

"Here?" she said. "In our back garden?"

"Let me think," Lauren said. "Let me think . . . Yes. We can put a marquee over the tennis court. Have the sit-down there. Then we can do drinks closer to the house—Yes! We can get a smattering of bandstands erected across the lawns where people can shelter if it rains. That gives us something to decorate with flowers. I can see it."

Just before Lauren started telling me which flowers she thought would be best, my father joined us.

"Congratulations to the happy couple," he said as he

approached with a bottle of champagne. "Let's all have a drink."

It was only then that I focused more clearly on what had been set up in the garden. There were ten round tables set out on the lawn, all decorated differently with flowers and chairs and from what I could see from here, china. They had wanted to kick off wedding planning already. My heart sank. I was happy my mom and Lauren were happy for me, but I felt bad that this wasn't a real wedding. This time next year, I'd be divorced.

My father poured us all some drinks and raised his glass. "Here's to my darling daughter and your fiancé. Parker, you're one of the sweetest, kindest, most generous people on the planet, and I'm very proud of you. I'm happy and relieved that you've found a man who will put you first, even if you won't do it for yourself. Tristan, you're focused and clever and I know you to be a man of honor. Welcome to the family."

I scooped an arm around my father's waist and leaned into him. I'd never had any doubt my father loved me. I just hoped he forgave me when Tristan and I divorced as quickly as we'd decided to get married.

"Now we all have drinks," Lauren said as she strode across the lawn toward the prepared tables. She waved for us to follow. "If we're having the engagement party right here, then it's a great time to look at table decoration and settings. I've set up some options so you can get a feel for what you like."

I sighed and Tristan squeezed my hand. He was so much better at faking this than I was. "Sounds great," he said as he followed Lauren, pulling me with him.

"The baby pink roses are always a popular choice but —" She held up her hand. "I know you don't necessarily follow the most popular route on these things, so I also have other designs with more of an eclectic look.

"Look at this one," Lauren said, guiding us toward the table under the willow tree where I used to practice my handstands. "This is dried flowers and grasses. It's a very new look. Not something that would appeal to everyone but I thought you might like it."

I nodded, trying to be enthusiastic. "I like it."

"I'm not so keen," Tristan said. "There's something wrong about surrounding people with dead flowers at a wedding."

Lauren gave a nervous I-don't-agree-but-whatever-you-say laugh and took us over to the next table. "You might feel the same about this one." She led us to a table set up in front of the summer house. "It's paper flowers and paper mâché sculptures. Everything's recyclable." It looked like the art classroom of a kindergarten.

"It's very colorful," I said, trying to sound positive. Lauren had us choosing flowers and centerpieces when we hadn't even decided the number of guests that would be invited.

"But other than the more traditional tables, this is my favorite." She arced her hand toward the next table with a flourish, like she was the prima ballerina at the Royal Ballet.

I had to hand it to Lauren, the table looked amazing. Instead of the usual pale pinks and creams, the table was covered in bright blue and purple flowers.

"It's a little more informal than the traditional look. The moss, together with the verbena and the blue boy, gives the feeling of summer meadows."

"I like it," Tristan said.

I looked up at him and he looked genuinely enthusiastic. "It's very you," he said and he bent and placed a kiss on my forehead. If I hadn't known it was an act, I would have fallen hook, line, and sinker for the way he looked at me.

"Well, we don't have to decide now," I said. "We don't even know if we want a sit-down meal at the wedding—"

"These table settings are for the engagement party but of course you'll have a formal meal at both of them," Lauren interrupted. "There are a lot of people who've waited a long time for this moment, Parker. People will want to celebrate with you."

"But you're not suggesting that we marquee the tennis courts just for the engagement party?" I turned to my mother for backup, then glanced at my father. I should have known better. He wasn't going to veto my mother on this kind of thing. And my mother loved to throw parties at the best of times, let alone when her daughter got married. Bloody Sutton, if it wasn't for her, I wouldn't have even suggested the wedding thing to Tristan and we wouldn't be stood around my parent's garden planning a wedding that would rival Will and Kate's.

"What about a compromise?" Tristan suggested. "Either a small, intimate engagement party with a sit-down dinner and then a large, informal wedding, with just drinks and canapes. Or a large engagement party with a very small wedding?"

"Or what about no engagement party with a very small wedding at a registry office," I countered.

"Absolutely not," my mother said. "Think of your father's business. Just with his top associates at the bank and then some of his major clients, that's eighty to one hundred people."

I groaned. "This isn't a business event. This is my wedding."

"I agree," my father said. "We can get that number down significantly."

"How many people do you want to invite?" my mother asked Tristan.

"Twelve," Tristan replied.

My mother stole a glance at my father who was nodding.

"Just twelve?" Lauren asked. "Is that just family and then you want friends and business associates and—"

"Twelve people all together at both the engagement party and the wedding."

Lauren sighed. "Well, that does free up some space. Perhaps we can pare things back a little and—"

"We could do twelve as well," I suggested. "Then it's evenly matched."

My father started to laugh. "Good luck with that."

"Either way, we don't want some ridiculously big do," I said. It was going to be embarrassing enough to tell everyone we were divorcing.

"I know you don't like being the center of attention," Lauren said. "But it's your *wedding* day."

Silence descended on the group like a grey cloud in a summer sky.

"I've got it!" Lauren clicked her fingers in the air like she'd just performed magic. "The engagement party is held here at the house. We go all out. Outdoor chandeliers, live music, ice sculptures, flowers wherever you look." This wasn't sounding like the small, intimate gathering I'd hoped for. "We call it a party to celebrate your marriage. It's not an engagement party. It's not a wedding. It's just a party. But it's big, and fun, and informal. And then you have a small wedding of twenty—or maybe fifty of the people closest to you."

Tristan squeezed my hand. "How do you feel about that?" he asked, his tone hushed, and even though my parents and Lauren could all hear, I appreciated him making it just about the two of us for the first time since we'd stepped through my parents' front door.

"How do you feel?" Not only did I not want to make a big fuss about marrying a man who I'd be a stranger to once our divorce was finalized, but I didn't want to put Tristan through it. Our relationship was faked and Tristan seemed like a good guy. I wanted to downplay this entire thing.

"I think it sounds like a good compromise," he said. "I like the idea of the actual wedding being small."

"Okay," I said, nodding. "Okay," I said to Lauren. "Big party. Small wedding. But the wedding has got a cap of twenty-five—including everyone standing right here."

Lauren opened her mouth to speak and my dad cut her off. "Good, glad that's sorted out. Shall we all have another glass of champagne? It's not every day that I gain a son-in-law."

"Yes," Lauren said. "Another glass of champagne will help loosen everyone up. I thought we might take a couple of pictures that we could incorporate into the invitation boxes."

"Pictures? Invitation boxes?" We should have eloped.

"Pictures of the happy couple. We don't have to use them but they'll be nice sentimental keepsakes if nothing else. I've set up my camera down by the willow trees—as you know I'm quite the amateur photographer since I did that evening class with the WI. I'm confident I can capture the love you have for each other in the lens of my camera."

It took everything I had not to groan. Photographs? Really? I felt terrible lying in ordinary conversation to the three people in front of me. I wasn't sure how I was going to pose with Tristan and make everyone believe we were in love. "We were thinking of getting something professional done."

Lauren scowled at me. "Oh you don't need to bother. The lighting here is just beautiful this afternoon and we can make them black and white—they're going to look just as good as the professionals. I've gotten really quite good, even if I do say so myself."

"Sounds fun," Tristan said from beside me.

He couldn't possibly be serious.

Lauren beamed at him and she led us back to the willow tree, my parents following us.

As Lauren fiddled with her camera, Tristan bent and whispered in my ear. "Stop freaking out. It won't take much to be convincing. Follow my lead and everything will be fine. People believe what they want to believe." He snaked an arm around my waist and I tried to ignore the heat of his large hand on my hip. As he pulled me toward him, I stumbled and fell into him. My hand reached for him to stop myself from falling. It was like pressing my hand into a tree trunk. I guess that's why it felt like I was running into a wall when I bumped into him in the hotel lobby.

"Oh that's a lovely shot," Lauren called. "Hold that pose."

Tristan grinned down at me.

"Does she know I tripped?" Neither Lauren nor my parents could hear us—they were a few meters away and chatting amongst themselves.

"You're adorable," he said, circling his other hand around my waist and bringing me upright and tight against his oh-so-hard body.

"You're hard." I prodded my finger into his chest.

I glanced up at him and he was chuckling. "Not a problem yet, but the afternoon's not over."

I rolled my eyes and hoped it took his attention from the blush I felt burning into my cheeks. "I didn't mean—you know what I meant."

"You're particularly adorable when you're blushing."

"I don't blush," I said.

"Oh I disagree. You blush a lot. It's one of my favorite things about you."

One of?

Before I had a chance to respond, Lauren marched over and began to manhandle us. "Such a gorgeous couple." She lifted my arm and placed my hand flat on Tristan's rock-hard pec and then did the same with the other hand. "Now look into each other's eyes."

Tristan grinned like he knew what we were doing was absolutely insane but he was enjoying himself anyway and I couldn't help but smile at his amusement. The laughter lines around his eyes were out in full swing and without thinking, I reached up and smoothed my fingers over them.

"Absolutely gorgeous," Lauren shouted from some-where. "You two are perfect together."

Despite the fact that we weren't together, there was something about that moment with him that did feel abso-lutely perfect. He was so calm and relaxed and so completely at ease; it felt like all of that was somehow seeping into me, making me believe we could actually pull this fake marriage thing off. It was me that had initiated this entire fake proposal, but it was Tristan who was making sure it happened. Like he was invested in this just as much as I was—like he was my rock-solid partner in crime.

TWELVE

Tristan

I watched as Parker fiddled with the flowers she'd put in a vase I didn't know I owned. Her apron was lower than her very short black skirt and for a flash, I wondered if we were a real couple, was this the time—just minutes before guests arrived—when I'd sneak up behind her, smooth my palm up her inside thigh, push my fingers into her folds, and take her right up to the brink before the doorbell went. She'd have to spend the rest of the evening wondering when she'd finally get her orgasm.

"What are you thinking?" she asked. "What have I forgotten?"

I wasn't about to confess I was wondering how easy it would be to bring her to the edge of her climax. "The table looks great. You need me to help with anything?"

"I don't think so."

"You didn't need to go to all this effort, you know." She'd spent most of the day cooking while I worked. I'd offered to help but I got the impression cooking was how she worked things out. That and eating chocolate-covered raisins. "We could have called caterers. Maybe you're a bit more like Lauren than you think."

"Believe me, if Lauren was hosting this dinner party, there would be an ice sculpture somewhere and we'd be having at least five courses. I've made soup and roast chicken. No one's going to be impressed."

"I will be. My friends won't care what we serve, and their wives and girlfriends will just want to snoop around my house. They always complain they don't ever get invited over."

She nodded and tucked her hair behind her ear, betraying her nerves. "At least we don't have to pretend."

"Right. It's not like anyone is going to ask us about wedding planning." Last Saturday at her parents' place was the first time I saw Parker really wound up. Her mother and Lauren had acted like it was their wedding. I didn't ask why they had to be involved at all, since it was clear they had more than an equal say in the wedding. Didn't make much sense to me, but I stayed quiet because it wasn't my battle to fight.

She groaned. "Speaking of, Lauren called me today to ask me if we wanted to do a tasting of the canapes being served at the party."

"Okay," I said, treading carefully. "You want me to come with you?"

She shook her head and peeled off her apron. "No. I told her to send us the menu. She doesn't know it yet, but I'm going to just pick whatever we need without tasting. Does anyone really care what canapes taste like? It's one mouthful."

She'd read my mind.

"If you don't care what they taste like, you could tell her you value her input and ask her to pick for you."

"Which she will do anyway unless I'm prepared to throw down."

"Exactly. Save your energy for your charity and compliment her at the same time."

"I'd like to, but I've not been in the office for a week now. Can I go back in on Monday?"

Lucky for me, before I could answer, there was a knock at the door. "Our guests," I said.

"Tristan. Can I go back in on Monday?" She followed me down the hallway.

The fact was I'd not discovered anything more about the fraudulent withdrawals from the charity account or the potential break-in at her flat. I'd broken into the local street CCTV and next door's cameras, and nothing looked odd or out of place. Either there was nothing to worry about because the payments and the incident at her flat were coincidences, or the fact that everything looked like a series of coincidences was cause for serious concern. Someone could be going to great lengths to maintain Parker's illusion of safety while behind the scenes, they chipped away at the charity she'd worked so hard to support. Either way, I couldn't keep her a prisoner at my place any longer.

"Tristan," she said as I reached the door. "Don't ignore me. I want an answer."

"Yes," I said. "Yes, you can go back to work."

She grinned up at me and lust crawled up my spine. That smile. That red lipstick. That beautiful mouth.

"Thank you. You see? Our first engaged-couple spat and we came out the other end. Oh hang on. Shoes. They're going to think we're the most ridiculously ill-matched couple." She slipped into higher-than-high, shiny black shoes and finally gave me the nod to open the front door.

"Hello!" Hollie said. "You must be Tristan's fiancée." She completely ignored me, pushed past me, and flung her arms around Parker. "I'm Hollie. And you're a shortie, too. These men are so tall. It's insane. I have a permanent crick in my neck."

"We're all the same height lying down," Dexter called from behind Hollie. "Let her go. She's British and not used to all your American effervescence."

Hollie released Parker and Dexter leaned in to give her a kiss on the cheek. "I'm Dexter."

"Hi, both of you. Oh, and Dexter, you're the man to thank for the ring. It's going to be hard to give up when the time comes."

"If," Hollie said.

"I'm sorry? I didn't hear you," Parker said.

Did Hollie just say "if" as in *if* the time comes? Had Dexter not told her our arrangement?

"Oh nothing. I didn't get to see the ring." Hollie glanced down at Parker's hand. "You don't have it on?"

I began to usher everyone through to the kitchen. "Everyone here tonight knows the deal. Parker doesn't need to wear the ring. She's among friends."

"Of course she is," Hollie replied. "But why wouldn't she wear the ring? It's gorgeous. And she's your fiancée."

Parker glanced back at me and I rolled my eyes. "Ignore her."

"Do you know," Dexter said, "you're going to be the third guy in our group to get married, despite Gabriel, Joshua, and Andrew being engaged for longer."

We arrived in the kitchen and Parker handed out

glasses of champagne. We were celebrating, after all. Sort of.

"Well, they've always been a little slow," I said.

"Apparently Hartford and Joshua want a venue that's booked up two years in advance," Dexter said.

"You mean Joshua does. Why doesn't he pay someone to cancel?" I asked.

"The kind of people who have their wedding at Claridge's don't appreciate a payoff," Dexter replied. "No one in June would move, apparently."

"London is nice in June," Dexter said. "Not too hot. Less chance of rain. People haven't started taking their summer holidays. June is good. I suppose that's why everyone wants it." Dexter nudged Parker. "Honestly, looking back, I wish we'd just eloped. Planning is so bloody stressful."

Parker groaned. "Tell me about it. We're not even properly getting married and it's already too much."

I shrugged. "Happy to elope."

Dexter chuckled. "Words I never thought I'd hear coming out of your mouth."

"Exceptional circumstance," I muttered.

"Yes," Hollie said. "You're an exceptional man for an exceptional woman." She turned to Parker. "You're gorgeous, by the way. That blunt black bob and red lip combo is hot as."

I leaned over to Parker to loud whisper in her ear. "American. She can't help it."

"Hey, Tristan," Hollie said, glaring at me. "I hope to God you're not saying that Parker isn't gorgeous and I know for a fact you're a sucker for red lipstick."

Hollie had backed me into a corner and she knew it. Of course Parker was gorgeous but to admit that would be playing into Hollie's hands. Before I knew it, she'd be trying to turn my fake relationship into something real. But if I denied it, I'd be lying and might upset Parker—neither of which I wanted to do.

"I'm not saying another word about anything because I know you'll use it against me." The doorbell went. "Saved by the bell."

I glanced over at Parker to check she was okay that I left her to fend for herself. She nodded, her nervous tic—tucking her hair behind her ears—noticeably absent. I headed back out into the hall. Sofia, Andrew, Joshua, and Harford were on the step.

"Remember, we're doing this so you're all introduced before the wedding party so it doesn't look weird that my friends don't know her. You're not meeting my fiancée."

Andrew barged past me, not saying a word, and Sofia followed. "It'll be fine, Tristan. You don't have to explain anything to us. We're going to make your girlfriend feel super-welcome."

I groaned. Had they not all read the memo? Parker and I weren't really together. This was not a real thing.

"She cooked, Tristan. Did you see this?" Hollie said. "This is like the second time I've been over the threshold in your house and the first time it didn't really count because I let myself in to get that tool thingy Dexter wanted. This time, not only have you invited me, but I'm getting fed and being handed wine. I always knew you'd mature as soon as you got a serious girlfriend."

I wondered if it was even worth responding. I needed to distract them all so they weren't focusing on me and Parker.

"How's the baby?" I asked Sofia.

"Urgh. I hate being pregnant. My feet are swelling and so is my ass."

"You look fantastic," Andrew barked, rubbing his hand over Sofia's ever-expanding stomach. "Went for a scan today. She looks bloody beautiful even now."

"When are you due?" Parker asked, handing Andrew a glass of champagne and Sofia a glass of something nonalcoholic she'd had delivered by Uber Eats about an hour ago after I'd mentioned that Sofia was pregnant.

"I have four and a half months to go. Can you believe it? Already some days I want to reach in there and get her out already."

"It will go by in a flash," Parker said.

"That's what everyone keeps telling me," Sofia said. "Hopefully the wedding will distract me. It's only five weeks away. You're both coming, right?"

"Wouldn't miss it," I said. Five weeks? Parker and I would probably be married before Andrew and Sofia.

"Tristan and Parker first," Dexter said, reading my thoughts. He chuckled and helped himself to a top up. I was being the worst host. I just wasn't used to people in my house for dinner. I was used to going to Beck and Stella's or Gabriel and Autumn's and having everything laid on. "And you said you'd never get married. I always knew you were full of shit, Tristan, but this just proves it."

"Slightly different circumstances," I replied. I'd expected a roasting from my friends about marrying Parker, and I didn't mind their ribbing. I just worried Parker would. She didn't know that taking the piss was Dexter's love language. He didn't need to tell me he loved me for me to know it. Parker didn't know him like I did.

"Give him a break," Hartford said as she took a glass of champagne from Parker, who was being the perfect hostess.

It was sweet of Hartford to stick up for me and I winked at her, trying to communicate that their joshing was like water off a duck's back. I appreciated her support, but it really wasn't necessary. My friends were all incredibly driven, successful people and roasting me was the way they let off steam. It had been the same since we were all teenagers. It didn't bother me one bit. I knew they didn't mean it and even if they did, I knew most of what they were saying wasn't true.

"You're Arthur Frazer's daughter?" Andrew asked and my jaw tightened. Sometimes Andrew could be fucking insensitive.

"She's Parker Frazer. Try talking to her to find out who she is rather than who her father is," I said, shooting Andrew a warning look. Me, they could pick on. Parker was off limits. "Don't mind Andrew, Parker. He's insensitive to anyone's emotions and completely focused on himself, but I love him just the same. He's my Lauren-equivalent."

Parker gave me a small smile and I pushed a glass of champagne into her hand.

"Yes, I'm Arthur's daughter," she said.

Andrew nodded. "He's a good guy. Came across him a few times over the years."

"You're right," Parker replied. "He is a good guy."

"And he seems reasonable. Why has he made it a stipulation of your trust that you be married? That seems entirely unreasonable."

Trust Andrew to be so bloody blunt.

"Andrew," I said, wanting to distract his attention.

"It's fine," Parker said, tucking her hair behind her ear. "He did it a while ago. I had a . . . boyfriend that turned out to be a bit of a shit. I think this was his way of encouraging me not to turn my back on a serious relationship."

This was the first I was hearing about this. I was pretty sure I'd asked her why Arthur had made the marriage stipulation, but maybe I hadn't. "You were serious with the guy who was a piece of shit?" I asked.

"Yeah. I mean, he proposed and I said yes and I thought he was going to be the man I'd spend the rest of my life with, so I think that qualifies as serious."

The room was entirely silent now, everyone's gaze fixed on Parker. My heart was pounding in my chest for reasons I couldn't fully explain.

"What happened?" I asked.

She glanced over to the kitchen like she was looking for an excuse not to have to answer any more questions. "Turns out that he was after my money. Or my father's anyway."

What?

The cooking timer in the kitchen went off. Parker set down her glass and went to see to the food. I followed. "Why don't you all take a seat at the table," I called over my shoulder.

Even though we were only meters away from each other, I wanted to be closer to her—for her to know I was there if old wounds had been opened up.

"You okay?" I asked.

"I'm fine," she said, tucking her hair behind her ears and not meeting my eye. "Can you pass me the soup bowls?"

"I didn't know you were engaged," I said, setting the soup bowls beside her.

She shrugged. "It was a long time ago. I'm over it." There was an edge to her voice that told me that wasn't entirely true.

I searched for some words to make it better. She deserved someone who was with her because she was funny and kind and a great cook. Not someone who was just after her money. "He was clearly an idiot."

She nodded and began to ladle soup into the bowls.

"You're better off without him."

She nodded again and reached for another bowl.

"If you give me his name, I can make life pretty difficult for him. Impossible even."

She laughed. "Thank you." She turned and squeezed my arm. "I appreciate that, but really there's no need." We locked eyes and it was a moment of such intimacy that it took me by surprise.

She glanced away first. "You mind putting out the soup?"

"Absolutely. Smells delicious."

In some ways I felt as if I knew Parker better than I knew most people, but I'd just been reminded that there were a lot of things about her I didn't know. But the more I found out, the more I wanted to know.

THIRTEEN

Parker

I'd been engaged a grand total of nine days and was now just minutes away from the first guest arriving for our engagement party.

If only I'd stop sweating long enough to actually put my dress on. If only my heart would stop pounding so I could take a breath. If only I had a shot of tequila.

Someone knocked on the door to my old bedroom in my parents' house. "I'll be out in a minute." It was a lie. I figured I'd need more like forty-five to have a panic attack, recover, reapply my makeup, get dressed, and make it downstairs.

The door opened, just a crack. "Are you decent?" Tristan asked and I sent up a small thank-you to the gods that it was neither my mother nor Lauren.

"It depends if you have tequila or not."

He chuckled, that deep sound that seemed to make my bones shake, and gently pushed the door open with his foot. "I thought you might need a shot of courage." He held up a bottle and two shot glasses. He looked phenomenal. Tristan was one of those men who would look good whatever he wore, but in a bowtie and a dinner jacket, he was insanely attractive. His slightly too-long hair always looked like he'd been styled for some Gucci modelling shoot, but I knew this was how he looked about ten minutes after getting out of the shower after he'd towel-dried his hair.

"Get in here and lock the door."

He glanced behind him. "There's no lock."

I pulled open my dressing table drawer and brought out the rubber door stop I'd stolen from the school music room and wedged it under the door. "Wrong," I announced. "Get me some booze, like yesterday."

Tristan set down the glasses and poured us two shots of tequila and handed me one. I tried not to look at his long, tanned fingers as he reached out. His hands were enormous, with a smattering of hair on the back. His nails looked like he had regular manicures, although I couldn't imagine Tristan getting a manicure any more than I could imagine my father getting one—they both had far more important things to worry about. Tristan was just one of those men who made zero effort in his personal appearance but looked like he spent eighty percent of his time preening. It wasn't fair.

"We should cheers to us—the happy couple."

I groaned. "Tristan, come on."

"You need to get over yourself. So what if you're telling all your friends and family a gigantic lie." Tristan was grinning like someone who just had twenty-five million pounds land in his lap.

"It's not funny. Are you trying to make me feel worse?"

"It's a little bit funny. Take your shot. You'll feel better."

He clinked his glass to mine and tipped back his drink. I had nothing to lose at this point.

"No one is going to believe this. A month ago, I didn't even know you."

"When you know, you know." Tristan's cocky grin unfurled on his face like he hadn't a care in the world.

"How can you be so relaxed about this?"

"It's a party. The people here know and love you. What's to be stressed about?"

I put my head in my hands. What wasn't there to be stressed about? "Well if we skate past all the lying and deceit, what about the tens of thousands of dollars this party cost to put on?" I said. "For a lie."

"But your parents paid for it. They wouldn't accept anything from me."

I lowered my hands and looked at Tristan. "Wait, what? You offered to give my parents money?"

"For the party," he said. "It's my engagement too."

Getting to know Tristan these past days had been a revelation. At first pass, he was just some pretty computer geek who didn't have a care in the world. It didn't take long to discover there was much more to him than that. He was thoughtful—to his friends and to me. He was broad-shouldered in every sense of the phrase. And he was so kind.

"You are ridiculously kind. Stop that. It doesn't help."

"I think we need more tequila."

Maybe another shot would help. Maybe by the time I got downstairs I'd be a dribbling drunk mess and wouldn't care about any of this.

He poured out two more shots and took his immediately.

"I'm having a meltdown. What's your excuse for shots before a party?" I sipped my shot this time.

"Lying to people isn't my favorite thing to do in the world either, Parker. We've just got to keep our eye on the end game—twenty-five million for Sunrise. Speaking of . . ." He reached into his trouser pocket and pulled out a business card. "I asked Lauren to put one of these on each person's place setting." I took the card from him. "I thought Sunrise might get a few donations from it."

I looked down at the card and flipped it over. There was a QR code and a line that said, *Sunrise does important work for children with congenital heart defects. It's a cause important to Parker and Tristan. Every donation helps.*

A lump formed on in my throat and I swallowed. "That's really nice of you, Tristan." He was so kind. Why had I roped him into this crazy scheme? It was ridiculous.

He shrugged. "It's a very worthy cause." He sat on my childhood bed. "Are you going down in your robe?" He nodded toward the pink toweling robe I was wearing. I'd had it since I was fifteen.

"Maybe."

"You're going to have to put a smile on your face or everyone is going to know something is up."

"I know."

"So apart from the lying and the cheating and all the money your parents have spent on this party, what else is the problem?"

"Apart from all that?" I took the rest of my shot and leaned against my dressing table. "You know that every single person at this party is going to be staring at me. You too."

Tristan shrugged. "Who cares?"

"There will be no excuse to leave early and you won't be able to hide up here and avoid everyone."

Tristan stayed silent for a beat. "That wasn't my plan, but it sounds like it might have been yours."

"I just don't like parties."

"I gathered."

"And my mum told me she's got us a cake—can you believe that?"

"How terrible. What an awful mother, getting her newly engaged daughter a cake. What could she be thinking? We should call the police and have her arrested."

He might think it was no big deal, but I knew a cake meant a cake *cutting*. And that meant—urgh. I'd have to tell everyone I had a virus or something.

"I can see your mind ticking over. What aren't you telling me? This can't just be about the fact your mum bought you a cake."

"Put two and two together, Tristan. We're going to have to cut the cake. Together. And then people are going to expect us to kiss." I leaned against my dressing table.

Tristan raised his eyebrows. "Okay so . . . we'll kiss." He stood up and I looked away, embarrassed that we were having to discuss kissing like we were talking about groceries.

"In front of *everybody*." He clearly hadn't understood we were going to have to kiss for the first time in front of about four hundred people.

"Right. But unless you're telling me we're going to have to do that naked, I'm not quite sure what the problem is."

"We've never kissed before. We're probably going to bump noses. Or worse, I'm going to topple over because I'm bent over backward so you can reach me from up there."

Tristan stood and put his hands in his pockets. "I see the problem. Good thing there's still time. We can make a run for it. We can pretend we forgot a pair of shoes or something —leave them all to it. They won't miss us."

I growled and Tristan stepped nearer.

My heart began to rev like a Formula One racecar. I slid to the far side of my dressing table, but he just came closer. Then he stepped one leg over mine so my legs were trapped between his and slid his thumb under my chin.

"What are you doing?" My voice came out weak and unsteady.

"I figure since we've never kissed before, you might want to practice." My breath caught in my throat. I needed to inhale or I was going to pass out.

"See here, when you're leaning, you're even lower than when you stand—which is saying something, Cream Puff. But the amazing thing about human bodies is that they're meant to fit together." His voice had lowered and it felt like we were underwater. I couldn't hear properly and couldn't move. "I can still lean down to you like this." Slowly, he bent and lifted my chin so our faces were just millimeters away from each other. His breath was hot and fresh, and I shouldn't want him to kiss me as much as I did. There wasn't anything I wanted more in that moment. He was so calm and calming—his touch was lavender oil and a warm bath, sunshine and a glass of wine—yet he was in complete control at all times. He took my bottom lip in his mouth and clasped my face in his hands, his long fingers sliding into my hair as he guided me to my feet. All I could do was relax, knowing that Tristan had this. He knew what he was doing. I simply sank into his touch and enjoyed the firm press of his lips, absorbing the heat that spread from him to me and back.

I would have happily stayed like that for a thousand years, but we were interrupted by a knock at the door.

Tristan slowly pulled back. "You taste great." He fixed me with a look that said everything's going to be fine, then he headed to the door, removed the stop, and opened it a crack. "Hi, Michele. She's just getting changed. Do you need anything?"

I stood and tightened my robe like we'd been doing something we shouldn't.

"Nothing at all," my mom trilled from the hall. "I'll leave you lovebirds to it. I just wanted you to know that people will be starting to arrive in less than ten minutes."

Tristan nodded, shut the door, and turned to me.

"I should get changed," I said.

He pushed his hands into his pockets and looked at me from under his eyelashes, giving me a sexy, slightly dirty grin—like maybe I'd given him a little more than a kiss. "I'll leave you to get changed."

Just as he was leaving, he turned back to me. "Next time you want to kiss me, Parker, there's no need for a borderline anxiety attack. You just need to ask."

FOURTEEN

Tristan

I was about to head into my engagement party, holding my fiancée's hand. On the list of things I thought I'd never do, this would make the top three.

We reached the top of the stairs and I squeezed Parker's hand as if to say, *are you ready?* But she didn't respond. Instead she seemed transfixed by the people rushing in opposite directions below us. I was pretty sure she was going to bolt for the loo in three . . . two . . .

"You look beautiful," I whispered, hoping to put a halt to the thoughts I could practically see racing through her mind. We were already a few minutes late to our own party. But there was no doubt what I said was true.

"You look fantastic," she said. "But then again, you knew that already."

"I did?" Living with Parker, even for only a week and a half, meant I'd gotten to know her probably better than any other woman I'd ever been in a real relationship with. The more time we spent together, the more I liked her. Not only was she a fabulous cook, she was honest and driven to make things better for people.

She rolled her eyes. "Of course you did. You always look fantastic."

"You always say the nicest things to me." If I was going to get married for real, Parker Frazer would make a really great fiancée. I always felt better when she was around.

I squeezed her hand. "Don't let go. Together we've got this."

She nodded like she wanted to believe me but wasn't sure.

Tonight would be easier for me. My friends were here but they all knew what was really going on. Okay, I had to deal with my mother—my father was away on business and couldn't rearrange, which was an undisguised blessing. My mother was just happy as long as I was happy. All the pressure was on us to convince Parker's family and friends that we were in love.

"Parker!" Lauren shot out of nowhere to meet us at the bottom of the stairs. "You look gorgeous. Your guests have started to arrive. Quickly, out into the garden."

"I think we need a glass of champagne, Lauren. Do you know where we'll find one?" Two shots clearly hadn't been enough.

"Yes, yes. This way."

We stepped out onto the patio and the smattering of people on the lawn all turned in our direction. A waiter to our left held a tray of champagne. Without dropping Parker's hand, I handed her one glass and then took one for myself. "Remember, this is for twenty-five million pounds," I said under my breath.

She nodded. "Yeah. And the lucky thing is you're a nice guy, so it's not that difficult to pretend."

"Nice guy?"

She didn't hear me because someone enveloped her in a hug. "I'm so happy for you," the woman said. "I never thought I'd see the day when you got married. Especially before me."

I could tell the smile Parker wore wasn't genuine. "Katie, this is Tristan. Tristan, Katie is my oldest friend from school."

"Parker was always the groom to my bride when we were playing with her mum's veil. She never wanted to be the bride."

"It was a hard job trying to convince her," I said. "But I won her over in the end."

Katie's grin was wide and genuine for her friend and she urged me on. "Tell me how you two met. This is quite the fairytale whirlwind."

"I won a date with her at a charity auction," I said. "I saw her earlier in the evening and I thought she was beautiful, but she disappeared like Cinderella before I had the chance to win her over and convince her to come out with me. When she appeared on stage and people were bidding to take her out—well, I just knew I had to give fate a little helping hand."

"Swoon," Katie said. "That's a story to tell your grandchildren."

"Happy memories," Parker said almost convincingly.

"I'm just so incredibly delighted for you," Katie said. "After everything that's happened, I'm glad you have someone who deserves you. Let's double date. Can you do dinner soon? Tristan, you're going to love my husband, Nick."

"Sounds good," I said. Luckily, Lauren interrupted us before Katie had us cracking open our diaries on the spot.

"Katie, my love, I have to have the happy couple circulate. You don't mind, do you?" Before getting a response, Lauren dragged me by the arm across the lawn to meet more people I didn't know and would likely never see again. During the following hour, we must have hugged seventy-five thousand strangers.

Parker was clearly uncomfortable with the congratulations and good wishes from all the people gathered here—and it was little wonder, as I was pretty sure Lauren hadn't stuck to the agreed number of guests. There looked to be seats for about a thousand people around the tables. Lucky for me, she didn't have access to my contacts or everyone I'd ever met would probably be here today, including the obstetrician who delivered me. Things only got worse when Lauren guided us to our seats for dinner. Neither Parker nor I had taken much interest in the seating plan. We certainly hadn't expected to be seated on our own, just the two of us, elevated to the rest of our guests at one end of the marquee.

"Is she serious?" Parker hissed from beside me as Lauren beckoned us up the three steps to our table.

"Isn't it pretty?" Lauren said. "Very common in America to do a sweetheart table and with Tristan's parents divorced, I thought it would be more comfortable than having the usual top table."

"Please shoot me," Parker muttered under her breath. "This isn't a wedding," she continued, loud enough so Lauren could hear. "We didn't need a top table."

There was no point complaining. We were here and we had to make the best of it.

"Lovely idea, Lauren," I said, trying to hide the fact that Parker was freaking out beside me.

"Is it usual for these tables to be on a stage?" Parker asked.

Lauren's smile blazed. "*That* was my idea. Thought you could see everyone much better from here. And everyone can get another look at the happy couple."

I squeezed Parker's hand before releasing it and holding out her chair. "Wife-to-be?"

Lauren took a couple of paces back, like she was enjoying a painting in a gallery, almost jumped for joy, and then left us to it.

"Can you believe this?" Parker asked. "It's like we're an exhibit at a museum. You're going to have to stop me from killing her. Like, that's your job today. Once I get my hands on the knife, we're going to cut the cake with, I will have very little self-control. If you don't want to be married to someone doing life for murder, you'll have to hold me back."

I chuckled, glancing out and down to our guests that filled the marquee. "It's just a couple of hours. No one's getting murdered. If I have to hold you down and feed you chocolate-covered raisins to prevent a bloodbath, I'll do it."

"Thank you. Your first duty as my fiancé—make sure I don't kill anyone."

"I had hoped taking your virginity would be my first assignment, but needs must."

Parker laughed and warmth filled my ribcage at the sound of her laugh. "I hate to break it to you, but that ship has sailed."

"Shame."

The servers presented the first course. It occurred to me I had no idea what we were eating.

I glanced over at Parker.

"Don't ask me," she said, reading my mind. "I left it to Lauren."

"I think it's duck," I said.

Parker started to laugh. "Never in the world have two people been less interested in their engagement party."

"People say it's stressful planning a wedding," I replied. "I have no idea what they're talking about."

To anyone looking at us, we were thoroughly enjoying ourselves. Lucky for me, I genuinely liked my fiancée. At least I wasn't faking that bit.

The meal was delicious and the sounds of chatter and laughter filled the tent. Even Parker seemed to relax. I managed to make her laugh at least three more times before we'd finished.

"I actually think just the two of us on this table was a great idea," Parker admitted. "At least we haven't had to keep up any kind of pretense between ourselves. It's been a welcome break."

"Every cloud has a silver lining."

"The cake, my lovely couple. The cake. Everyone," Lauren bellowed, "gather round. We're going to cut the cake."

Parker groaned beside me. "I spoke too soon."

"Come on," I said, standing and taking her by the hand. "The sooner the bit where you get your hands on a sharp knife, the better."

Parker laughed and it lit up her entire face. I couldn't help but smile. "Is it me or is it weird to have a cake cutting at an engagement party?"

"Just go with it," I said through my grin. "No one else seems to think it's weird."

We stood by the two-tiered cake as people started to congregate around us.

"Thank God they've all agreed to a small wedding," Parker said. "Can you imagine if this was a three-day thing?

My mother would have people releasing doves and the Pope sending a message of congratulations."

"Are you Catholic?"

"No. But that wouldn't stop my mother when she sets her mind to something."

"I'm more concerned about Lauren. We're going to need to keep an eye on her. I know everyone agreed on a twenty-five maximum for the wedding, but it wouldn't surprise me if the guest list suddenly ballooned."

"Already ahead of you. I insisted on a restaurant that had a maximum capacity of thirty."

"Smart."

"Thanks. We're a good team."

That's exactly how it felt—like we were a team. Aside from my best mates, I'd never had that with anyone. Certainly no one I was dating. Or fake-dating. "Absolutely we are."

People seemed to surge toward us like a bunch of hungry hyenas who had spotted their prey. Parker looked like she just knew she was about to get eaten.

I muttered under my breath. "Eyes on the prize. Twenty-five million."

Lauren handed Arthur a microphone and my stomach plummeted into the earth's core. What the hell was he going to say? He knew Parker and I were faking it. I knew that he knew. I hoped he wasn't about to embarrass anyone.

"Ladies and gentlemen, thank you all for coming out this afternoon to celebrate the engagement of my beloved daughter, Parker, and the man who will soon become my son-in-law, Tristan Dubrow. I've known Tristan for around ten years now and during that time, I often considered introducing him to Parker. I like to think I'm a pretty good judge of character, and I knew as soon as I met Tristan that he was a man who could be trusted. A man who cared. Loyalty is at the core of who he is and I admire that about him. When I invited him to Parker's charity gala, I confess I hoped to do a little matchmaking between him and my daughter."

I wondered if it was Arthur's plan all along that I be the winner of the bid for a date with Parker. But it couldn't have been; he hadn't even mentioned her before the auction started. "But I didn't need to. Fate took the reins and without Tristan knowing Parker was my daughter, he made a scene-stealing bid to take her to dinner."

I couldn't decide whether Arthur's speech was genuine or whether he was just trying to help add meat to the bones of our super-speedy engagement. Either way, he was convincing.

I could feel Parker's eyes on me and I turned to meet her gaze, which was full of questions. But about what? Arthur wasn't saying anything she didn't already know.

Arthur wrapped up his speech wishing us a lifetime of happiness and moved out of the way so we could cut the cake. At least no one had asked us to make a speech.

Parker took the knife and I clasped my hand over hers as we slid the knife into the cake. In a little under a month, we'd be doing this again with our wedding cake.

Lauren started clinking her fork against her champagne glass and everyone followed suit. I couldn't do anything but smile at the ridiculousness of the scene. I wrapped my arm around Parker's waist and pulled her close. "Good thing we practiced." The kiss back in the room had meant to relax her, or so I told myself, but as our lips touched, I'd stopped kidding myself. There was no doubt about it—not only was Parker beautiful and clever and had an adorable addiction to animal print pajamas and chocolate-covered raisins, she was also sexy as hell and I'd *wanted* to kiss her. I'd managed to convince myself that it was in her best interests that we have a practice kiss. Who was I kidding? I just wanted an excuse.

As I dropped my mouth to hers, I paused, just for a fraction of a second, breathing in this moment in case it was the last chance I had to kiss her. Then I pressed my lips against hers for a little too long. She tasted sweet like summer and smelled of spice. My favorite combination.

She reached her hands into my hair and moaned quietly, so quietly that no one but me would hear. She was enjoying this just as much as I was.

As if she suddenly realized where she was, she slid her hand onto my chest and gave me a little push. As I stood, I realized we'd not only kissed in front of an audience, but we'd garnered enthusiastic applause.

I slid my hand around Parker's waist and pulled her toward me. I glanced over at my group of friends, who were smiling like this was really my non-fake engagement party and they were so happy for me. Like I really had just kissed my fiancée and pulled her toward me. Like they were overjoyed at finally seeing me in love.

I'd have to set them all straight.

FIFTEEN

Parker

So far, so good. We'd gotten through my dad's speech, cut the cake, and had a very public kiss. Luckily, Tristan's arm around my waist had compensated for my inability to hold myself upright while he kissed me. Back in my room, I'd been leaning on my dressing table when we kissed, so I had grossly overestimated my limbs' ability to operate normally when Tristan was so close. My heart might still be hammering, but at least I was upright. It was all I could hope for.

"You look beautiful," Stella said as she approached me. Tristan and I were still holding hands, despite my Aunt Maddie only having eyes for Tristan. She was lecturing him on the secrets of a happy marriage and he, very sensibly, wasn't trying to make a contribution as she set out her three-thousand-point plan.

"Thanks, Stella. Honestly, I feel more than awkward."

Maddie maneuvered between me and Tristan, breaking our physical connection.

"Well you don't *look* awkward. You both look great. Like the perfect couple."

"Tristan gets up in the morning looking great. On the other hand, I'm a magnet for spillages whenever I dress up."

Beck came up behind Stella and wrapped his arm around her waist. "How are you getting on?" he asked.

All I could do was shrug.

"You should know Tristan wouldn't do this thing for just anyone. That's not to say he's not a great guy. He is. And I know it's an excellent charity that Tristan feels strongly about, but he must like you a lot to do this. You should know that."

I didn't know what to say. Was Beck disapproving of what we were doing? "It's really good of him."

"You're supportive, though, right?" Stella asked her husband.

"Sure," Beck said on a shrug. "Partly because it's a great cause and partly because . . . Well, I hope you both keep an open mind."

Stella laughed. I got the distinct impression I wasn't in on the joke.

"Did I miss something?" I asked.

"It's just that Beck and I started out pretending to be together," Stella explained.

"You and Beck?" I glanced between them. They were both grinning.

"Yes, Stella made me pretend to be her boyfriend," Beck explained.

"A very small price to pay for accompanying you to the wedding from hell." Stella shook her head as if she couldn't believe what she was about to say. "My newly ex-boyfriend's wedding to my newly ex-best friend." She groaned. "I have no idea how you talked me into it."

"That sounds . . . horrible and messy and oh em gee, I can't even imagine," I said.

Stella laughed. "It was all those things. But out of it, I ended up with this guy, so all's well that ends well. You never know when an awkward situation will lead to something great."

My cheeks flushed like I had my head a foot away from a roaring fire. When I heard my name called across the grass, I'd never been so happy to be interrupted. It wasn't like that between me and Tristan. Yes, Tristan was gorgeous and I was attracted to him, but I was only human. There wasn't a single girl at this party who didn't feel the same way.

I glanced away from Stella and Beck, trying to see who had called my name. Tristan's mother, Eileen, came barreling toward us.

"Hello, you three," she said, grinning so wide she looked like she must have a jaw ache. "How's my lovely daughter-in-law to be?"

My stomach plummeted into the lawn. I hated lying to her, especially as she was just so happy for us. She grabbed my hand and squeezed it between both of hers. "I'm so happy he found you. He's so very lucky. And the work you do—Tristan told me about how you're launching a program to help the families." She shook her head and her eyes went glassy. Without a word, Beck smoothed his hand over her back. "It's wonderful," she said, her voice shaky and weak. "It would have made such a difference."

I was used to people being moved by the work Sunrise did. Vulnerable, sick children fighting for their lives melted the hardest of hearts, but we weren't discussing any details and Eileen was still moved to tears. And then Beck was very quick to comfort her—it was almost as if he expected her to be emotional. Maybe she was always like this. Not for the first time today, I felt like I was missing something.

"Can I get you a drink?" Stella said.

Eileen shook her head, dropped my hands, and pulled out a tissue from her bag before dabbing at her eyes. "I'm fine, thanks." She plastered on a grin. "This is a joyous day. My son is getting married. You two are going to have a wonderful future together." Her voice cracked at the end of the sentence. She was really upset. I scanned the party, wanting to find Tristan and call him over to help comfort his mother. I reached out for her but she lifted her hand. "I'm sorry. It's an emotional day. Excuse me." She rushed off in the direction of the luxury loos Lauren had arranged to be craned into the garden yesterday.

I turned back to Beck and Stella. "Should I go after her?"

Beck shook his head. "I don't think so, but let's tell—Oh, here he is."

Tristan's arms snaked around my waist and he pulled me toward him just like a fiancé would.

"You're mum seems really upset," I said.

"She got a bit overcome when she was talking about Parker's charity," Stella added.

Tristan nodded as if he wasn't surprised.

"She raced off to the loo. Shall I go and check she's okay?" I asked

Tristan pulled me closer to him. "She'll be fine. She won't want a fuss made. She'll be embarrassed."

"It's totally understandable," Beck said. "Big family occasions are bound to bring up memories."

What sort of memories? Was Tristan's mother upset about Sunrise, or was there a traumatic family party in the past no one had yet filled me in about?

Tristan cleared his throat. "Absolutely. You look like you need a drink, Parker. And you, Stella." He craned his neck to locate a waiter before releasing me and grabbing two glasses of champagne as someone came by with a tray full.

Tristan's eyes crinkled from his smile. He bent and placed a reassuring kiss on my head, as if to tell me that I didn't need to worry about a thing. But it wasn't me I was worried about.

Being with Tristan's friends was more relaxing that it should have been, considering I was lying to everyone I loved and cared about apart from Sutton. Lucky for me, after being introducing to Hartford, she seemed to be getting on like a house on fire with all Tristan's friends. Being with the group felt borderline enjoyable, probably because I wasn't lying to any of them.

But it didn't last long as I heard Lauren shouting my name. I turned to find her burrowing through the crowd toward us.

"She's coming for us again. Let's escape," I said, pulling on Tristan's hand. I wasn't quite sure where I was going; I was just heading the opposite direction of Lauren's voice.

"Where are we going?"

"Anywhere. The loo! We can lock ourselves in! I was just starting to relax. God only knows what Lauren has in store for us now." I fixed a smile on my face at the people we passed without stopping to chat. I caught Katie's eye as I passed her. "Sorry, Katie. Just off to the loo! Tristan's helping me with the buttons on my dress." I didn't stop until we were upstairs and in the family bathroom. I ushered Tristan in and shut and locked the door.

"We're safe in here, I think."

Tristan was chuckling.

"I have no idea why you're laughing. We just escaped

Lauren Flowers. Do you know how difficult that is to do? I might sign up for the SAS or something. I've clearly got skills I didn't know I had."

"You're funny," Tristan said, smiling at me and taking a seat on the side of the bath. Now we were here, what were we going to do?

"Sorry, I just couldn't take anything else."

"I've actually had more fun than expected," he said. "I think the sweetheart table was a blessing in disguise. Took the pressure off a little."

"I'm not sure about that. All those people staring at us? I feel like we disappointed them because we didn't recite any Shakespearian soliloquies or break into song or something."

"Singing is not a skill of mine. I think I would have driven everyone from the marquee. The food had them distracted mostly. I'm not sure they needed entertaining."

I nodded. "Yeah, the food was great. Did your mum enjoy it? How is your mum? Did you catch up with her?"

"She's fine." He stood from the bath and pushed his hands into his pockets.

"She seemed pretty upset."

He paused and then said finally. "We had a family member die of congenital heart disease. Mum still gets very upset . . . You know."

"I'm sorry." I reached for his arm and he froze.

"It's fine." He pulled his hands out of his pockets. "You've had your time-out. I think we should get back to the party. Lauren has probably found something else to focus on by now."

I didn't know Tristan that well but I could tell he was trying to change the subject away from one he clearly didn't want to talk about. Maybe it wasn't just his mother who was upset at the thought of the death of his family member.

I certainly didn't want to upset him.

"Sure," I said. "You're right. Let's go back. But if you spot Lauren, promise we'll duck or find another hiding spot?"

He shook his head. "I never pictured my engagement party. But if I had, it absolutely wouldn't have been anything like this."

"I'm taking that as a compliment," I said, unlocking the bathroom door.

"Go ahead and do that."

SIXTEEN

Parker

I swept my finger down the screen of my phone to read his message again. It was cute that Tristan had texted to let me know he'd arrived in New York, but still more than a little weird that we barely knew each other and were acting like a married couple. I stuffed my phone back in my pocket as Sutton headed back from the loo. We'd come to Tate Britain to see the Turner. We always did this before Sutton sat her exams or went for a job interview or did anything that was going to cause her stress-o-meter to go to one hundred. She said it was like smoking a joint, but the buzz lasted longer and was better for her IQ and criminal record. To be honest, I needed to de-stress too. I had to go wedding dress shopping this afternoon, and my mum had insisted she and Lauren come with me.

"So did he kick you out while he went to New York?" Sutton asked. "Worried that you'd discover his sex dungeon while he was gone?"

"Actually, he wanted me to stay. I'm going to pack up

the flat, take the stuff to storage that I'm not going to use for the next couple of months, and then rent the place out."

"On Airbnb?"

"Or something," I replied. "I feel like this is the perfect opportunity to take stock. Maybe look at my life differently."

"I suppose when you're getting married to the hottest man alive, it's time to reassess where your life is going." Sutton chuckled to herself.

"We both know Tristan and I won't know each other this time next year."

Sutton went uncharacteristically silent.

"What?" I asked. "Spit it out."

"Well, you know how I'm a doctor now? I can diagnose illnesses, even without you having to ask."

"You're not a doctor yet. Are you?"

She shrugged. "No one knows. If I get a placement in one of the London hospitals I've applied to, come September, I'm hoping someone will explain it to me. But doctor or no doctor, I could spot the chemistry between you and Tristan a mile away. When he kissed you the other night at your engagement party, it was like your father had shelled out a hundred grand for a fireworks display. You two lit up the party."

"Don't be ridiculous," I said. "You know the deal. I'm just doing what I need to do to get my hands on my trust fund."

"And what is it exactly that you're *doing* to the hottest man alive, also known as Tristan Dubrow?"

I elbowed her in the ribs and took a seat on the long oak bench set in front of one of my favorite landscapes. "It's purely platonic. You know dating isn't my priority."

"But you're not actively *not* dating, are you? You're living with this guy. You must spend a lot of time together."

"A little. But the house is pretty big. We're not tripping over each other." The fact was when Tristan wasn't in his office—which was a lot of the time—we were usually hanging out in the kitchen, eating and chatting. I found I preferred cooking for two rather than one, so had been working my way through my grandma's recipes. Tristan was my very willing guinea pig when I tried new things in the kitchen.

"Are you really telling me the kiss at your engagement party was the first time you'd locked lips?"

I blushed as I remembered my legs threaded through his and his body pressed up against my flimsy robe in my bedroom. "We sort of had a quick practice before we came down."

"A quick practice? I have to tell you, nothing about that kiss looked rehearsed. What about the wedding night, have you been practicing that too? You know the wedding's not legal unless you two sleep together?"

"No one is going to know we're not sleeping together. Unless he or I spill the beans, there's no evidence. Anyway it is *legal*. It just could be annulled if either of us applied for it. Which we won't." I'd looked into it. There was no way I wanted to go through the trouble of getting married and then still have my trust fund denied me on a technicality.

"I suppose it's difficult to prove a negative," Sutton agreed. "But you might just do it once, so your case is water-tight."

I laughed, but since our engagement party, I couldn't deny that I'd imagined Tristan naked, under the sheets and between my thighs. "Why don't *you* sleep with him? You seem pretty obsessed."

"Of course I'm obsessed," Sutton replied. "Have you seen the guy? He's like a wall of muscle topped by a movie-star smile and hair that's begging to be tugged. Like, I wish I'd met him before I graduated. I would have dragged him into anatomy lectures and had him strip. He's magnificent. Have you seen him coming out of the shower in a towel? Does he look as good as I think he does?"

From the hair on his hands, I imagined he'd have chest hair—which was likely to be soft and spread across his muscles like the grass on the Umbrian mountains.

Not that I'd been thinking about it.

"Well, have you?" Sutton asked.

"No, of course I haven't. It's not like we share a room or anything. This is an arrangement. Any hope of it being anything else is your vivid imagination running wild."

"If you say so. I just get a vibe from the two of you. He's single, right?"

Cold hit me like a snowball to my chest. We'd never discussed our relationship status prior to our scheme. I'd just assumed he was single. He'd never mentioned having a girlfriend. "I guess."

"You guess? You've not asked him? If your dad was to see him in town having dinner with his girlfriend, he's going to figure out your plan. You need to ask Tristan—and make it a condition of your arrangement that he doesn't fool around with anyone else for as long as you two are married. Or at least until you separate."

Sutton was making sense, but Tristan was doing me a huge favor. "I'm not in a position to make demands. This is as inconvenient as it gets for him. I don't need to make it any worse."

We'd discussed that after we were married, I'd continue living in the house. Up until now, I'd never seen a hint of another woman. Maybe when the papers were signed, he'd bring women back to his place?

My jaw clenched and I turned my mobile over in my hands, itching to message him and ask whether he had a girlfriend. But it was none of my business. We weren't in a relationship. I had no right to ask him probing questions or make demands on him.

Tristan and I had an arrangement—one that meant that I finally would get access to my trust fund and get to help hundreds of families in need. That's where our relationship began and ended—even if a small, insistent part of me regretted there couldn't be more between us.

SEVENTEEN

Parker

I'd never felt more ridiculous in my life. Standing in front of at least twelve mirrors, my mother and Lauren were clinging to each other with one hand and a box of tissues with the other.

"You look so beautiful, my darling," my mum said through her half sobs.

"You've found your dress," Lauren said, dabbing her eyes. "It's perfect."

How was I going to break it to them that I'd rather march naked down the aisle than wear this meringue of a dress?

"Can we see it with the veil?" Lauren said to the sales assistant, Shayna.

"I'm not wearing a veil," I said. I'd only agreed to try on this ridiculous dress because I thought they'd both agree it was over the top and awful.

"Don't be silly, darling. This is your *wedding*."

"Exactly. *My* wedding, and I don't want to wear a veil. I

certainly don't want to wear this dress. The whole point in having a small wedding at a registry office is that it's low key. This"—I swept my hands down my body—"is very *high* key."

My mother looked like I slapped her and instantly, I felt terrible. She thought this was the real deal and was just trying to make things nice.

Lauren cleared her throat and stood. "If you don't like this dress then we must find you something you do like. There are lots of beautiful dresses here. It's the best bridal shop in London. What kind of thing did you have in mind?"

"Just something . . . less."

"Okay," Lauren said, nodding at Shayna to come and help us. "We'd like something a little more understated. What about a Monique Lhuillier without a train? Something that looks more like evening wear?"

The assistant set to work going through the racks of gowns, pushing the dresses apart to find more options.

"I'm going to change," I said.

"We'll find something you're going to love," Lauren called after me. "Don't you worry."

Thank goodness for Lauren. If she hadn't been here, I would have either ended up wearing this poufy gown or we would have left the shop and my mother and I would have never spoken again.

I shut the dressing room door and pulled out my phone. There was a message from Tristan asking how the dress shopping was going.

I replied saying that I wanted to shoot myself. My finger hovered over the send button. After my conversation with Sutton earlier, I really wanted to know what Tristan's deal was. He was gorgeous and successful and thirty-four—I couldn't expect him to be celibate. But over the last few weeks, he'd never mentioned anyone. Neither of us had. Not to each other anyway.

If I was going to be made a fool of in front of my friends and family, I had a right to know. I deleted the message and wrote out another.

Are you single?

Then I deleted it. Too many loopholes in that one.

Are you seeing anyone?

Deleted. Way too vague.

Are you sleeping with anyone?

It was concise, direct, and the answer would tell me exactly what I wanted to know.

I pressed send and chucked my phone on the bench next to my handbag. If he replied at all, it wouldn't be any time soon.

I'd just begun to fold my arms around my back, origami style, to unhook the dress, when my phone beeped. It was Tristan.

Not even with my fiancée.

Warmth and relief swirled in my stomach. I knew we had a deal. For both of us, getting married was about getting my trust fund. Except there was a part of me—two percent, perhaps three—that couldn't help but think that the things I felt during our two kisses the day of our engagement party were . . . real. I'd never felt anything close to the heat, chemistry and connection I'd felt when Tristan had his hands in my hair and his lips on mine. Sutton talking about fireworks was just her typical hyperbole, but her description underplayed how it felt to be kissed by Tristan. Three-point-five percent of me hoped that he'd felt something real too.

I didn't respond to the message. Tristan wasn't a liar. If he said he wasn't sleeping with anyone, he wasn't sleeping with anyone.

Just as I'd freed myself from my dress, my phone buzzed again.

Tristan again.

Unfortunately.

Heat chased up my spine. Unfortunately, he wasn't sleeping with *anyone*? Or his fiancée?"

Was Tristan Dubrow flirting with me?

I tried to bite back a smile but before I had a chance to consider my response, Shayna knocked at the dressing room door and swept in, holding an armful of gowns which she placed on the freestanding rack in the changing room.

"These are more popular with our brides having more intimate affairs," she said. My phone buzzed again. Was that Tristan? Despite not being a real bride, I started to feel a little giddy at the thought that my fiancé was messaging me. "Shall we start with this one?" She held up a strapless satin gown.

It was pretty and a lot more subtle than the last dress I tried on. I just wasn't sure it was me.

"What else do we have?" My phone buzzed again.

"Now your mum and her friend aren't here, how about you tell me exactly what you're looking for?"

I sighed, not quite sure how to put it into words. "I don't know. Something a little less bridal?"

Shayna frowned and then held up her finger. "Give me a minute." She hurried out like she'd just had a flash of inspiration. The moment she left, I grabbed my phone.

A message from Tristan.

Are you sleeping with anyone?

I typed out a reply. *Not even my fiancé. Unfortunately.* And then I deleted it. I might have misread what he was saying. If I hadn't, then flirting with Tristan felt a little like playing with fire. And I wasn't looking to get burned.

Instead I replied, *Not unless you count the cows on my pajamas.*

As I pressed send, a second one came in from Tristan.

Sounds weird, but it would feel like cheating.

My stomach tilted. I knew exactly what he meant. Yes, this entire palaver was a ruse to get hold of my trust fund, but we were in this together. We had each other's backs. I shouldn't have even asked the question of Tristan. He wouldn't be sleeping with someone else when he was engaged to me, even if our engagement was just for show. He wasn't that kind of man.

I sent my reply. *I know what you mean.*

He responded right away. *I'm missing your cooking here in New York. You'll have to give me lessons when I'm back.*

Shayna knocked on the door, holding up the first dress that I'd been excited to try on since I arrived.

I nodded. "Let's try it."

It was cream silk, with a high neck and midi-length skirt.

Shayna unbuttoned the back and held it out for me to step into. "We call this our skater skirt wedding dress. Being honest, most of our brides choose this as a second dress—one to put on when the dancing starts—but I think it might be just what you're looking for."

It was simple and elegant, and the fabric felt soft next to my skin. It didn't feel that different to putting on a dress for cocktails with Sutton.

"Gosh, you look like a forties pin-up girl. The neckline is perfect with your blunt bob and I could see you with just a flower behind one ear, no veil." She finished buttoning me up and turned me to face the mirror.

I exhaled. I looked normal, but slightly better. "I love it," I said.

"Think your fiancé would approve?" she asked.

I shrugged. "It's very me. I think as long as I'm happy, he will be too." It wasn't a lie.

"Sounds like you picked a good one," she replied.

"No complaints so far." I twirled slightly in the mirror and the dress rose up.

"It fits like it was made for you," Shayna said. "I'm not sure we're going to need many alterations, if any."

Double points for this dress. "We're getting married in ten days, so if I can buy off the rack, even better."

Shayna gave a laugh which was half-deranged panic and half relief. "Looks like this is the one. We've just got to convince the two ladies out there now."

"Can't I just buy it and tell them it's decided?" I asked.

"We can, but in my experience—and I've been doing this a long time—if you go out there, delighted with your dress, they'll come around. And that's much easier than enduring any bad feeling because they weren't involved."

I sighed. It was good advice, though I knew the next half an hour was going to be spent trying to convince them that this was the right dress. It was time I'd rather spend texting my fiancé.

EIGHTEEN

Tristan

I wasn't sure I'd ever been so eager to get home from a trip to New York. The wedding was a week away. Parker had her dress, the venues were booked, and I still hadn't tried on my suit. I didn't *have* to get a new suit for Saturday—it wasn't like I was going to be showing my grandchildren the wedding photos—but I wanted Parker to know I was making an effort. If she'd had the strain of picking a dress for our weird wedding day, I shouldn't escape unscathed.

My phone buzzed. It was a text from Parker saying yes to my question about whether she'd left the deadbolt off the front door.

Hey, you're awake early, I replied.

Still in bed.

I chuckled. Parker spent a lot of time in her bed. She said she could do everything she needed to in pajamas and under a duvet. I couldn't argue with that.

Back in a min. Cab around corner.

I'm at my flat, she replied.

Really? I typed out, slightly concerned. *Thought you were only spending one night there?*

I waited as the phone showed she was typing and then she stopped.

Is everything okay?

My mind began to wander to worst-case scenario. Had there been a break-in at her place? Had her ex turned up at her work and dragged her back to her flat? Had he broken into her place as soon as she got back and wasn't letting her leave? I was being ridiculous but I needed her to tell me that.

I pressed call on the phone but she didn't answer.

I leaned forward to speak to the driver. "Change of plan. You need to get to Maida Vale. There's a big tip if you can get there in less than five minutes." She'd probably just gone to the loo or run out of battery or something, but it could be more serious. I still hadn't discovered who had been taking the payments from the charity bank account, and although I set up a permanent hack into her building's security cameras, nothing had come up. Maybe whoever had been targeting her had been waiting for me to be out of the country.

I rang her again but it kept going straight to voicemail. Fuck. I checked the time. Six thirty in the morning. Her phone should be fully charged. Why hadn't she called me back? My paranoia grew, crawling into my chest and circling its hands around my heart.

At least there was no traffic. I pulled some cash out of my wallet, ready to press into the driver's hand as soon as we arrived.

The minutes seemed to extend into hours. I kept trying her phone over and over until we pulled up outside her building. I thrust the money at the driver and opened the door before we'd come to a stop. If she didn't answer the buzzer, I was going to have to break down the front door. I didn't have the fob with me.

As luck would have it, someone was just exiting the main doors dressed in running gear as I sprinted up the path to meet him.

I caught the door just before it shut, thankful and furious at the same time that he hadn't waited until the door closed. People just weren't focused on security.

I didn't bother with the lifts, opting instead to take the stairs two at a time to the third floor. I pounded on Parker's front door. There were no signs of a break-in. That was something at least. "Parker, it's Tristan. Let me in."

Just as I was about to shout again, I heard the turn of locks and the door opened. A red-eyed, pajama-clad Parker saw me and promptly collapsed.

Shit.

I barged through the door and crouched down beside her, feeling for her pulse. Her heartbeat was strong, and as I glanced up and down her body, wondering what to do next, her eyelids fluttered open.

"Parker," I said. She gave me a weak smile.

"I think I'm sick."

I scooped her up off the floor and headed to her bedroom. "What kind of sick?" I asked. Was it serious? Why hadn't she said anything? We'd texted every day that I'd been in New York.

"I'm so cold. Can you put the heating on?"

She was in the middle of some kind of delusion or something. The place was stifling. "Parker, it feels like the fucking Sahara in here." I set her on the bed and placed my hand on her forehead. It was like touching a pan that had just come out of the oven.

"You have a temperature."

"I just need another blanket," she said.

I pulled off my coat and went to get her a glass of water. When I came back, her eyes were closed. Her shiny black hair was splayed across the pillow, and despite having just collapsed and having the temperature to end all temperatures, she still managed to look beautiful? "Do you have a thermometer?"

"Lips," she said, her eyes still closed. "I have lips."

She certainly did have lips. She might be gaga, but she was also adorable.

I took a seat next to her bed and felt her forehead again. She was still scorching hot.

"And so do you. Such great lips." She made an *mmm* sound, the sort I'd make after a spoonful of crème brulee.

I chuckled to myself. Was she dreaming? She'd been awake thirty seconds ago.

"I need you to have a drink. Can you sit up a little?"

"What are you doing here? You're in America. Is this a dream? Am I dreaming? If I'm dreaming, can you kiss me again?"

"I'm back from New York," I said.

She pushed herself up from the mattress so she was sitting, opened one eye and then fell back to the mattress. "It's so hot. Can you open a window? It's so hot." She moved to strip off her cow-print pajama top, but I pulled it back down.

"Wait. Let me get some fresh air in here and then we need to get some fluids into you."

"No," she yelped. "I'll vomit."

I stood and opened her window a little, just to let a little fresh air in, then reached around her and pulled her to a sitting position.

"You smell so, so, *so* good. Not me. I smell of vomit. You. Do. Not."

One-handed, I grabbed pillows from where they were scattered across her bed and propped her up.

I sat opposite her and leaned forward. "Parker, I'm serious, I need you to take a small sip of water. Do you understand me?"

Both eyes open, she nodded. "As long as you understand I will vomit."

I wasn't sure if she was serious or whether she'd lost all mental capacity. Either way, I had to try to get some fluids into her.

I helped put a glass to her lips and she took two sips before I put the glass down. "Tastes so good." She lay her head back on the pillow and then began to clutch at her stomach. "I'm—"

She sprinted out of the bed like she'd been set on fire and skidded into the bathroom. The clunk of the toilet seat was followed by the sound of Parker fulfilling her promise, retching the contents of her stomach into the toilet bowl.

Shit. Maybe I shouldn't have told her to drink. But she needed hydrating. I texted Gabriel. He'd know the number of a doctor who would make house calls. Maybe she needed an IV.

I hovered outside the bathroom door while I called the doctor Gabriel recommended.

"Parker, I'm coming in," I said as I opened the bathroom door.

She moaned an incomprehensible response from where she was on all fours on the bathroom floor. I scooped her up and took her back to bed, then returned to the bathroom for a couple of face cloths, which I wet with cool water.

"Tristan," Parker moaned when I approached her bedside. "You need to get out of here."

I chuckled. "I'm not going anywhere."

"I'm probably contagious," she said as I began to wipe her face with one cloth and then the next.

"Well, unless it's Ebola, you can return the favor when I'm rolling on the floor, covered in vomit."

Her shoulders slumped. "I should feel humiliated, but I'm too exhausted to care. I'm glad you're here."

She had no reason to feel humiliated. She was ill. It happened to all of us. And she was still cute—with or without the vomit.

"I've called the doctor. He should be here soon. Just rest." I stroked her forehead and she closed her eyes in a lazy blink.

"Can I get you anything?" I asked.

"Is a new body on offer?"

"You don't need a new body. We'll get this one fixed up and it will be as good as new."

She offered me a small smile before she started to shake and turned translucent white. Christ on a bike, I hoped the doctor got here soon.

"Let me get the window." I shut the window in her bedroom, turned the heating thermostat down in her hallway, and then opened a couple of other windows in the flat to get some air circulating. How long had she been like this?

"Have you had some paracetamol?" I asked.

"Can't keep anything down."

I took her hand between mine as she lay against the pillows. "Sushi," she said.

I was pretty sure a snack of raw fish was the last thing she needed. "Maybe later."

"No." She moaned and hitched up her legs, like I was a bucket of slime she was trying to avoid.

"Let's wait and see if the doctor thinks sushi is a good idea."

Before she could make any more sushi demands, the buzzer went. I let the doctor up.

"She's in here," I said, and led him into the bedroom. "I got here an hour or so ago and she fainted. I got her to sip some water but she threw it up."

"You're her boyfriend?" he asked.

"Fiancé," I replied without thinking.

He set about taking her temperature, pulse, and blood pressure. "How long have you been feeling like this?" he asked.

"Hours," she replied. "After the sushi."

"You ate sushi?" he asked and she nodded. "Last night?"

Ohh, she'd been trying to tell me it was food poisoning.

"Late. Delivered about eleven."

"Bad sushi is more common that you think," the doctor said. "If it were up to me, no one should be allowed to serve takeaway raw fish. It's too easy for it to go wrong." He pulled out a telescopic drip stand from his bag and set up an IV. "You're dehydrated. I'm going to give you some antibiotics as well. If you're still vomiting in twelve hours, or you see blood in your stools, you're going to need to go to hospital." The doctor glanced at me and I nodded.

Sushi? Who ate raw fish that was off? Surely it would be too easy to smell it? While the doctor set things up, I headed to the kitchen to see if there were any remnants of the takeaway. I pulled open the fridge door and found a half-eaten sushi platter. I took it out, slid it on the side, and popped off the lid.

I took a step back. It stank. But not of fish. It smelled

more of . . . chemicals. Not the kind of chemicals you get from a plastic box, but of stuff you would find under the sink. That couldn't be good. I took out my phone and texted a contact I knew who worked in a lab. They owed me a favor. *I'm sending some sushi over to your lab. I think it's been tampered with. Please test it.* What was I asking her to test for? Poison, I guessed. There was every chance run-of-the-mill food poisoning was the culprit here, but with the weird payments and suspected break-in, I couldn't shake my suspicions that something more sinister was going on. Was I an idiot for not getting the police involved sooner? Did they need to be involved now?

I found a food bag, slid the leftover sushi inside it, and called a courier. The sooner it got to the lab, the sooner we'd know.

It took about thirty minutes for the IV to finish. After the doctor had packed everything up, he followed me out into the hallway. "I think she'll be fine now she's had some fluids, but if she gets worse, or she doesn't get better by this evening, take her to A&E."

"Say it's not food poisoning. What if she accidentally ingested a hazardous substance. Would the symptoms be the same?"

He scowled. "Most probably. But it's like to be food poisoning. Unless she's got some kind of weird connection to Russia."

"I know. But you're saying this is how she'd be feeling if it was something more nefarious than food poisoning. Is that right?"

"It would depend on the poison, but so long as it was meant to kill her, then yes, it's likely that the symptoms would be similar."

"Thanks, doctor."

"If you hear hooves, don't assume zebras."

I wasn't quite sure what he meant but I nodded anyway.

"Like I said," he continued, "if she starts to vomit blood, you see blood in her stools, she loses consciousness or if she's still being sick in eight to twelve hours, take her to accident and emergency. But with the drip and the antibiotics, she should start feeling better in an hour or so."

"Understood," I said. Hopefully by then I'd have the results back from the lab and Parker would be feeling a lot better.

I let him out and then closed and locked the door before going back into Parker's bedroom. "Can I get you anything?" She looked a little brighter and she was sat up, not a groan or a mention of my lips in sight.

"Some brain bleach?"

I frowned. Whatever she was describing didn't sound healthy. "Brain bleach?"

"Yes, so I can use it on you to erase the ramblings of this crazy person and the images of my clinging to a toilet bowl."

I chuckled. Parker was back. "Aha, I have a button for memory wiping. I just pressed it and I have no memory of anything before the doctor arrived."

"Thank God," she said. "I was worried I might be so embarrassed that I'd never be able to look at you again."

Why would she be embarrassed? She'd been sick. I smiled. "Can I get you anything?"

She shook her head. "I'm just so tired."

I pulled up the duvet and swept the hair from her eyes. "You should sleep." How did she manage to still look pretty when she was so poorly?

"You're a kind man, Tristan. Thank you."

"Don't forget my great lips."

Her eyes widened and then she closed them again, as if

being so shocked had simply taken up too much energy. "You promised me no memories of anything before the doctor arrived."

I stroked her forehead. "Oh that button has a loophole. If I don't want to forget something, it malfunctions."

She sighed but didn't reply, already asleep. While Parker slept off the effects of the sushi, I was going to poke around and see if there was anything that seemed out of place. If it turned out the sushi had been poisoned, I wanted to be as prepared as I could be. I wasn't sure what I was looking for, but I'd know if I found it.

I started in the kitchen. Parker's entire one-bedroomed flat looked like it had the contents of a three-bedroom house squashed into it. There was just so much stuff everywhere. Cookery books lined the back of the work surfaces. Overspill crockery was piled up in front of the cookery books, leaving little room for actual food preparation. Even floor space had been commandeered by freestanding storage for more stuff. Even every electrical socket had something plugged into it—three phone chargers, the kettle, the toaster and an abandoned hand whisk. No wonder she liked my kitchen so much. I couldn't think in here, let alone cook. Maybe because everything was so cramped, Parker had put her sushi on the counter and had inadvertently contaminated the food herself. The place wasn't dirty but everything was so close that it was possible she used the draining board to unpack the takeaway and had knocked into something.

I continued to survey the kitchen but nothing stood out. I moved into the small hallway. There wasn't much to see— the coatrack, the skirting. No new marks or holes or anything that would arouse suspicion. The bathroom was more calming than the kitchen. It suggested that if Parker didn't have so much stuff, this place could be really nice. Three glass shelves above the sink had been carefully displayed with perfume bottles, bath oils, and candles. On the windowsill sat three glass jars containing bath salts, cotton wool, and in the last one, something that smelled of Parker and looked like cold porridge. A small cupboard under the sink had all the usual things: backstock of shampoo, razor blades alongside bleach, cleaning equipment, and a random plastic plant. Nothing stood out to me as suspicious or not belonging to Parker. But poking had given me some more information about the woman in the room next door. It felt like there were two Parkers. Bathroom Parker who enjoyed peaceful, well-organized pretty space who also liked to cook in my house, and Kitchen Parker who seemed to be in a competition to fit as many things as possible in a very tiny space.

NINETEEN

Tristan

Standing in my new French blue suit, I tapped on Parker's bedroom door.

"How are you getting on?"

"You can come in. I could do with a hand getting the last few buttons on this dress done up."

The first thing that caught my attention were the bright red strappy heels she was wearing. Then I trailed my gaze up to the white dress that emphasized her tiny waist. "You look . . ." Beautiful wasn't a good enough word. Lots of things were beautiful—women, good gin, the feeling you got when you made your first hack. Parker was so much more than any of those things.

She glanced up at me. "You think it's bridal enough? My mum told me everyone was going to mistake me for one of the guests."

"I think it's the perfect dress for you. And the shoes are . . . They're the kind of shoes that make a husband very happy."

I enjoyed her blush a little too much.

"Well, I had to get something to match my lipstick."

"Lips look great."

She rolled her eyes. "Thank God I wasn't hospitalized."

"I was worried there for a moment. I thought you were going to throw up a major organ at one point."

She laughed. "Me too."

"That doctor deserves a mention in the speeches today. Without him, I'm not sure we would have a wedding today. You were not in good shape."

"Agreed. I don't think I'll be eating sushi in a while."

"You know I told you that I'd sent the remnants of the fish off to a lab."

She shook her head like she couldn't believe we were discussing this again. She'd thought I'd been overreacting to think that what had happened was anything more than food poisoning. "You know what the doctor said himself—he'd like to have takeaway sushi places banned."

"I told you, a mate owed me a favor; it's not like I went to a lot of trouble. But what's interesting is that the results from the lab showed traces of detergent."

"Detergent? Like from the box or something?"

I shook my head. "Nope. It was on the fish. It wasn't a lethal dose—just enough to cause vomiting and diarrhea. Could have been an accident in the restaurant kitchen, or basic carelessness by one of its employees. Maybe even you knocked the soap at the sink when you were unpacking it."

"That's weird that I didn't taste anything. Probably all the soy sauce."

"Of course it could be more nefarious. It's impossible to be sure."

"Nefarious?" She laughed. "If someone wanted to kill me, there are better ways, I'm sure."

I didn't say what I was thinking—that someone might have just wanted her sick so she couldn't go through with this wedding. Or maybe someone wanted her ill so they could look after her. It was better to drop it. She was on edge today as it was. There was no need to make it worse.

"Will you do one thing for me? Change the locks."

"On my flat? Why?"

"For me, Parker. I know you think I'm paranoid, and that's fine. I hope I am. But I'm asking you to change the locks."

She shrugged. "Why is it such a big deal to you?"

"Better to be safe than sorry. Please promise me?" I asked.

"Fine. I'll have the locks changed. You're getting plenty of promises out of me today." She smiled at me and then her face fell. "Are we crazy to be doing this?"

I stepped forward, turned her around and took over buttoning her dress for her. "Maybe a little." The skin of her back was as smooth as the silk she was wearing. My fingers lingered a little longer than they should have.

"You getting cold feet?"

I finished the final button and our eyes met in the mirror. "Six months ago, hell, two months ago, if you told me I would be getting married any time before now and the turn of the next century, I would have told you that you were betting on the wrong horse. I've had the odd girlfriend here and there but no one who's made me want to get down on one knee. Not even close. Marrying you? To help as many families as I know you're going to? I can't think of a better reason to get married. And getting a hot bride is just a cherry on the cake."

"Hot bride?"

I shrugged. I hadn't said anything that wasn't true. "Hot

bride who thinks I've got good lips. Pucker up, sweetheart, you know I'm using them on you later."

She spun and pushed me. "You're ridiculous. I was hallucinating. I mistook you for Val Kilmer in *Batman*. Now, that's a man with good lips."

"I like my dark knights Christian Bale-sized, as you know."

"Yeah, because you wish you had Val Kilmer's lips."

"You want a reminder of just how good my lips are?" I stepped forward and she tipped her head back to look me in the eye. "Our last unmarried kiss before we leave?"

She shook her head. "You wish you got to kiss me again."

A smile tugged at the corners of my lips. "Maybe I do, Cream Puff."

My phone buzzed, interrupting our little dance. "It's the car," I said.

"Then we better go." She picked up her bag and skipped past me, the skirt of her dress lifting to show off her perfect legs as she did. I had to fight the urge to catch her hand and pull her back toward me, push my hands into her hair and kiss all that cherry red lipstick off her. But as usual, she was two steps ahead of me.

In under an hour, that woman was going to be my wife.

TWENTY

Tristan

I took Parker's hand as we got to the front of the oak-paneled room where we were going to be married.

My parents and all my friends—together with their partners—were gathered to witness my marriage. The irony wasn't lost on me that Parker and I were going to be married before some of my friends who were desperately in love. It wasn't love that drove Parker and me. It was need. Although over the last weeks, we'd transitioned from near strangers to partners in crime, housemates, and friends. And now we were about to become husband and wife.

I'd agreed to Parker's plan before I knew much about her, but now I was about to promise to love, honor, and cherish her. It didn't feel as alien or uncomfortable as I'd expected it to when she'd first suggested it. I liked Parker. I respected her. I admired her passion for what she did and the way she worked so hard to achieve great things, despite having a father as wealthy and powerful as Arthur Frazer. She could have spent her time making charitable donations and flitting from party to party. But she hadn't taken the easy route. She'd worked hard to create a legacy as hard won as her father's had been. He should be so very proud of her and by the look in his eye, he most certainly was.

The registrar cleared her throat and quiet descended on the room.

My heart thudded against my ribcage and unexpectedly, I was a little nervous. Not because I didn't believe we were doing the right thing. Not because I thought anyone was going to object when the time came. It just hit me that, whatever the motivation, I was about to be married.

I was about to be someone's husband.

Parker was going to be my wife.

The officiant started to speak and I looked over at Parker. She must have sensed my gaze because she looked over at me and as she did, my heartrate evened out. When we were asked whether or not we knew of a reason we shouldn't be married, we both answered that we didn't.

We had chosen the simplest, most straightforward vows. There would be no honoring or obeying. No til-death-us-do-parts.

I agreed to take Parker as my wedded wife.

She agreed to take me as her wedded husband.

We signed the register and just like that, in less time than it took to eat lunch, we were married.

It felt completely natural and unforced, but I swept my thumbs over Parker's cheekbones and pressed my lips to hers.

I pulled back slightly and whispered, "You have great lips, wife." I enjoyed her blush at the memory of the night she'd given me the compliment, but before I could tease her about it further, we were surrounded in a circle of handshakes, hugs, and congratulations. My heart swelled in my chest as I felt the love and good wishes from the people around us. I didn't drop Parker's hand for a second.

We were in this together.

The next twenty minutes were a blur as we were ushered out of the registry office and walked the five minutes to the restaurant where we were going to break bread with the people most special to us.

The wedding might have been just for show, but it was a truly wonderful feeling to have so many people rooting for our happiness.

"We're lucky to have so many people who love us," I whispered to Parker as we took our seats in the private dining room of the restaurant Parker had picked.

"We really are. And I'm lucky I married someone who appreciates it. Thank you."

I pressed a kiss to her temple.

Arthur took a seat next to Parker at the long table and leaned in to us both. "You're officially family, Tristan. And I can't think of a better son-in-law." He was father of the bride, so I supposed that it was only appropriate that he say something to his future son-in-law. But he knew this was a marriage in name only; he didn't have to be quite so generous to me.

"I have something for you." Arthur pulled out a cream envelope from his inside breast pocket. "Your mother and I didn't have a clue what to get you. Tristan's got a house and I know it's impossible to buy my daughter anything without her telling me how my money would be put to better use as a charitable donation. So we decided to get you something money can't buy—more time together."

Was he sending us to jail?

He handed the envelope to Parker. "Ten days in Mexico. You leave tomorrow night."

A holiday? Together? Alone?

Parker's mother, who was seated the other side of her husband, clasped her hands together, delight radiating from her smile as she leaned forward to see our reactions. "It's the most beautiful hotel," she said. "Rumor has it, the Obamas holiday there."

"That's so kind, really, but I have to work," Parker said. "And so does Tristan."

"Tish tosh," Parker's mother said. "You two need a holiday. You just got married, for goodness' sake."

"But—" Parker started to protest but I silenced her with a squeeze of her thigh under the table.

"We'll figure it out," I said.

"Honeymoon? Are you serious? I've seen how hard you work. And I have a thousand things to do at the charity."

"I know." I skirted my hands over her back, rubbing circles across the silk of her gown. "Don't worry about it. I can take my work anywhere and we can find someone to cover you at your job."

She opened her mouth to protest.

"Parker," I said, a warning in my tone. "Don't worry about this now. We can deal with it later. Let's enjoy lunch with our family and friends."

Her shoulders dropped beside me and I moved my hand from her back, down to link my fingers with hers. "This is our special day."

"You're ridiculous."

"You're beautiful."

"You win."

TWENTY-ONE

Parker

My mother had taken her interfering to a new level and bought me an entire new wardrobe to take to Mexico with me, which was the only thing to explain the mammoth-sized suitcase being wheeled to our room by the smartly dressed porter. Of course Tristan insisted on carrying his own.

"You think you can stay awake until we make it to the room?" Tristan asked.

I elbowed him in the ribs. "You're hilarious." I'd spent the entire ten hours on the plane asleep. "I was tired."

He grinned at me. "I think we were meant to join the mile-high club, not the passed-out-snoring club. Great start to the honeymoon, wifey."

"I'm not a good flyer. I think the anxiety sends me to sleep."

"On the upside, I got more work done than I expected," he said. "Which means I have more free time now we're here."

"You're not exhausted?" I asked. I could sleep right now in the corridor if I lay down.

"Well now that you mention it, it's close to midnight and we're being shown to our hotel room. I'm guessing they've got a bed in there somewhere."

I don't know why it hadn't occurred to me before, but it suddenly struck me that we were about to enter a room—most probably the honeymoon suite—which meant we were going to be faced with just one bed.

"Tristan," I said, "there'll be a bed. *One* bed."

We came to a stop and the porter let us into the room. "Welcome to the honeymoon suite. You can't see the view at the moment, but you're on the beach and you have one hundred eighty-degree views of the ocean."

I smiled, hoping he wouldn't see me stressing about the fact that one of us wasn't going to have a good night's sleep tonight, or for the next nine nights.

"This is your living area," he said as we came out of the hallway into a large, bright room with a dining table and chairs at one end, a small kitchen at the other, and to my everlasting relief, two sofas—large enough to sleep on—in the middle. "You have a large terrace out of these doors, with a private plunge pool, a spa, and dining area. You also have a terrace outside your bedroom window."

"It's beautiful," I said.

"Lovely," Tristan said.

"We have champagne for you," he said, stopping at the kitchen counter, opening the bottle and then pouring us our second glass since we'd crossed the threshold of the hotel.

We clinked glasses and continued the tour into the bedroom.

"The bed is an Alaskan king-sized," he said with a glance at Tristan's tall frame.

"It's a big bed," I said, wondering what he was expecting us to say.

"A very big bed," Tristan agreed, grinning.

"The bathroom has a steam room, a jacuzzi bath as well as a double-headed shower," the porter said. "You're going to have a great time."

After the porter had showed us how to work the air conditioning, told us where the room safe was, and then gave us the number of our personal butler, Tristan assured him that we didn't need any room service, tipped him, and closed and locked the door.

"I thought he was planning to stay for the week," Tristan said as he collapsed on the couch. "Why is travelling tiring when you're doing nothing but sitting?"

"Because you didn't nap on the plane?"

Tristan laughed. "No one can categorize nearly ten hours of sleep as a nap. Whatever the reason, I'm exhausted."

"You should sleep. You take the bedroom. I'm fine here on the sofa."

Before I could move to dig out my toiletries from my case, Tristan scooped me up in his arms and padded into the bedroom. "This is what people do on honeymoon, isn't it? The groom carries the bride over the threshold?"

"I think that last happened in 1947, but okay."

He threw me on the bed like I was five years old and playing aeroplanes with my dad.

"Unless there's a good reason, we can share a bed. We won't even be able to see each other from our respective sides."

The idea of ten days on the sofa wasn't massively appealing. It didn't take much to sell me on the idea. "I suppose we are married now."

"You better have packed those cow pajamas, or I won't forgive you," Tristan said as he pulled his case open.

"Isn't this insane?" I asked as I watched Tristan unpack from where I was lying on the bed and definitely not wondering how long it would be until I saw him in a towel.

"The room? It's nice."

I propped my head on my hand. "The fact that we're on honeymoon. Together. We've only known each other a little over a month."

"I'm not sure 'insane' is the right adjective. 'Unusual' maybe. We should just make the most of it. I know you didn't want to come, but we're here. We have this beautiful room. In this beautiful hotel, in this amazing country. Let's just enjoy it."

"I suppose we're stuck here for the next ten days. There's no escape."

"Honestly, Parker, I can't remember the last time I went away on a trip that wasn't business related. I can't wait to drink margaritas and lay out in the sun. I figure you owe me a night nursing me and my hangover after your sushi experience."

I covered my ears with my hands. "Don't say that word!"

"What word?" He turned to me from where he was putting his t-shirts onto hangers. "Sushi?"

I groaned. "No. I can't even think about it without smelling vomit."

"Then you won't be pleased to hear about the Japanese restaurant just off the lobby. You could eat sushi for breakfast, lunch, and—"

I threw a cushion at him and he finally stopped talking.

"I'll hold your hair back as you vomit from one too many

cocktails and too much sun. Even if you hadn't done it for me, it feels like it should be my wifely duty."

Tristan chuckled, stalked out of the bedroom, and came back rolling my case in front of him. "You going to unpack?"

"Maybe in the morning," I replied. "I can't move. I'm just going to fall asleep right here."

He shook his head and heaved the case onto the stand. "I'll unpack you," he said.

"You don't have to do that," I replied on a yawn.

"It's my husbandly duty. Do you mind?"

That was the thing about Tristan. In some ways he bulldozed obstacles and objections, but in other ways he was tremendously reassuring and respectful of my boundaries. If I had designed a man who would fit me, Tristan would be it.

"You really don't have to."

"I'll take that to mean you don't mind." I did nothing but watch as he untangled my messy packing and arranged things into drawers and wardrobes.

"You're very organized," I said.

"It's all relative. You're very disorganized."

"Am I?"

"Have you seen your flat?"

"Hey! It's small. There's just not enough space for everything."

When he finished, he shut my case and tossed it into a cupboard I hadn't even noticed. "Tell me something." He lay opposite me on the bed, his long legs stretched out to the end like a desert road you couldn't see the end of. His hips mirrored mine, lying sideways on the bed, and my stomach swooped at how near he was. It made no sense. We'd spent ten hours on a plane sitting hip to hip, but somehow the thirty centimeters between us now made me feel closer to him than I ever had.

"What?"

"Why don't you get a bigger place?"

I pulled in a breath. "I don't need a bigger place. It's only me." I didn't want anything to draw attention to my family's money. It wasn't important. It wasn't who I was.

"It feels like it means more than that."

I shrugged as I watched his body shift. I'd never had an excuse just to sit and stare at Tristan before. Obviously I'd seen him and been around him, been closer to him than this, but I'd never had the chance to stare—to notice how flawless his skin was, the two freckles on his jaw, how his eyes narrowed when he was frustrated. "My flat doesn't define me."

"Of course it doesn't. But like it or not, the things that surround us reflect who we are. Do you not like being Arthur Frazer's daughter?"

"I adore my father," I said. "I'm proud to be his daughter."

"Too proud to accept your parents' help?"

I rolled onto my back to stop myself from staring at Tristan. It wasn't doing anything good for my heart rate. "It's not about being proud. I moved into this place because it's just the right size for one person." My flat was cramped, there was no doubt about that. But it suited me. "I don't need a bigger place. A big flat or a fancy car aren't important to me. You were right. I'm not into flash."

Tristan didn't say anything, but there was something in his silence that told me we weren't through with this conversation. So I added, "Money can be a magnet for the wrong type of people."

"What does that mean?"

I rolled back to face him. The gap between us seemed to have closed ever so slightly. His hand was placed in front of him, just as mine was, and our fingertips were just centimeters away from each other. "I don't want people in my life who like me because my father's rich."

"Surely people like that are easy to spot."

I shrugged. Maybe for some people. Looking back, there were clearly signs I missed.

"I don't think moving to a slightly bigger flat would make much difference. A two-bed place would mean you had somewhere to store your chocolate-covered raisins."

I grinned. "Turns out my husband has a wine cellar with lots of extra storage space."

"So taking help from your husband is fine. But not from your father?"

He splayed his hand and the tip of his little finger touched mine. A crackle of electricity sizzled between us.

"Being Mrs. Tristan Dubrow changes things a little."

One corner of his mouth curved into a smile. "Believe me. It changes things a lot."

TWENTY-TWO

Tristan

As I drifted back into consciousness, I was vaguely aware of the warmth of a body in front of me. I pulled her tighter toward me, filling my lungs with her sweet scent. Was I dreaming? Who was I holding?

Oh yes, that would be my wife.

I opened one eye and realized we were spooning in the middle of the enormous bed. I chuckled to myself. I was pretty sure that was the most chaste first night this suite had ever seen. Parker moved in my arms as she woke.

"Good morning," I whispered.

She froze and when I tried to pull her closer to relax her, she placed her hands over mine and opened them to free herself, rolled over, and then sat upright. She looked at herself up and down, presumably to see if she was still dressed. "Is it morning?"

"The clock over there says eight fifteen and there's light coming through the curtains, so I'm going to go with yes, it's morning."

She stared at me like I'd just told her we were about to embark on an ascent of Everest.

"What's the problem?" I asked.

"You were spooning me," she said.

"Apparently, I like to spoon my wife in my sleep. And given the way your arse was nestled in my crotch, I'm thinking you liked it too. Is that a problem?"

"We need to get some pillows for down the center of the bed," she said, leaping to her feet. "I'll call room service. Tonight should be better." She was a little on edge for my liking. She'd woken up in my arms, not naked with my head between her legs.

I needed a shower. Preferably a cold one.

I groaned and rolled out of bed. "I'm going for a shower. There's room in there for two if you're up for it."

She gave me an eye roll any seventeen-year-old girl would be proud of. I stripped off my t-shirt as I headed into the bathroom.

"You should probably wait to be in private before you change," she called after me.

"Can't handle it?" I asked her.

Parker had been stressed before the wedding. I wasn't sure what was up with her. Sometimes I wondered if she just didn't like to enjoy herself. But I was determined to enjoy myself this holiday. We were here for ten days. We might as well make the most of it.

I had a long, hot shower, pulled a towel around my waist and went to check out the view. On the way, I picked up a brochure of activities. Parker was on the terrace with a pot of coffee and two mugs, so I slid open the doors and stepped out.

She turned, her sharp black bob slicing the thick, hot air,

her eyes covered with large, black sunglasses. "Are you really going to walk around like that all holiday?"

I glanced down at my towel. "What are you talking about?"

"Never mind. I ordered you coffee." She nodded to the coffee pot.

"What a good wife you are." She shot me a look that told me if she thought she could take me in a fight, she would. I chuckled to myself, topped up her coffee then poured out a fresh cup for myself.

"So what's on the agenda today?" I asked. "You seem like you're in a feisty mood. Maybe a little shark wrestling?"

"Agenda? We have an agenda?" She glanced down at the brochure I'd put on the table.

"Not a formal one. I just wondered what you fancied doing today. Cocktails on the beach? A boat trip? Or maybe you just want to ogle me in a towel for the rest of the day?"

"You wish I wanted to ogle you in a towel for the rest of the day." I swear I caught a flicker of a grin at the corners of her mouth. "I was just planning on reading my book here on the terrace. Taking in the views. Maybe having a dip in the plunge pool. But if you want to do something a little more adventurous, don't let me stop you."

I took a sip of my coffee. "Absolutely not."

"You don't like the coffee?"

"The coffee's just fine. The idea of you holing up here on your own with a book is absolutely not okay."

She lowered her glasses to the end of her nose and stared at me. "I'm not asking you to stay. You go wrestle sharks or whatever other adventurous activity you want to participate in. I'll stay shark-free, if you don't mind."

"Nope. Nope. Nope. This is *our* honeymoon. I'm sure we can find something we *both* want to do."

"If you want to stay here and read, then we found something. Otherwise, we can agree to disagree."

I watched as she pretended to read. It was obvious she wasn't *actually* reading, but something was off with her and I didn't know what. I'd seen her overwhelmed before. I'd seen her feeling guilty for lying to everyone she loved. But I hadn't seen her like this.

I sipped my coffee and took in the view. I didn't want to leave her for the day. Not when she clearly wasn't happy. I wanted to understand. I wanted to make it better.

"Tell me what's going on?"

"Nothing," she replied and my gut churned in frustration. For some reason, I could lie to her family and I could watch her do the same. But I just didn't like her lying to me. "I just want to read my book."

"But you're not reading your book. You're just staring at the page. Parker, we might not be really husband and wife, but you should have realized by now that I'm a really good friend. Tell me what's going on?"

She slid her book onto the table and pushed up her sunglasses. "If I tell you, will you leave me alone?"

I winced. "Not promising anything."

She laughed. "At least you're honest." She smiled a long, lazy smile. "I'm straight-up exhausted. I thought the wedding was the end of it—you know, the push and pull with my mum and Lauren, worrying about the questions I was going to get asked, having to choose my dress, flowers, venues. I thought that after we were married, I'd finally be allowed to relax, but then I had to run around and organize work so I could come to Mexico and we had to race to the airport and—I'm just sick of having everyone's eyes on me. If we go down to the pool or we go on a boat trip or whatever, we're going to be the honeymoon couple in the honeymoon suite and I'm just . . . sick of people looking at me. I'm sick of people talking to me. I'm sick of talking. I just want to hole up and not speak to another living soul for the entire time I'm here."

It made sense. She wanted to hibernate. No doubt she'd be happier if she was at home in her messy little nest of a flat, behind a locked door with nothing but a book and Uber Eats for company. But we could do a little better than that. We were in Mexico, after all.

"Well, given I'm your husband and I'm in charge of making you happy—especially on your honeymoon—I'm going to make that happen. With one exception."

She groaned.

"I'm sorry," I continued, "but you're going to have to look at my face. I promise I won't talk to you and you don't have to talk to me. I'm just not leaving you on your own. Not during our honeymoon. It doesn't seem right."

"Okay," she said. "You're going mute for this entire holiday, are you?"

I shrugged.

The silence had started.

"Tristan, don't be an idiot. You can talk. I just might not talk back. For a few days at least. But I don't mind if you want to go out and explore—do water sports, get drunk at the bar, go eat sushi— Scratch that, don't eat sushi if you want to share a bed. At this point, any hint of sushi breath will guarantee you a lap full of vomit."

I shook my head and pointed to the ground, indicating I was staying put. I wasn't going anywhere without her.

She shrugged and went back to her book. I went inside, slid on some shorts and grabbed my laptop. I started going through my emails. After about an hour, I moved to one of the sun loungers just along from where Parker was sitting.

About forty minutes later, Parker joined me on the lounger next to mine. It felt like a kind of victory, but maybe I was reading too much into it.

Just before eleven, she pulled off the white dress she'd been wearing, revealing a red bikini that showed off all her curves. She pulled on an oversized sun hat and wandered to the plunge pool. My mouth dropped open like a lovesick, cartoon puppy. The parts she kept hidden were just as mesmerizing as everything on display.

She was gorgeous.

We spent the rest of the day not exchanging a word. At around one, I asked our butler to create a small buffet. When it arrived, I made her a plate and put it on the table next to the lounger. Our butler mixed up some drinks and left them in the fridge, so I made sure both our glasses were kept topped up.

At just before three, she tried to apply sunscreen to her back, so I took the bottle from her and slowly rubbed in the lotion to every exposed part of her back. She thanked me with a smile.

By seven, long after the sun had set, Parker closed her book, picked up the array of glasses and plates we'd gotten through and took them inside, then headed to the bathroom.

I took a quick shower after her and at eight thirty, handed her a glass of champagne. In my head, I wished her a happy honeymoon. After dinner, she put on her pig pajamas and slid under the bedsheet. I got in the other side and faced her.

She reached over and stroked her palm down my face. "Thank you for today." My heart thundered in my chest at the sound of her voice. It was like I hadn't heard her speak for weeks. "It's the nicest gift anyone ever gave me."

I was more than happy she was happy, but I wasn't quite sure what I'd done.

"It means so much that you listened to me and gave me a chance to recharge. And I'm also pleased you didn't listen to me and leave me on my own."

I trailed my fingers up her arm. "There's no one I'd rather say nothing to than you." It was true. Today had been the most comfortable I'd ever been in silence. Most comfortable I'd ever been with any woman.

She blushed at the compliment. "You sleepy?" she asked.

My hand slipped down her back and began to trace the outline of her spine. "No. You?"

She slid her leg between mine and shook her head.

My hand snaked lower and smoothed over her bottom. Her palm trailed down my chest.

We continued to slowly circle each other, caressing each other's bodies, exploring every line and surface like we were two animals who just met after thinking they were the only one of their kind. It was an exploration full of curiosity, reverence, and intimacy, and neither of us wanted to rush it.

"What are we doing?" she whispered.

"What do you want to do?"

"I want you to kiss me," she replied.

She wasn't going to have to ask twice. I rolled her onto her back and slid on top of her, caging her with my arms. I trailed my teeth along her jaw and took a deep breath to try to steady my racing heart. God, she smelled so good. She tasted of margaritas and sunshine, and I wanted to swallow her down. I took her top lip between mine, savoring the sweetness, and groaned as she pressed her tongue into my mouth.

My cock sprung to life between us and I circled my hips, grinding into her, our clothes still separating us. God, it felt so good to be touching her, so right, like something had been missing and now had finally slotted into place.

Her nails bit into my shoulders and I groaned at the unexpected sensation. She hooked her legs around my waist, shifting my cock so it connected to her clit, and moaned into my mouth.

Fuuuck. I wasn't sure I'd consciously been waiting for this moment, but it was like I'd been let off a leash and I was finally free. "I think I wanted this all along," I said as I pulled back to look at her. Her normally sleek bob was a little mussed and her lips were red because of my mouth rather than any lipstick.

"You wanted to kiss me with tongue and dry hump me in front of my family?"

I laughed. "If I knew it would be this good, then probably."

I leaned up, creating space between our bodies, and Parker unbuttoned her pajama top. At the sight of the flesh of her stomach, I sunk down to lick and suck and kiss my way up, up, up to her neck. "You have the most gorgeous skin," I said.

"Must be all the cream puffs," she said, and I couldn't help but grin like the cat who got the cream, licked the bowl, and got a refill. "What?" she asked.

"You," I replied.

"What about me?"

"I like you. I like talking with you and I like saying nothing with you. I like being with you."

She trailed a finger down my chest and it was the most seductive touch I'd ever felt. "I like you too."

I shifted to pull off her pajama trousers as she slipped off her top. I took in her body in its full glory. "You're so beautiful."

"No, *you're* so beautiful." She sat up and smoothed her hand down my arm. "It's like you're made from velvet-coated steel or something."

I exhaled at the sight of her shifting breasts and the feel of her fingers tracing every bump and curve of my body. "You feel as good as I thought you would when I first ran into you."

"You taste just as good as I thought you would covered in cream."

"I like your thumb," she said, cupping my hand in hers and raising it to her mouth so she could press a kiss to my skin. "And your hands." She turned my palm down and kissed my knuckles. "This trail of hair seems like a tease, a promise of something more." She shifted to sit in my lap and pressed her hands over my chest. "Like it's protecting something precious that not many get to see. Or feel. Or experience."

We both looked down and saw my erection protruding up and out of my boxers, flat against my stomach. I lay back on the pillows and she pulled the material down and off my legs before crawling back over me, her legs either side of my waist.

We locked eyes as she shifted further up, her folds dragging up my thickness. She stopped and huffed out breath.

"What are we doing?" she asked.

There were so many right answers, I didn't know which one to pick.

Doing what felt good?

Acting on instinct?

Exploring our feelings?

Instead of giving her an answer when I wasn't sure, I smoothed my hands over her waist and locked them over her hips. I didn't want her to do anything she didn't want to, but she had to know I wanted this too.

She started to shift, little movements up and down, the drag of her over my cock sending electric pulses to my balls. The knowing smile framed by that sleek, black bob chased my heartbeat around my body.

Ever since bumping into her in the hotel lobby, I'd thought Parker was fun and intriguing and completely gorgeous. It was why I bid on her. But how had I never focused on her body more? Her breasts were perfect and round, with dusky pink nipples that jutted forward like they were begging to be tasted. The flare of her waist, the sweep of her neck, her soft, hot skin. Her lips, that smile, the way I could tell when she was looking at me. It all cranked up my desire into the red zone. She was the kind of woman who lived in every man's fantasy.

How had I held off until now? Now she was naked and on top of me, I felt like a bloody idiot for not making a move sooner.

She leaned forward and arched her back. The way her fingers curled against my chest and her arse widened was too much. I sat up and captured her nipple in my mouth, curling my tongue, sucking and pulling.

Her hands thrust in my hair and she moaned. "What are we doing?" she asked again.

I pulled back, replacing my mouth with my hand as I reached behind her and my fingers found her wetness. "We're rutting, fucking, making love." We locked eyes and I slid my hand back to her hips. "Is it okay?" I asked.

"Don't stop. I want this."

I rolled her onto her back and pressed my lips to hers—my tongue finding hers—exploring her mouth like I wanted to swallow down her words and store them in a secret place where I'd have them forever.

She reached between us, circling my cock and pulling her hand up to my crown then pressing it down on her clit. She lifted her head to look at me and her eyelids fluttered closed.

Adrenaline rushed through me at the thought that I got to make her feel so good and I shifted back onto my knees, grabbed my wallet from the bedside table, and pulled out a condom. Christ, I only had three. It wasn't going to be enough.

She watched as I rolled it over my cock

"You're beautiful," I said.

"You're beautiful," she whispered.

I bent over her and pressed inside.

"More," she sighed. "Deep."

"More?" I asked. I was doing everything I could to hold back.

"I want you so, so deep."

Fuck. Whatever self-control I had left dissolved and we locked eyes as I drove into her slow and oh so deep.

"Fuck, Parker, I think I'm going to pass out. You feel so good."

She stroked her fingers up my back and I groaned.

"Everywhere you're touching me. It feels . . . like I'm going to explode."

I'd never felt anything like it. Yes, we were in a beautiful place, and yes, we'd had the most relaxing day. Yes, she had the perfect body and the perfect smile, but they couldn't be the only reasons this felt so bloody fantastic. It wasn't just good sex. This was something else I couldn't put words around.

"I know," she said. "How have we not done this before?"

I chuckled as I started to move over her. "I don't know, but I'm not going to waste a single moment from now on."

I was wondering whether Amazon Prime delivered here, and whether I could order an industrial-sized box of condoms. We were going to need it.

As I thrusted in a steady rhythm, Parker continued her exploration of my body. Her fingers pressed into my collarbones and over my pecs. Her feet swept up my thighs and over my arse.

I lifted her leg up and over my shoulder and groaned as I drove in again from a different angle.

"Just like that," she whispered as I clenched my jaw, trying to fend off an orgasm charging toward me like an armed battalion. "Shit, Tristan."

Her expression was panic and desire. I leaned forward, pressing my forehead to hers, wanting to reassure her that whatever she was feeling, I was right there with her.

"Tristan," she called out. She began to tighten around my cock, and she dug her nails into my chest. "I'm—"

I kept pushing into her, wanting to prolong her pleasure, however painful it was for me. She arched into me and I was gone. I thrust up into her, wanting to get closer, deeper, wanting to share everything with her.

Her entire body shook beneath me. With my head bowed, I smoothed my hand over her legs, trying to soothe her. Eventually she stilled and I leaned and pressed a kiss to her lips.

"What was that?" she asked.

I rolled off her, discarded the condom, and pulled her

toward me, our bodies intertwined as we continued to settle and subdue each other.

I couldn't answer her. Whatever we just shared was unlike anything I'd ever experienced before.

"That was honeymoon sex," I said.

TWENTY-THREE

Parker

I shuffled out of the bathroom like a ninety-year-old who'd lost her Zimmer frame. "You've broken me." We'd done nothing for the last thirty-six hours other than have sex, sleep, eat if we remembered, chug glasses of water, and have more sex.

In bed. In the shower for two. In the plunge pool. On the sofa. Back in the bed.

Tristan chuckled. "I have to admit, I'm exhausted. It's like our own version of circuits."

"It's a lot better than circuits. Although my body would disagree with me right now."

"You want to leave the room?" Tristan asked as I lifted the sheet and scooted into his arms—one of my favorite places to be.

"I mean, no. But if we don't, I think I might endure permanent damage."

"We could go and sit out by the pool. That way we'd be forced to—"

"Your penis would be forced under cover and I'd be safe?"

"For a while at least."

"I should catch up on emails." It was the first time I'd thought about work since the wedding.

"I think that's the last thing you should do," he replied. "Let's get out of here and go have some fun." He threw back the sheet and I watched while he got out of bed and headed to the bathroom. Sutton was right, Tristan was like a page out of an anatomy textbook.

"I'm getting in the shower." He narrowed his eyes. "Alone. You're going to stay there until I get out. Then you're getting in the shower. And then we're both going to leave this hotel room and go find something to do that's not sexy and just about having fun."

I fake pouted and watched his perfectly peachy bottom head into the bathroom.

Maybe he was right and it was time for a little fun.

Within the hour, we were both dressed and in the lobby, ready for our nonsexual fun. Everyone looked so happy and relaxed, and I realized it had been a while since I'd left London. Years more than that since I'd been away on a holiday that wasn't about meeting donors for the charity.

Maybe my father knew exactly what he was doing when he gave Tristan and I this trip.

"We're too late for Chichen Itza today," Tristan said as he came back from the concierge desk. "And I wasn't sure whether or not mountain biking was your jam."

I grimaced. "No, it's most definitely *not* my jam, my marmalade, or my chocolate spread."

"Chocolate spread?" He raised his eyebrows in a suggestive pulse. "Now that gives me some ideas." I elbowed him in the ribs. "You're cute when you're grumpy."

"You're *not* cute if you make me go mountain biking."

He shook his head, slung his arms around my shoulders, and guided me out into the Mexican sunshine. "I have something much more fun planned. "You have a swimsuit under your dress, right?"

We headed toward the ocean, silky sand slipping between our toes. Tristan led me to the jetty that stretched out into aqua-blue ocean.

"What do you think. Can you handle it?" he asked as we got to the water's edge.

"Handle what?"

He pointed toward a couple of pedalos that were tied to the timber piles.

"I've never been in one before. Is it fun?"

He shrugged. "No clue. Let's find out."

An employee of the hotel appeared and untied a bright yellow pedalo. "Your paddleboat, miss." He helped me in from the jetty. "You know where you're going?" he asked.

"Yup, we got it," Tristan replied like he was a master pedalo rider.

"Where are we going?" I asked.

"Just going to explore the coastline for a bit and enjoy the sunshine. Is that okay?"

I shrugged. "At least my body will have a chance to recover from thirty-six hours in bed with you."

"We don't have to talk if it makes you feel any better."

I laughed. "You know how to make a girl happy."

"So many years wasted on building an armory of seduction techniques when all I needed to do was shut my mouth."

We pedaled out from the jetty. Tristan steered us across the bay to where there were some rocks jutting out into the water.

"It's really beautiful here." The green water, bright blue sky, white sand—it triggered something in me. "It's like how we're programmed to find puppies cute. It's the same with this place. It would be impossible to find anyone who didn't think this place was glorious."

I glanced across at him, his aviators covering those pale blue eyes, his tanned skin that looked even more golden than usual against the white of his t-shirt and the glare of the sun. He looked like he belonged here, in a place where no one could say anything other than how beautiful, how relaxing, how completely glorious he was.

"What are you looking at?" he asked, his gaze straight ahead.

"You," I replied. "You think we can have sex on a pedalo?"

We were just about to reach the rocks and Tristan nodded past them. "I've got a better place."

Behind the rocks was a small secluded cove that sheltered a white sand beach.

"You knew this was here?" I asked as we peddled closer to the shore.

"They told me back at the hotel."

"Wait, is that—oh my gosh, Tristan, did you arrange this?" To the side of the cove, under the shade of a collection of palm trees, was a low table covered with a pink-and-green tablecloth.

"I may have mentioned we were going to stop by."

I glanced over at him and I could tell by his shy smile that he was happy he'd surprised me.

As we got nearer the shore, Tristan jumped out of the pedalo and pulled me onto the beach. A waiter sprang into action, ran over and grabbed the rope, and wrapped it round a rock that protruded from the water. Tristan rounded the pedalo and scooped me out of the contraption and carried me to dry land.

"It's like you're my knight in shining armor. Or swimming trunks." I pressed my lips against his jaw. "How romantic."

We both took a seat overlooking the ocean as the waiter poured us drinks, uncovered platters of food, and then called a speedboat to come and collect him. We were left with a radio and strict instructions to use it if we needed anything at all.

"This is amazing," I said. "You arranged all this?"

"It's very peaceful. And I need you to regain your strength."

I circled the back of his neck with my fingers. "Same," I said. "But it would be a shame not to take advantage of such a secluded spot." I reached under his t-shirt and stroked my hand down his abs.

"You're insatiable," he said, shaking his head. "I need food and water before you have me again."

"I knew you couldn't handle me."

He grinned as he dished up lunch for me first and then himself.

"I can't believe you did all this."

"It's our honeymoon. If I can't be romantic here, then when?"

"I know the wedding is a means to an end and everything, but is it weird that it feels less and less . . ."

"Like we're pretending?" he asked. "Maybe because we're not."

I leaned and placed a kiss on his arm. "If that's the case, then I'm pretty sure we can get creative with lunch." I kneeled up, stripping off my dress and bikini top.

Tristan looked me up and down and groaned before reaching for his t-shirt and pulling it off.

"Oh no, Mr. Dubrow. You said you needed food and water first. So, food and water it is." I lay on the sand and placed a row of sliced fruit from my collarbone, between my breasts, over my stomach, and down to where my bikini bottoms started.

"You look good enough to eat, Mrs. Dubrow. Or is it Frazer-Dubrow. Did you decide?"

Before I could tell him I was keeping my own name, Tristan bent and took a bite of melon from my stomach, his tongue lingering on my skin and making it tingle. He moved up to the next slice and the next, then trailed his tongue between my breasts for some pineapple.

I clenched my hands at his breath on my skin and tried not to arch my back at the feel of his tongue. With his teeth he trailed a piece of cold melon from the center of my chest across to circle my nipple, toying with it and turning it hard and sharp.

"Hey, you're meant to be eating," I admonished him.

He swallowed the piece of fruit and began feeding on my breast, his teeth replacing the cold, hard melon. I shuddered and he gasped and sat back on his knees.

"I'm leaving you sticky," he said. "That won't do." He retraced his steps back down my body, sucking and licking. I had no idea if it was the juice of the fruit he was after or whether he was just trying to drive me wild. He arranged himself between my legs, eating his way down, down, down until he reached my bikini bottoms. "I'm not quite done feasting," he said, his breath hot over my sex. He rolled down the fabric and his tongue continued the trail down until it hit my clit. I couldn't help but moan. I'd been left waiting too long. He chuckled and began to lick and flick and circle, my hips swaying as if trying to escape because the pleasure was just too much to bear.

His large hands grabbed the fabric of my bikini bottoms and stripped me of them in one swift movement before pinning my hips to the sand.

"You're not going to escape." He bowed his head and licked me from back to front almost perfunctorily, like it was a recce for a future mission. I almost came on the spot.

He chuckled. "Oh, Cream Puff. Not so soon."

I tried to take a deep breath to push back my climax but it was as if I had rocks in my lungs and I was trying to race up a mountain. "Tristan."

"I'm right here," he said, before plunging his tongue into me.

I cried out and a growl of pleasure echoed from between my thighs, travelling like a wave up my body and down my limbs. His tongue pushed firmly up and down my folds and another burst of pleasure set off a tsunami of bliss, followed by another and another until I was crying out because I just couldn't take any more. I thought I might just burst with how he made me feel. Just before I passed out, my orgasm ripped through me like a dam had burst and I reached for Tristan, needing him to hold me.

As I floated back down from my climax, he pressed a kiss between my collarbones, one on my neck and another on my forehead.

"You're delicious," he said as he arranged himself on the sand next to me and rested my head on his chest.

I didn't have the energy to respond. My legs were boneless and liquid. My voice had been carried out to sea.

We lay like that for what seemed like hours until I became aware of the seagulls overhead. "I have my hearing back," I said.

"And you're talking. I was worried there for a while."

"Me too. I thought maybe that was it for me."

Tristan chuckled. "We should eat. There are wraps in the cooler. And we both need to drink."

"I suppose," I said, unmotivated to do anything. "I'm not sure I can move."

Tristan went to retrieve some food and water and I managed to sit up and look around at the cove we were in.

"It's beautiful here." I wasn't sure if lust had dulled my senses earlier or whether the orgasm had heightened them, but the cove seemed more beautiful, the sea greener, the sand finer and peppered with jewel-like shells.

"It is," Tristan said, sitting down opposite me and placing our lunch and some drinks between us on a cloth. "You need to drink." He opened the screw cap of the bottle and handed it to me.

"Thanks." Is that what relationships were meant to be—someone focused on your welfare and happiness as much as their own?

"I can tell by your smile that you're thinking something interesting. What is it?"

"My smile told you that? I'm always thinking about something interesting."

He fixed me with a *be-careful-or-I'll-kiss-you* look and bit into his sandwich.

"I was just thinking how pleased I am that you bid on me at that auction." So many coincidences and almost-didn't-happens had led us to this exact moment. How easy would it have been for us never to have even met?

He nodded. "And to think, I wasn't supposed to go."

I frowned. "What do you mean?"

He shrugged. "You know, most of those charity things, I

just write a check and send my apologies. If Arthur hadn't been the one to ask me, I would . . . Never mind."

"If it hadn't been for Arthur asking, you would never have come to the gala? I get it. That doesn't bother me."

"That wasn't what I was going to say."

I tilted my head to the side. I wanted to hear him uncensored. "So tell me."

The waves lapped at the shore of our private cove and a cloud settled in front of the sun, cloaking us in shade for the first time today.

"If I'd bothered to look more carefully at the invitation and seen that it was a gala supporting Sunrise . . ." He glanced at me, held my gaze as if he was deciding whether or not to continue, and then looked away. "If I'd know the evening was raising money for a charity helping children with congenital heart defects, I would never have attended."

I tried to cover my shiver. I knew Tristan wasn't a bad man. I knew he wasn't ungenerous or unfeeling, so why would Sunrise's mission have stopped him coming to the gala?

"When I was eight years old, my parents had another a child. A girl. Her name was Isadora. Issy."

He didn't need to say anymore. The haunted look he wore told me everything I needed to know. I dropped my sandwich and moved to sit next to him, my arm hooking around his waist. He didn't move.

"She died when I was eleven after years of hospital visits, treatments, pain and suffering." His sister had been the family member who died that he spoke about in the bathroom at our engagement party. It all made sense why his mother would have been so emotional about guests being asked to contribute to Sunrise.

I pressed my head against his shoulder. I wanted to climb inside him and hug him from the inside out.

"She was beautiful and smiley and never pronounced the R in my name. It was always Tis-tan. You know?"

I nodded, trying not to let the tears slip from my eyes.

"She had these blonde curls that would bounce back no matter if you brushed her hair or if she was just out of the bath."

I could see her as if she were right in front of me.

He took a breath and continued. "Her illness consumed all of us. I would creep into her bedroom at night to make sure she was still breathing and find my mother or my father in there weeping. And then when the time came and she died, it was like our world stopped. I remember feeling such guilt when I felt anything but grief. My parents were so miserable for so long, I thought that was how I was meant to be feeling. I felt disloyal for any happiness that crept in through the crack of my broken heart. It was almost unbearable. Looking back, they were navigating the breakdown in their marriage. They split up the following summer and . . ."

His confessions were like blades slicing through my stomach. Painful beyond belief but only a fraction of how Tristan must feel. I wanted to stop it, make it better for him, pull out those memories and drown them in the sea-green ocean.

"I'm so sorry," I said. He'd suffered so much pain and it was buried so deep, I'd had no idea. It made sense now how emotional Tristan's mother had been at the engagement party, the QR code he'd arranged for donations, and why he'd agreed to marry me.

"I hope the money from your trust fund will make it easier," he said. "Hopefully take the pressure off and keep other families together."

"I hope so too," I replied. "You lost more than a sister when Issy died."

He nodded, his head falling into his hands, his fingers sliding into his hair. "My whole family died with her. At least, the family we were before we lost her. We've never been the same."

I couldn't bear seeing him in so much pain. I climbed into his lap facing him, wrapped my arms and legs around him, and held him. And held him.

He buried his face in my neck His breathing never stumbled but he didn't try to pull away. We sat there, entangled in each other, closer than ever.

"I don't talk about it. Not ever. Not with anyone. Thinking back to that time is too painful."

I wanted to say that he could tell me anything, that I was his safe space, but there was no need. He knew it already.

TWENTY-FOUR

Tristan

The alarm on my phone went off and I reached across the bed, just like I had every morning in Mexico. Except this morning, my hands didn't find Parker. I opened my eyes to find the other half of the bed empty.

We'd gotten home last night and she'd fallen asleep on the sofa in front of the TV. I'd carried her upstairs to bed.

"Parker?" I called out, but there was no reply.

I staggered out of bed and into the hallway, where I saw her bedroom door ajar. I pushed the door open to find Parker fast asleep.

What was she doing?

I scooped her up and, as I was laying her down back in my bed, she opened her eyes. "You're always carrying me places," she said, her voice full of sleep.

"It's because you're so tiny—it's easy and quick." I slipped back under the sheets, lying on my side next to her. I propped my head up on my hand. "Why did you go back to the guest room?"

She dragged her hands down her face and groaned. "I don't know. I suppose I didn't want you to wake up and wish I wasn't next to you."

Now it was my time to groan. "Why would you think that?"

She propped herself up onto her elbows. "If this was my house, I might feel that way if you woke up in my bed. You know I like my space."

I chuckled. "Oh how I love your truth bombs, Parker. But for the record, I didn't want to wake up to an empty bed."

"You sure?" she asked. "I'm a grabby sleeper. I like to starfish."

"I noticed. I might have to invest in an Alaskan king." My phone buzzed on the nightstand. "It's Gabriel," I explained. "He wants to catch up for dinner. Are you free tonight?"

"He's inviting me?"

"He's inviting us."

Parker sighed. "Tristan, he knows we're not a real couple. He'll be inviting you, not us." She sat up properly this time and looked me right in the eye. "We've been thrown off course a little. Maybe it was the sunshine or the margaritas. Whatever it was, we're back to real life now. And in real life, we're not a real couple."

She was starting to piss me off. If she was trying to dismiss what had happened between us as a holiday romance, I was going to get irritated.

I knew how good Mexico had been.

I knew how close we'd gotten.

I knew she felt it too.

I swung her legs around and shifted her onto my lap so she was facing me. "Stop freaking out, Parker."

"I'm not freaking out. I'm being practical."

"No, you're freaking out. We're not going back to how things were before Mexico. Even if we wanted to—which neither of us do—it would be impossible. Too much has happened."

"You're telling me what I want and don't want?" she asked.

My jaw was tight and my heartbeat thundered in my chest like horses' hooves. I wanted her and I knew she wanted me too, but something inside her was trying to sabotage us before we'd even got going. "Actually I am. And I'm right, too. But I want to understand why you're pulling away."

"It's just so complicated. What do we do, file for divorce in ninety days and then start dating? It's too weird."

"We'll figure out ninety days in ninety days. Between now and then, we're going to enjoy being with each other. Waking up together. Going to bed together. Eating together and socializing with each other's friends."

She tucked her hair behind her ear. "I don't have a good track record with boyfriends," she said, glancing up at me sheepishly.

I wanted to tell her I was already president of the Bad at Relationships Club, but something told me there was more she had to say.

"I told you that I was engaged once. A while ago."

I held my breath. I wanted to hear more about it but I hadn't wanted to ask.

"It didn't last long." She let out a bitter laugh. It was a tone I'd never heard from her before. "Right around the time he found out I didn't have access to any money of my own, he . . . left me."

"What happened?" I didn't need to know. I could guess

the rest, and it made me want to punch the guy's lights out. What a weak dickhead. Couldn't make his own money so wanted to live off someone else's.

"It took him a while to realize I had no money of my own, and it took me more than a while to figure out who he was." She sighed and tucked her hair behind her ears again, though it was already there. "I lived in a bigger flat then. A place in Mayfair. I ran in a different circle. I suppose he thought I was rich—after all, I'm Arthur Frazer's daughter, aren't I? But I wasn't rich. Dad gave me money if I asked, but I didn't ask very often. Day-to-day, I lived off what I earned. My bank account was in the black but it wasn't overflowing. Looking back, he was always disappointed when I gave him handmade gifts at Christmas or his birthday. I missed all the hints he'd drop about expensive watches or gadgets. None of it means anything to me, so I just . . . didn't pick up the signals. And then one day he straight-out asked for a camera for Christmas and pointed out the model. I laughed and told him I couldn't afford it. It was something like five thousand pounds. Would have been a drop in the bucket if I had the Frazer money he thought I did."

She looked up at me.

"Five thousand pounds is a lot of money on a Christmas gift, regardless of how wealthy you are." I wanted to buy Parker a bath full of diamonds and it still wouldn't be enough, but everything was relative.

"Right," she replied. "And I didn't have it."

"Your father doesn't strike me as a man who would keep you short," I said.

"Of course not. He's more than generous, but I never expected him to supplement my income. He bought me a house. I left university without any debt. It wasn't like I didn't get help; I just didn't get an allowance. Because I was a grown woman. He would offer from time to time, and he talked about setting up a trust fund, but I wasn't interested. I always said I would go to him if I needed anything, but I was comfortable with what I had. And you know me well enough to understand that paying my own way felt . . . important, somehow. Anyway, Mike got really upset with me when I said no to the camera. I tried to talk to him about it and suggested something cheaper, but he just got more irate. He told me I should speak to my father and that I was being selfish."

It took everything I had not to ask for this guy's surname and cause him some serious problems online. I could have his bank account drained within ten minutes. Give me a day and I could have his passport cancelled. A colorful criminal record is a lovely gift at any time of year, and priceless, too.

"So you dumped him?"

She hung her head. "No. I bought him the camera."

My stomach plummeted into the floor.

"I put it on my credit card. Looking back, I realize what an idiot I was, but at the time I just wanted to make him happy. Before then everything had seemed so perfect. I just wanted to go back to that. I thought the camera would do it. A few months later, he suggested a trip—he said it would help us relax before the wedding preparations got underway. We hadn't landed on a venue or anything, in part because we wanted really different things. He wanted a destination wedding where everyone was flown out to the Maldives and put up in a resort. I wanted something more . . . intimate."

"Something more you," I said.

She shrugged. "Anyway, for this pre-wedding trip, he

wanted to go to Dubai. He'd planned out luxury accommodations and a private plane to get there. But I had work and we were short staffed, and I told him I couldn't make it. So he said he could make it a boys' trip. I wasn't thrilled because it was meant to be our pre-wedding trip, but I accepted it. And then he asked for my credit card." She gave a half laugh. "What an idiot."

"You gave it to him?"

She shook her head. "No. It was maxed out from the camera. I told him that. So he told me to go ask my dad. I refused. And then over the next few weeks, he started to question me about whether or not I had a trust fund and if I was the beneficiary of my dad's will. Finally I told him that my father was leaving everything to charity and that he didn't believe in handing wealth down through the generations."

"What did Mike have to say about that?"

"He didn't even try to pretend. He just looked me in the eye and told me he wanted my engagement ring back."

I cupped her face in my hand, trying to erase the expression of sadness she wore.

"I'd been lied to and manipulated. I'd fallen for his charm and compliments and . . ." She shook her head. "I was such a fool."

"No," I said. "He was the fool."

"Anyway, apparently he's in Monaco now. No doubt trying to land a rich wife."

"Something tells me you didn't bounce back quite so easily." Perhaps she still hadn't, given I'd found her sleeping in the spare room this morning.

"You were the first date I'd had since it all happened."

I frowned but she answered my question before it had fully formed in my brain. "It was six years ago."

Things started to slot into place. Arthur happy to have me take her to dinner. Gifting us the honeymoon. He wanted his daughter to trust someone again.

I sat and pulled her onto my lap. "He's the one to blame in all this."

"I know. But now I never know if someone likes me because of who I am or because of what they think I can give them."

I sighed. "Everyone wants something."

"Exactly. It's impossible to know who to trust."

"That's not what I meant. More that anyone in your life will have expectations—maybe it's loyalty. Compassion. Maybe it's protection. Friendship. A shoulder to cry on. A good time. Sex. Status. Money. Whatever it is, we give and we take. That's just human nature. It's more that he pretended to be different than who he was. And deep down, his values—what he wanted from you—didn't align with yours. And vice versa. He couldn't offer you what you needed."

She snaked an arm around my waist and pressed her cheek against my chest. "I've never thought about it like that."

We lay in comfortable silence for what felt like hours. "I like talking with you," she said finally. "You're not meant to have abs like this"_she prodded my stomach—"and be wise and thoughtful. It's strictly forbidden."

"You can trust me," I said. "You can have my shoulder to cry on any time you need it. I promise you honesty. And friendship. And—"

"Good sex?" She laughed, and I felt every muscle in my body unlock.

"I'm not Mike," I said.

She sucked in a deep breath. "I just don't know how to navigate this."

"What about one step at a time?" I suggested.

"You think it's going to be easy?"

"I think every day with you is easy. Much easier than a day without you."

She shrugged. "So we just . . ." She grimaced. "Go with the flow?"

I laughed and pressed a kiss to her lips. "Try it. You might enjoy it."

Her hands smoothed over my shoulders. "Does that mean I get to touch you like this for the next ninety days?"

"I positively encourage it."

She took my hand and slid my fingers between her legs. "Does it mean you get to touch me like this for the next ninety days?"

I pushed my thumb over her clit and dipped two fingers inside her as she met me with a swivel of her hips. "Oh absolutely. There will be lots of that."

I caught her nipple between my thumb and forefinger and began to squeeze and roll and pull. "And there will be some of this." I shifted and pushed her back onto the bed, the angle giving me better access. I pushed my fingers deeper. "And more of this."

I lay down between her thighs and replaced my thumb with my tongue. I began to lick and flick and grind into her. "And don't forget this." By the time I was done with her, she'd never dare leave my bed again.

"Oh god, it's not enough," she groaned. It wasn't exactly the phrase I liked to hear in bed. I lifted myself up on my hands to see her face. "I need you inside of me." That was better. "I want to be full of you." That was much better.

I couldn't help but smile. I liked her needy and pleading. It was so different from the capable, independent woman she was at every other moment of the day. Seeing both sides of her, and knowing I was the only one to do so, was intoxicating.

I kneeled up, rolled a condom over my straining cock, and without warning, pushed into her, trying not to explode as she arched off the bed. "Like this?"

"Oh god. I can't breathe," she gasped. "I actually can't breathe. You feel so good."

"You like me deep inside you, pushing into you like this?" I started up my rhythm, trying to ignore how she grabbed at the sheets, pushed her hands into her hair, bit down on her lip. Like she was possessed. By me.

"Always," she huffed out. "Always so good."

I pushed her knees to her chest so I could get deeper and she screamed. The vibrations nearly exploded my balls and I paused for a second, just to regroup. Everything this woman did turned me on. Every smile. Every glance over her shoulder. Every shade of lipstick. Every scream. It all made me want her more often and for longer. She made me insatiable.

I picked up speed, pounding into her, over and over. Knowing she was vulnerable with me, giving me permission to do what I wanted to her—and I only wanted to make her feel good—was like a drug for me.

And her. It was like she was high on me.

On us.

On what our bodies could do together.

I glanced down to where we were connected—where I slid into her hot, wet pussy—and my vision blurred. She was so beautiful. Her heart, every angle of her body. I'd never known a woman could be so fucking compelling, could have me coming undone like this. There was no part of her I didn't want to possess.

She reached for me, fingering the beads of sweat gathered at my hairline. She wanted to possess me too. I could feel it. See it in her eyes.

"Parker," I said, wanting her to know that I knew how she felt—like I wouldn't stop fucking her if a hurricane tore through the building. Like there had been nothing close to this feeling my entire life and I knew there never would be. Like nothing could tear us apart.

"Tristan," she called out, her voice full of concern.

I'd been too rough. Fuck, it was like I was trying to nail her to the bed. Her nails bit into my shoulder and she bit down on her lip and I realized, far from me going too far, I'd pushed her right to the edge of her orgasm.

Her entire body began to shake and I couldn't stop. Instinctively, I knew that she wanted me to keep fucking her, deeper and deeper. Silently she cried out, her back arched and her entire body shook.

I stilled, the blood in my veins dancing with impatience.

"I need more," she whimpered.

Fuck. I knew it. She wanted what I wanted. She needed what I needed. We were twinned. Aligned. We were bloody perfect for each other.

I plowed into her again, fast and deep, as if I were mining for her very soul.

She started to shake again, her body contracting around my cock. So soon?

"More. Don't stop," she cried out.

I clamped my hands over her shoulders and kept fucking and fucking and fucking until it was like I'd run out of oxygen. A flash of white light tore through the room like lightning, a guttural roar ripped out of my throat, and pain bit into my muscles. Something buried deep inside me, that had been sleeping for a lifetime, had been awoken. My orgasm stretched into life, rumbling deep inside me, then chased through my body. I'd never felt anything like it.

Parker began to shake underneath me again and I collapsed onto her, needing to be closer, wanting to protect her and share with her everything I was feeling.

She sighed and I moved to her side, suddenly worried I had squashed her.

"You okay?" I asked.

"Think so."

I swept my hand down her body. We lay like that until I could summon up the strength to move. I grabbed a bottle of water by the bed, unscrewed the cap, and held it out for her.

"I can't," she whispered.

I set down the water, moved around the bed and pulled her up so she was leaning against my chest. Then I held the bottle to her lips. She took a sip. And another.

"You're amazing," I said. She really was the most extraordinary woman I'd ever met. Not only was she deliciously sexy, but she was so much more. She was insightful. She was strong, sweet, and vulnerable. She was kind and clever and thoughtful. It made me want to be all those things too. I wanted to be good enough for her. She deserved a man who would strive to be her equal. A man who'd take care of her.

"I can hear you thinking behind me," she said after a few minutes. "Penny for them?"

"We need a shower," I replied.

She shook her head. "I can't make it."

I scooped her off the bed and carried her through into the bathroom, then set her on the built-in bench in the shower.

She looked exhausted. As if I'd wrung her out and there was nothing she had left to give. Once the water was warm, I stepped a couple of feet away, grabbed some shampoo, and lathered my hair. I'd wash myself and then her. Then I'd wrap her in a towel, dry her and dress her. She wouldn't have to lift a finger. I rinsed off my shampoo and then set about soaping my entire body, massaging the overworked muscles as I worked my way down my body. As I got to the base of my stomach, I glanced over to find her watching me. A hint of something in her eyes made me stop.

I knew that expression.

She was as insatiable as I was.

Despite the rush of the shower, I could hear her heavy breaths. She liked to watch. She wanted to know what happened next. I didn't take my gaze from her as I pushed my hand down and circled the base of my cock. Her pupils dilated and her tongue darted out and licked her lips. Fuck, she was so sexy. Slowly, I began to drag my fist up and around my length, massaging the soap along my hardening erection.

I continued to watch her take in the sight of me stroking myself up and down, rounding over my crown and changing the angle as I grew harder.

She snaked a hand down her body and between her legs and I groaned, tightening my fist. She really couldn't get enough. Her fingers dipped between her folds and she parted her knees.

I stepped toward her. I didn't want to miss anything.

My skin buzzed as the water fell. I knew I could stop touching myself and still come like a freight train watching her break apart, but it wouldn't be as good. It certainly wouldn't be as good as being buried in her.

I released myself and her gaze shot to mine. She must

have known what I was thinking as she moaned out, "Please . . ."

I pulled her to her feet, spun her around, had her kneel on the bench and placed her palms on the marble of the shower wall.

I was so hard, just the spray of the shower on my shaft made me tighten my jaw and hiss through my teeth. I needed to fuck. I needed to fuck her. My animal instincts took over. I pressed my front against her back and sank into her.

Oh, the relief.

It had just been minutes since the last time I was inside her, but it felt like a lifetime of wanting had been for this moment. I placed my hands over hers and buried my face in her neck. I wanted to get as close to her as I could, our bodies melded together like we were one person. I started to move slowly, wanting to take my time so these moments would last forever. I couldn't ever have imagined myself being so fucking full of adoration for someone else. So fucking needy for more of her, desperate to give her everything I had. It was almost overwhelming.

I linked my arms around her waist and pulled her closer still.

Our movements were slow and sleepy as we both seemed equally content to stretch these minutes into hours.

"You always feel so good," she whispered.

"You make me feel so good," I whispered back.

She twisted her hips as if trying to drive me deeper, trying to get closer. It was like a daylong rain shower had suddenly morphed into an impending storm. The beginnings of my orgasm had rumbled into life like a distant clap of thunder.

"Parker," I groaned out.

She pulled away from me and swiveled to face me. Taking my face in her hands, she guided my face down, pressing her lips to mine, pushing her tongue between my lips to meet mine in a way that said she was half drunk on lust.

I knew the feeling.

I reached behind her thighs and lifted her, pressing her back against the wall before ramming into her, high and fast. She cried out as if it were the first time she'd ever felt me inside her. I didn't know what it was about this woman, but she always knew exactly how to rachet up my lust and desire.

My hands underneath her, my fingers found her folds and she gasped. She pressed her hands into my shoulders and pushed herself flat against the wall as if she were trying to create some distance between us, like she thought she couldn't handle the onslaught of sensation.

But she would.

"Tristan," she called out.

"It feels so good, doesn't it?"

She began to shudder and writhe right in front of me, impaled on my dick. I was doing that to her. I was making this phenomenal woman feel like the sun was rising just for her and that felt fucking incredible.

The waves of her orgasm brought me to the brink and despite denying myself the orgasm of the fucking century, I pulled out just before I came.

She reached around my chest and I wrapped my arms around her neck, and we held each other, letting the spray cover us as we recovered.

Although I wasn't sure I ever wanted to recover from Parker Frazer.

TWENTY-FIVE

Parker

It felt like I had a thousand tiny bruises all over my body. Not that Tristan wasn't careful with me—he was, but I'd never had so much sex in my life. I couldn't go near him without wanting to touch him and touching him led to more touching, which led to naked touching, which led to my body feeling like I'd been run over.

"You look beautiful." Tristan squeezed my hand as we stood on Gabriel and Autumn's doorstep. "You have nothing to be nervous about."

"These people have known you forever and love you. I know I've met them before, but that was different. We weren't . . . I didn't care before. Now I want them to like me."

"They will like you. Because I like you."

I groaned. "That's a terrible thing to say! I want them to like me because I'm a likeable person, not just because—"

"Sorry. I didn't mean it like that." He turned me toward him and cupped my face in his hands, my anxiety draining away. I was safe, without a care in the world. "They're going to like you because you're kind and funny and a great listener, and for all the reasons I like you. Not just because you're my wife. *That's* what I meant."

"Well, when you put it like that, maybe it's okay." I grinned up at him like he'd just said exactly the right thing. Because he had. "Do they know that we're . . . whatever we are?"

He knew without me having to explain what I meant. "I imagine so. They know most things about me before I realize it."

I laughed. "The best kind of friends."

"You're going to have to stop wearing lipstick so I can kiss you without looking like I'm into drag."

I shook my head. "Not going to happen."

Autumn threw open the door, looked at Tristan then at me, then at our joined hands, and squealed. "I knew it." She gathered us both in a hug before releasing us and racing into the house. "Gabriel! Hollie!" she called over her shoulder. "I told you it would happen in Mexico. They're holding hands."

"Does she know we can hear her talking about us?" I asked.

"The good thing about Autumn is that whatever she's thinking comes out of her mouth. And the bad thing about Autumn is that whatever she's thinking comes out of her mouth."

We wandered into the living room, where Gabriel, Dexter, Hollie, and Autumn were all staring at us.

"I'm so excited for you guys," Autumn said. "You seem so perfect together."

"Autumn," Gabriel practically growled, "leave Tristan

and Parker alone. If they want to talk about it, they'll talk about it."

Autumn looked at us hopefully. "You want to talk about it? Please God, tell me you want to talk about it."

"I'm hungry," said Tristan, taking a seat and pulling me down on the sofa next to him. "And Parker and I are a real couple now. We're taking each day as it comes."

That was short and to the point. Hopefully the explanation would satisfy everyone and we could focus on having a pleasant evening.

Hollie sat and sucked in a breath, clearly trying to decide whether or not she had something to say. My heart sank when she began to speak. "But there's no reason why you have to get divorced in ninety days, is there?" she asked. "If you're a couple, and you're happy, why would you get divorced?"

"Exactly," Autumn said, taking a seat next to her sister. "You'd only have to go and get married again later."

"Which could be fun." Hollie and Autumn exchanged a mischievous glance.

They didn't need anyone else to participate in their conversation.

"You two are going to get deported if you don't watch it," Tristan said.

Gabriel stood up. "Yeah, you should both be careful, because if anyone can make it happen, it's Tristan. He'll put you on Interpol's most-wanted list and you'll end up in a maximum-security prison serving life sentences."

"Do lifers get conjugal visits?" Autumn asked, squeezing Gabriel's bottom as he passed in front of her. "Did I mention I made sticky toffee pudding and it looks phenomenal?"

I could barely keep up. We'd covered our relationship, prison regulations, and baking in a two-minute window.

Gabriel came back into the living room, carrying a tray of champagne glasses. "I thought we'd celebrate the happy couple," he said, easing the tray onto the coffee table.

The happy couple? I supposed there were two of us, and we *were* happy. I took a glass and clinked it against everyone else's.

"How's that table coming on, Gabriel?" Tristan asked.

"I'll show you if you like," he said.

Tristan slid his hand around my waist. "I'm just going to have a look at something in Gabriel's workshop. You want to come?"

"I'm okay here," I said, although I wasn't quite sure if that was true. He pressed a kiss against the side of my head and stood.

"Tell us all about Mexico," Hollie said as the door closed behind Gabriel and Tristan. "I've always wanted to go."

"It was beautiful," I said. "The beaches were incredible."

"Tristan's so attentive to you," Autumn said. Her eyes were bright and excitable, and she kind of bounced in her seat when she talked. "It's adorable. I just knew he was going to fall hard when he finally found someone worthy of him. He's such a great guy and so clever and perceptive. It was clear the player stuff was just an act until he found someone he really cared about."

"Player stuff?" I asked.

"She didn't mean player—Autumn, did you?" Hollie asked.

"Sorry, no. Tristan is just always super flirtatious. Like, I think it's almost an addiction or some kind of game to him.

He likes female attention and he's very good at . . . getting women to fawn over him."

Fawn over him? Is that what they thought I was doing? I took a breath. I wasn't sure why I was in the middle of this conversation, but it didn't feel good. Tristan and I hadn't known each other long, but it felt like I knew who he was. I didn't want two near-perfect strangers telling me something about my husband that I didn't already know. I needed to be able to trust that the man I saw was the man he was. I'd had enough men pretending to be people they weren't to last me a lifetime.

"Autumn, you're making him sound like an asshole. And he's not. He's just flirtatious and he's never seemed particularly set on being a one-woman guy—"

I jumped to my feet, too uncomfortable to stay seated. "I think I'd like to see Gabriel's workshop after all."

"Oh God!" Autumn said and she rushed to the door. "Tristan! Come back here. I've upset Parker."

I tried to take some deep breaths. I was sure Autumn and Hollie were trying to be kind by pointing out how my relationship with Tristan was different from any he'd had before, but characterizing him as a flirtatious player wasn't the way to do it.

Tristan appeared in the doorway. "I was gone two minutes. What did you two do?"

"I called you a player," Autumn said. "I was trying to say you're different with Parker, but it came out . . . sideways."

"It's fine," I said. I just wanted everyone to stop talking.

"And I was trying to say how nice it is to see you reformed," Hollie said.

"Fucking hell, you two. Bloody Americans. I want to talk to Parker, privately."

"No," I said. "I'm fine." I didn't want to blow this up into some big drama.

"I'm so sorry." An alarm started ringing in the kitchen and Autumn ran past us both. "Shit, it's the chicken. Gabriel," she called out, "your dinner is burning!"

"Is this too much for you?" he asked. "It's not like this with Stella. She's less . . . boisterous. We should have gone to dinner at Beck's place."

"They're in Barbados," Gabriel said, striding out of his workshop. "You're stuck with us. Come eat some burnt chicken and we can unpick whatever Autumn has done." He guided us to the dining room and I let him, despite the fact that I had my metaphorical running shoes half laced up.

Tristan sat on the shiny oak bench and I slid in next to him. I felt like we were about to embark on group therapy, but I just wanted to forget everything. Autumn and Gabriel piled dish upon dish upon dish on the table, handed out plates, and everyone began to help themselves.

"Okay," Tristan said. "So what exactly did you say, Autumn? Let's deal with this."

Autumn and Hollie were like a double act, relaying what they had said to me in the living room. "It was meant to be a compliment," Autumn said.

Tristan shook his head. "I'm a pretty laid-back guy. I don't mind being roasted by you lot. I can take your jabs and your jokes."

"Yes," Hollie said. "You're lovely."

Tristan ignored her and continued. "But there are some things that I'm not laid back about. I'm not laid back about work. I'm not laid back about anyone who hurts my family. And I'm not laid back about people weighing in on Parker and me."

My stomach somersaulted at the idea that I was some kind of exception in Tristan's life.

"We weren't trying to hurt her, Tristan," Hollie said.

"Honestly we weren't," Autumn added.

"I know you meant well. You both have good hearts, but despite the fact that we're married, Parker and I are still getting to know each other." Tristan was calm but firm in his tone.

He squeezed my leg. "I've always been a flirt. I've always liked women. That's not to say I was shagging everything in London."

It felt like the entire table was watching for my reaction. I wanted to slide off the bench and under the table. "I flirt," Tristan continued. "Or I used to. I was single a long time before you."

I nodded. He never talked about a serious girlfriend, so what he was telling me shouldn't be news. He was hot and solvent—no doubt he had ninety percent of the single straight women of London panting for his attention. "Okay," I said. "It's fine."

"By getting married like we have, we've lied to a lot of people. But I've not lied to you. I promise."

"I'm sorry," Autumn said. "Tristan is a lovely, lovely man who takes more than his fair share of shit from these guys." She pointed at Gabriel and Dexter. "We're just so happy that he's found someone who makes him so happy."

Warmth thawed out my ready-to-run limbs and my shoulders unlocked. "He makes me really happy too," I said. "It's early days and the way things started for us—"

"The cream puffs!" Autumn said. "He told us all about how you peeled one from your dress and took a bite. He knew right then and there he had to take you out."

A smile unfurled on my face and I turned to Tristan. "That's when you decided to bid?"

"I didn't know you were being auctioned at that point. But I knew I wanted to get to know you. Any woman more concerned with enjoying a cream puff than preserving her dress is a special case."

I laughed. Tristan slid his hand over my leg and squeezed.

"I think what my beautiful fiancée was trying to say was," Gabriel said, his tone low and steady, "we care about Tristan a great deal. We just want to see him happy."

"I am happy," Tristan said.

"You hear that, Americans?" Gabriel said. "He's happy." He shot them a look that said they needed to watch what they said. From the way they responded, they'd had the look before.

It was no wonder Tristan was a flirt—it would be a waste if he wasn't. With his smile and those pale blue eyes, most people probably assumed he was flirting even when he wasn't. Now he flirted with me exclusively. I made him happy. The idea that Tristan's happiness was something I contributed to filled me with a warmth I'd not experienced before. It was like an ice cube, buried deep in my heart, that I'd resigned myself would stay frozen forever, had started to melt.

TWENTY-SIX

Parker

I hadn't been back to my apartment since before the honeymoon. I needed to collect my post and check that everything was okay—run the taps, grab a few items of clothes. I slid the key into the bottom lock and tried to turn it anti-clockwise, but it didn't work. I turned my key in the opposite direction and managed to lock it. It hadn't been locked in the first place.

That was the second time I'd left my flat's second lock undone. I was normally so fastidious. I must have just forgotten in Tristan's impatience to leave.

I opened the door tentatively and stepped inside. Everything was familiar, but I didn't feel the same vibe of coming home that I was used to feeling when I walked through the front door. In the last months, Tristan's house had been the place where I slept, showered, cooked. Despite having barely anything of mine surrounding me, Tristan's place had started to feel more than familiar, even if it wasn't quite home to me yet.

I picked up my post from the mat and plodded into the kitchen, where I glanced around for a phone charger. There was always at least one in here. I started to sort my post when something caught my eye. A single red rose sat in a mug on my kitchen table. It was very much dead. And it had very much not been put there by me.

Cold whooshed through my chest and I swallowed before asking myself a million questions. Had Tristan come in and put it there for me to come home to weeks ago and then forgotten? Had I absentmindedly put it there and not remembered? There had to be an explanation. Who else had a key to my flat? My parents had one, but I was one hundred percent sure that they hadn't used it. If my mother couldn't find a lead crystal vase, she would have dumped the rose in the bin before putting it in a mug. I pulled out my phone and took a picture, then sent it to Tristan, asking him if he put it there. I'd not told him I was coming today. The mysterious payments from the charity bank account had stopped and Tristan hadn't seemed concerned for my safety recently. I'd assumed everything was okay.

Tristan's name flashed up on my phone.

"You're back in your flat. Why?"

"I came home to check on things and collect my post."

He didn't respond, which was always the worst kind of response from Tristan. He always had something to say.

I heard the jangle of keys and rustling as if he were putting on a jacket. "Where are you now?"

I was just about to tell him I was sitting at my kitchen table when he said, "Don't say anything."

My heart began to race. Something in Tristan's voice worried me.

"Don't make any sudden movements, but go to the front door and leave. Don't argue with me. Don't say anything.

Please, Parker, just do this. Stay on the phone with me. Head to the stairs. Don't use the lifts."

My hands started to sweat but I picked up my post and stood. "Okay."

"Do you have a lot of post?" Tristan asked.

I glanced at the bundle in my hand as I headed to the door. "Not a lot. It's less than I expected. Mostly junk."

"Lots of circulars from estate agents offering you free quotations?"

"I guess." Why was he fixated on my post?

"Yeah, I get a lot of those too."

I stepped out into the corridor of my building and shut the door of my flat.

"Answer yes or no, are you out of your flat?"

"Yes," I said, my heartrate picking up again.

"Don't run but head to the stairs quickly and then get outside as soon as you can."

I did what Tristan said, walking briskly to the end of the corridor and out the emergency exit to the stairwell.

In less than a minute, I was heading out onto the road from my building. Tristan was coming toward me.

He saw me, hung up his phone, and sprinted toward me.

"You okay?" he asked, sweeping his hands down my arms and looking me over like I might be missing a limb or something.

"Why wouldn't I be?"

"You didn't leave a rose on the kitchen table. Neither did I. Was the door unlocked when you went in?"

"Yes, but we left in such a hurry that—"

"Did you change the locks like you promised?"

"I was planning to. What with the wedding and the unexpected honeymoon, I just hadn't gotten around to it—"

"So last time we were at your flat was when we came to collect some things for the honeymoon?" he asked.

I tried to think but I was struggling to focus. "Yes. I think so—yes, that's the last time I was here before today."

"We locked both locks. I took note. Someone's been in your flat. Don't go back there again."

A car was idling at the curb and Tristan ushered me inside before following me and telling the driver to take us back to Notting Hill. "I didn't mention it, but the payments started on your personal bank account a couple of weeks ago. I presume you didn't notice. They've been clever about it, camouflaging them to look like a payment to Amazon."

"Why didn't you say anything?"

"I didn't have much to say." His jaw was tense. The laid-back Tristan who normally inhabited his body had taken a day off. "I still haven't gotten to the bottom of who's taking these payments, but now, with the payments being taken from your personal account instead of the charity, and someone leaving you that rose—it's beyond creepy. We need to consider involving the police."

He was making me nervous. A dead flower on my kitchen table *was* creepy, no doubt about it, but calling the police seemed like an overreaction. More payments, this time from my personal account, were even more worrying. It was clearly *me* being targeted, not Sunrise. "You think the payments and the rose—they're definitely connected?"

"I can't assume anything. But I need you to work from home again—just until I know I can keep you safe. We can call the police when we get back to mine."

"I don't want the police involved. If you really think I'm in danger, then I'll be safe at your place," I said. "If someone wanted to find me, I've worked in the same building for years—they would have approached me there. I'm sure it's nothing."

He took my hand and squeezed it. "But things could be escalating. They clearly wanted to send a message by leaving the flower. They want you to know they have access to you."

It was hard not to be overwhelmed by what Tristan was saying. I appreciated him being protective but surely if I was in danger, they would have left more than a rose. The rose had been there for some time.

"I think we need to speak to your dad as well."

A dark thunk landed in my stomach. "I don't want to worry him."

Tristan nodded. "I know. But he would never forgive me if I didn't go to him at this point. And I hate to say this to you, but the most likely reason for you to be targeted is because of—"

"Who my father is." I sighed, resigned. "I know." Whatever I did, there was no way of getting away from the fact of whose daughter I was, and how much that meant to the rest of the world.

The screech of tires caught our attention. A car had pulled up behind ours and a man stepped out.

"This guy's name's Sergei. He's a friend of mine." Tristan led us back toward the car. "I trust him and so can you. I want you to stay here with him until I come back."

"Come back from where? Where are you going?" Panic began to rise in my throat.

"I just want to check some things out. I won't be long and I won't be far away. Give me your key and stay here with Sergei."

Sergei held the door to his car open. It had blacked-out windows and I couldn't see anything inside.

"You'll be quite safe," he said in a Russian accent.

Why was everyone telling me I was going to be safe like my safety was in question? A rose on the kitchen table was weird, but maybe Sutton had placed it there, or my mum. There had to be a simple explanation—and I was determined not to let Tristan get paranoid before I figured out what it was.

TWENTY-SEVEN

Tristan

I raced up the stairs to Parker's flat. Now I knew she was safe with Sergei, all I could focus on was finding out who was trying to send her a message and what exactly they were trying to say. If Parker refused to call the police, I couldn't make her, which meant I had to take matters into my own hands. In my gut, I knew the Amazon payments and the break-ins were connected. I just didn't have any evidence. And now, the rose? That was a message loud and clear. Whoever it was wanted to draw attention to themselves. I just wasn't sure what they were communicating or how dangerous they might be.

As I walked up the corridor to her flat, I glanced at the ceiling. I wasn't sure what I was looking for but I'd know it when I saw it.

Nothing seemed odd in the corridor so I took a close look at the front door. I pulled up the torch on my phone and peered into the lock. It didn't look like it had been forced. How had someone got in?

I let myself in with the key and shut the door behind me. I shrugged off the backpack I'd grabbed on my way out. It had a laptop in it and some equipment still good to have on hand in a security emergency like this. First thing was first, I pulled the rose out of the mug and put it in the bin. We had a photo. It was the cup I was interested in. Was it Parker's? Or had someone brought it in? There was no water in it—it was completely dry. But had someone brought a rose in bloom and put it on the table only for it to die before Parker had a chance to see it, or had someone put a dead rose in a cup? Both were sinister. I couldn't decide which would be worse.

I took some more photos of the cup, then rummaged around in a couple of drawers before pulling out a plastic sandwich bag. I slipped the cup inside, sealed the bag, and put it in my backpack.

If someone wanted to watch someone, where would they . . .

I stood and turned three hundred sixty degrees in the small kitchen, looking at the ceiling to see if there had been any disturbances. It would be too obvious in such a small space. I scanned the top of the kitchen cupboards and then ran my hand along them to see if anything had been left, but there was nothing. I checked under the kitchen table. Still nothing.

As I stood, something caught my eye but when I looked back, I couldn't see anything. What was it that had stood out to me? I took a step toward the toaster, which plugged into a double socket. A phone charger was plugged in next to the toaster, then next to it a pile of socks sat on top of what looked like a biscuit tin. God, she needed to tidy up or get a storage unit or something. I opened the tin. I wasn't sure what I expected to see, but other than a single digestive biscuit, it was empty. I slid the lid back on and paused, glancing back to the phone charger. Had that been there when she'd been sick? It was just a phone charger, but the cable seemed a little too short. I looked more closely and found a small hole in the base of the plug. That couldn't be right. I flipped it over, took a screwdriver out of my bag and opened the back. It was a camera. Whoever the fucker was that was messing with my wife had been watching her. Or had been planning to.

Working quickly, I pulled out some tools and set a tracer onto the counter underneath the camera device. I was going to try to hack into the feed from the camera and work out where it was going. Hopefully, I'd trace them before they saw me on the feed.

I checked all the other plug sockets but didn't find anything else.

I ran my hand around window sills and the top of book-cases, but came up empty. In the hallway leading to Parker's bedroom and the half bath, I felt around every doorframe and decorative arch. When my hand hit something the size of a pencil sharpener tucked above Parker's bedroom door, I knew what it was even before I pulled it down. Another camera. I left another tracer.

In Parker's bedroom, a mark on the carpet caught my attention immediately and my heartbeat cranked up a gear. The carpet was cream, but just below the picture opposite her bed was a white mark. If I hadn't spent so long in this room while Parker was sick, I may not have noticed it. I'd had far too long in here. I'd taken in every detail, wondering how it was possible to fit so many things into one room. She'd clearly moved from a bigger place after her engage-ment failed and tried to fit everything—was it her ex-fiancé doing this? An ex would be a likely suspect, especially since the rose had been left, but Parker had said that he was living in Monaco. Maybe something had brought him back to London? What had she said his name was? Details on his whereabouts couldn't be more than a Google search away.

The white mark was plaster dust. I took the picture from the wall to find someone had drilled a hole for another hidden camera. I taped another tracer onto the back of the picture and replaced it as if nothing had happened. Someone so lacking in attention to detail as to leave a pile of dust on the carpet just below where they'd drilled a hole to place a surveillance camera wasn't going to notice my thumbnail-sized tracer taped to the back of the picture.

I took a breath and scanned the bedroom. What else was I looking for? Ultimately, I just wanted to find out who was trying to terrorize my wife and bring them to justice. I didn't need anything more—I now had a link to them and I just needed to be back in front of my computer and figure this the fuck out. For the sake of thoroughness, though, I was going to put up some cameras of my own, just in case the fucker came back. I had a couple in my bag. If I set up one in the kitchen and one in the bedroom and pointed them both toward the hallway, no one would be able to move through the apartment without being caught on tape.

I worked quickly, at the same time, trying to figure out what I was going to tell Parker. Honesty was the only possible answer. I'd get the ex's name and then I'd get to work. We were due to go to New York the day after tomorrow for Andrew and Sofia's wedding. It would get us out of town, put some distance between us and whoever was so keen to keep an eye on Parker. By the time we were back, hopefully, I'd have traced the culprit.

TWENTY-EIGHT

Tristan

The timing of Andrew and Sofia's wedding couldn't have been more perfect. Parker was shocked and disturbed to learn about the surveillance equipment I'd found in her place, which made her especially quick to agree when I suggested we fly out early to NYC. We'd left later that night after speaking to the police. I was relieved Parker had finally agreed to involve them, though I wasn't going to sit back and assume they'd handle everything. Parker didn't know it, but I'd arranged for us to have discreet members of Sergei's team around us at all times. I still hadn't managed to trace the camera feed back to its source and I'd not been able to trace the whereabouts of Parker's ex. We'd been due to stay at the Mandarin Oriental with all the others, but I'd moved us to the Ritz. Whoever was surveilling Parker was an amateur in some ways, but I wasn't taking any chances. After all, I hadn't managed to track them down yet. And if the same person was responsible for Parker's food poisoning, I wasn't sure what their endgame was. I wasn't taking any chances.

"She looks beautiful," Parker whispered as Sofia walked down the aisle in front of close friends and family at the New York Public Library. It had been Sofia's choice of venue, apparently.

I nodded. "*You* look astonishing."

She rolled her eyes and I couldn't tell if it was because she didn't believe me or she was trying to focus on Sofia and the wedding. Honestly, if Parker wore fire-engine-red lipstick, her cow-print pajamas would look sexy. There was just something about her full, red lips.

It was a beautiful day with a perfect backdrop and I couldn't help thinking how Sofia had changed things for Andrew. This time last year, I would never have thought he'd be married with a baby on the way. Children were a huge responsibility. Creating a family was such a leap of faith. What happened if you got it wrong? Fucked it up somehow? Destroyed it?

As a child, my parents never spoke to me about the ups and downs of my sister's illness or their marriage. But I'd always been able to tell. The atmosphere in the house would tell me how bad things were and how sick she was. On rare occasions the thick tension would lift and smiles and tenderness would replace the tears, but it never lasted long.

After the divorce, things changed and life evened out, but the residue of that time remained tattooed on my insides. I could always read a room. I was always good at going unnoticed. And I was always prepared for the worst.

I carried the uncertainty of that time with me like a stone in my shoe that I couldn't get rid of. Most of the time, I forgot it was there. I just learned to live with it—knowing tomorrow could be very different from today. I took steps to ensure my world was as unchanging as possible. It was one of the reasons marriage had never appealed to me—why make a promise to love someone forever when it was an impossible promise to make? No one knew what the future held and it was foolish to tempt fate. Not that I wasn't happy for Andrew and Sofia—I couldn't be more pleased to see such a great couple, desperately in love and telling the world they were committed to each other. But today the stone had made a hole in my sock and was burrowing into my skin. Questions crowded my mind, and none of them had easy answers.

As Andrew and Sofia promised to love each other for the rest of their lives, the stone screamed, *what if things change?*

As Andrew and Sofia looked at gazed into each other's eyes like they would stand in front of a train for each other, the stone shouted, *how long will that last?*

As Parker squeezed my hand, the stone whispered, *how long until you have to give her up?*

After the ceremony, we were directed into another room, this one lined with books. "This is beautiful," Parker said, her head tipped back to take it all in.

We paused as we came to a waiter holding a tray of champagne. I handed her a glass and took one for myself before heading to where Dexter, Hollie, and Gabriel stood.

Parker tugged at my hand, pulling me down slightly so she could whisper into my ear. "Are you okay?"

I nodded, straightening. "Yeah. Just a bit of jetlag."

"Look at me."

I did what she asked.

"You don't have jetlag." She smoothed her thumb over mine in a movement so small but at the same time so deeply reassuring. That was the thing about Parker: she always wanted to make things better for people. I wasn't sure if that made me feel better or worse. I'd gotten used to relying on myself, living in the moment. But right now, all I could think about was her and tomorrow—what was going to happen?

I wasn't going to tell her I didn't know what the future held for us—that I couldn't see myself sharing my life with someone. It was driving me halfway to insanity not knowing who had broken into her flat. What if they were following her? Planning an attack? What if she got ill? How could I explain that I didn't know if we were going to last when the ninety days were up? I liked the now, but I knew better than to expect the now to last.

We looked on as the bride and groom were having pictures together. Parker tugged my hand. "Can I show you something?" she said. We excused ourselves from our group and retraced our steps to where the chairs were still in place from the ceremony.

"What did you want to show me?" I asked.

"I just wanted a few minutes alone with you. Thought maybe I could surreptitiously feel you up and at the same time, cheer you up."

I smiled at her plan. "Can you believe this place?" She thrust her hands in the air like she was trying to give the skyline a huge hug.

"It's pretty special."

She spun around and I snaked my arms around her waist.

"Ceremony was nice," she said.

I nodded, my chin resting on the top of her head. "Did I ever tell you how small you are?"

"Not for at least an hour and a half."

"I'm slacking. And you're very short."

She laughed and I felt the sound deep in my gut.

Quiet fell between us and we stood, her arms over mine, her hands stroking my arms, watching the hustle and bustle around us.

"You want to talk about it?" she asked.

"Nothing to talk about."

Silence ticked by for a few seconds, maybe a minute.

"Liar," she said. "You don't have to talk to me about it but I'm here if you want to. And you should know that I want to know what you're thinking. I want to understand when you're upset and why. Because I want to know you."

I pulled her tighter, and bent to press my cheek to hers. "I'm not sure I can put it into words. I'm just feeling a little unsettled. So much is changing."

She turned in my arms. "Because Andrew is getting married?"

Had that triggered these feelings of uncertainty? "Maybe." I pressed a kiss into her neck. "I feel like at the moment, I don't know what the future holds."

Her fingers smoothed around my neck. "None of us do."

I inhaled. "Relationships change things. When it's just me, I have some semblance of control over my future—I decide whether I'm going to go to the gym or take a trip or work the weekend. You know?"

She held my gaze. "And now we're together, you don't get to decide those things?"

I shrugged. "No. I do. But there are other variables at play that impact my day. Things that could change my future. Maybe you're working the weekend. Or we get into a fight. Maybe you get sick."

"We won't get into a fight as long as you keep me in chocolate-covered raisins and orgasms." She smiled up at me and I couldn't help but smile back. Her joy was contagious, but it didn't erase the uncertainty sitting like sludge in my gut. "But seriously, I think the idea is that we make peace with uncertainty. Any certainty in life is an illusion in any event. We think our lives are going to continue as they are, but there are no guarantees."

I nodded. "You're right." I wasn't stupid. I knew what she was saying was true. I'd just spent a long time making sure I controlled as much as possible in my life. I wasn't good with uncertainty.

"But you're still uneasy. Tell me why. Is it about the cameras you found?"

"Partly. I don't like not knowing what's coming for us. There are so many moving parts in our lives at the moment. The cameras. What's happening with us. Ninety days is nearly up and what then?" I paused. I didn't want to worry her, but she was asking to know me. "I've been like this since I was a kid. Sometimes I can sense something bad is going to happen. I just feel uneasy at the moment."

She looped her hands around my waist and squeezed me hard. "Because of what happened with your sister?"

"I think so. As a kid you don't expect your sister to die or your parents to divorce. You think that how life is today is how it's going to be forever. Of course, that's never the case, but usually, you learn the lesson a little later in life."

"It must have been so difficult for you. I can't even imagine."

Having Parker right beside me felt so good. So right. Like it was meant to be this way. But at the same time, feeling like that was terrifying. I'd always avoided having women in my life long-term because I never wanted to put stock in the notion that my today would be my tomorrow. There were no guarantees, and I couldn't bear the thought of waking up to a different future to the one I had planned out. As a single man with just me to worry about, my wife wasn't ever going to get sick or decide she wanted a different life without me. I never had to worry about that life-disrupting change. Parker had come along and shifted my possible futures, making me long for stability I knew didn't exist. I just didn't know how to reconcile this growing desire for forever with the truth I knew in my gut: forever didn't exist.

TWENTY-NINE

Parker

I had lunch to eat and a conscience to clear. Ninety days were nearly up but there was one more thing I needed to do before I got my hands on my trust fund.

"This is a nice surprise," my dad said as I popped my head around his office door.

"Maureen said you hadn't had lunch." I held up a Pret bag with his favorite egg and cress sandwich. "I thought we could eat together."

"Wonderful. Come in and sit down."

I took a seat and unpacked the sandwiches. "I got you water. No coffee. Mum says you're not allowed."

He sighed. "I'm on a complete coffee ban now. She said if I still want a glass of wine at weekends, the coffee has to be cut completely. Maureen won't even get me a cup."

"Maureen knows which side her bread is buttered. Mum is infinitely more terrifying than you are."

"Agreed." My dad opened his egg and cress sandwich

but before he took a bite, he looked me in the eye. "So, straight to it, why are you here?"

He'd not gotten to where he had by mincing his words. "I just want to talk about my trust fund."

He took a bite of his sandwich, giving me more time to elaborate. But I hadn't quite found the words.

"The lawyers are sorting out the paperwork. All funds should be in your name by the end of the week."

He wasn't telling me anything I didn't know and I should be deliriously happy with what he was saying. But it was like the lie I'd told him about Tristan and me had lodged in my chest and now was fighting to get out. "I wanted to talk to you about that," I replied.

He took another bite of his sandwich. Seemed like he was ready to listen.

"You know I thought it was a shitty rule that you made my access to the trust fund conditional upon me being married."

"This is not news to me, Parker. I get that you didn't like it. But you're married now. And you'll get access to your fund by the end of the week. So what's the problem?"

The problem was, I didn't feel right getting twenty-five million pounds under false pretenses, however much of a good cause I was going to donate it to. My dad wasn't a stranger I'd never have to face again. I loved him. And respected him. I had to come clean about what I'd done—even if it meant risking access to the fund.

"I didn't like it," I said, trying to buy myself some time. How did I tell my dad that I'd lied to him so he'd give me money?

"And I said, you're not telling me anything I didn't know. But I had my reasons, and I stand by them."

I sighed, put my wrap down, and sunk back in my chair.

"I don't see why you have to be concerned about my personal life. I'm twenty-eight years old."

"It doesn't matter how old you are. I'm your father and until the day I die, I will worry about you. I will continue to want what's best for you from beyond the grave."

"Maybe I know what's best for me."

He chuckled. "Maybe you do. Maybe you don't. I have a feeling we'll do this dance together, this little power struggle, until the day I die too."

"Will you stop talking about your death? You're vegetarian now, for goodness' sake." I gestured to the corner of his office. "You have a standing desk. You'll continue to rule London's financial world for a while yet."

He smiled at me. "When you were born, you came out holding your head up like you were determined to plow your own path. I love that about you. You have a fierce sense of right and wrong. You work hard. You're a good person, always far more concerned about everyone else than yourself."

I rolled my eyes. I'd heard this story a million times.

"I'm very proud of you, Parker."

"Daddy," I said, in a voice that implored him to stop being so kind. Was he trying to make this even more difficult for me than it already was?

"Spit out what you're trying to say."

There was no choice, I had to just come out with it and hope for the best. Worst-case scenario, he stopped me from getting my trust. At least I'd have a clean conscience. "I only married Tristan so I could get access to my trust fund."

He stayed silent, as if he hadn't heard me.

"Dad?"

"Go on."

"I wasn't in love with Tristan when I married him. He

agreed to be my husband for ninety days until I got my money."

My dad nodded like I'd just told him they were out of egg and cress sandwiches.

"Dad, I'm telling you I lied to you. My marriage to Tristan is just pretend."

My father steepled his fingers in front of him. "I've known you a long time, Parker. And I know you well. I'm well aware that when you married Tristan, you were just trying to get your hands on your trust fund."

It was as if he'd kicked me in the stomach.

"You knew?"

"You'd been trying to get me to change the rules of the trust for years. And then all of a sudden you stopped asking. I know you better than to assume you'd given up. This isn't my first rodeo. I knew you'd just changed tack."

"So you guessed about me and Tristan from the start?"

He shrugged. "You'd barely met when you announced your wedding. And anyway, if we're putting all our cards on the table here, when I saw Tristan after your auction dinner, he mentioned something."

My jaw dropped and I stood, my napkin tumbling to the ground. "Tristan told you I'd asked him to marry me?"

"Not exactly. I read between the lines. He confirmed it when I asked him straight out."

It was as if he'd pushed me over. I couldn't have been more shocked. My father and Tristan had been in on it all along. "So basically, you gave him your approval?"

Nausea swirled in my stomach. I couldn't even try to deceive my dad without him actually having orchestrated it. There was no escaping his reach.

"Parker." His tone was warning. "Don't overreact about this. Tristan was a virtual stranger to you when you suggested your little scheme. I've known him a long time. No doubt he felt obligated to let me know about your plans and frankly, so he should have. He's a loyal friend. He didn't know that I wouldn't mind if you were only getting married to get access to your fund. But he didn't tell me even though I'm sure he wanted to. He was trying to respect your privacy."

I sighed. I thought Tristan was . . . mine. I thought he was loyal to *me*. I got that we didn't know each other very much at the beginning, but we'd grown close. Feelings had developed. At least on my side. Our emotions might not be everything a married couple had between them, but real had replaced fake in many ways. Why hadn't he told me my father knew? There had been plenty of times when he had the opportunity. Our honeymoon—when we'd first slept together. Or straight afterward. He should have said *something*.

"So you gave him your blessing?" Earlier today, I'd worried my father would feel betrayed when he learned the truth. I didn't expect that I'd be the one to feel like I'd been lied to.

"I told him that if he married you—even if it was for the sole reason of getting your hands on your trust—it would fulfil the terms. And I thought it better him than someone I didn't trust."

"There is really no escaping your power, is there?"

"Don't be naïve. You're going to come into a great deal of money in a few days. And that money is going to make a huge difference to the people who benefit from it through Sunrise. You only have the ability to make that difference because you're my daughter—because of the money I've put in the trust. You're always looking at the downside, but there's a tremendous upside."

"I get it. And I'm grateful that you've given me that trust . . . It's just . . ." I loved my dad. I was proud of what he'd accomplished. Only sometimes, I wished I felt in control of my own life.

"I know I can be interfering," he said. "And I can't say that I didn't invite Tristan to come to the charity gala because I wanted you two to hit it off—"

"You were playing matchmaker?"

He shrugged. "Turns out I didn't have to try. Remember, he bid on you before he knew you were my daughter. You can't say that for any of the others who raised their paddles that night."

I sighed. "That's true."

"And you know Tristan well enough by now to realize he's not a man who gets serious about women at the drop of a hat. Fake marriage or not, I can tell by the look in his eyes he's serious about you."

"It doesn't matter how he feels. If he can't be honest with me, if he doesn't respect me enough to tell me the truth, then nothing between us is real."

I stood. I couldn't just sit here and chat. I wanted to go home. But I wasn't sure where that was. Tristan had made me promise not to go back to my flat. To a hotel? I needed to go back to Tristan's to collect some stuff. I supposed that would at least force me to confront him. I wanted to know why on earth he would keep something like that from me, especially when it seemed like we had been sharing so much—for real.

I headed out to my car. I needed time to process what my dad had said. I could do with a night away from Tristan before we had this conversation. I felt so hurt and betrayed by him—he and I were supposed to have secrets from the world. I was supposed to be his inner circle.

I pulled out my phone to call Sutton and saw I had an email notification. I swiped up to open my inbox and my stomach dropped through the seat of the car. It was an email from Mike, my ex. The man who'd only been with me because he thought I was rich. The man who made me look at every other man differently. Why on earth would he be emailing me? There was nothing he had to say that I wanted to hear. Was there? Only one way to find out. I opened the email.

Dearest Parker,

I wanted to vomit. I used to love when he addressed his notes to me that way.

A long time has passed since I last saw you and I have always regretted how abruptly we parted ways.

Regretted?

I think often about our times together. You were a kind, wonderful person and I was lucky that you loved me.

I didn't know whether to laugh or cry. He had been lucky to have me. But I'd been a fool to love him.

His email continued in the same way, repeating how he regretted he'd left, he'd never met anyone like me, he'd changed in the last few years. He'd grown up and realized how selfish he was.

Mike had always been good at saying the right thing at the right time. No doubt nothing had changed on that score. When at the end of the email, he said he was currently in London and would like to meet up to clear the air between us, I actually laughed out loud, tossed the phone on the passenger seat, and started the car. As if I wanted to waste a single minute on that guy. I pulled out of my parents' driveway and headed back to Tristan's place. As I drove, my thoughts hopped between Tristan and Mike. They were so different in so many ways, but wasn't I heading to Tristan's place to confront him about keeping things from me? Shouldn't I do the same with Mike if I had the opportunity? Maybe clearing the air with him would help me rebuild trust with someone who obviously hadn't acted maliciously. If I changed my mind, I could just not show up. It would serve Mike right.

I pulled over to the side of the road and grabbed my phone, replying that I could meet for coffee the next day at four. I gave him the name of a coffee shop around the corner from my office and didn't even bother to sign off. Maybe I'd go and give him a piece of my mind or show him how much better off I was without him. Maybe I wouldn't turn up at all. Either way, it felt good to be the one in control for once.

THIRTY

Tristan

Mike Wilson wasn't the only name Parker's ex-fiancé went by, but it was his legal name. He was also Giles Wilson and Michael Sanders. I'd found him quickly and uncovered a number of semi-illegal activities he'd participated in when he was fresh out of university. He'd refined his MO over the last decade and Parker seemed like his first attempt to marry for money. She'd been lucky to escape without Arthur having to pay him off. Earlier today, I'd tracked back the cameras in Parker's flat to a laptop used by Wilson and discovered what he was trying to achieve.

Tonight, I'd tell Parker. I wasn't quite sure what her reaction would be, but I knew she'd want to know. I'd picked up cream puffs from a French patisserie in Knightsbridge when I'd called round to see Dexter earlier and they were already in the fridge, along with bottles of wine and champagne I'd pulled from the cellar in case she felt like celebrating.

"I'm back," Parker called as she let herself in the front door. I stood, wondering where I should start.

I stepped into the hallway and watched as she took off her coat. I couldn't exactly put my finger on what it was, but something was up. She was tense. "Hey. Good day?"

"Hi," she said, voice a little more clipped than I was used to. She avoided meeting my eyes as she passed me in the corridor and headed into the kitchen.

"You okay?" I asked, turning to follow her.

She pulled the fridge door open and stared at the wine and the patisserie box. "I went to see my father today. He told me you both were in on our fake marriage from the beginning."

My body drained of heat. She was pissed off. I hadn't known what to expect this evening, but this wasn't it. "Yeah, he figured it out. He knows you pretty well."

"Why didn't you say anything?" Her voice cracked. Instinctively, I went over to comfort her. I slid my hand to her back but she shrugged it off and spun to face me.

"Parker, I'm sorry. He asked me not to mention it to you."

"What else have you *not mentioned* to me?" she snapped.

"Nothing." I pushed my hands through my hair. I hated seeing her so upset over something I'd done. "Seriously, Parker. I'm not keeping anything from you."

"I just need to know what's real after everything that happened with Mike. Don't you get that?"

The expression in her eyes almost killed me. "Everything with me is real," I said. I understood that she carried scars because of what Mike had done to her, but I wasn't him. "I barely knew you when you proposed. I'd known your father for years and owed him a great deal. Not only did I think he had a right to know you were prepared to game the rules of the trust, but I was worried about another man taking advantage of you. At the time, I didn't know I'd be the one to marry you. In my shoes, wouldn't you have done the same?"

"I thought you said he guessed what I was doing."

"He did." She wanted honesty, so I'd give it to her. "But if he hadn't, I'd have told him. Arthur Frazer is a good man and he deserves my loyalty. There's no way I would have married you under the circumstances without his blessing." My hands stung like I'd struck her. It was harsh but it was true.

Silence stretched between us like a glacier.

"Now you know," I said, still almost defiant.

"Now I know."

I sighed. "There are things I need to tell you. You need to sit down."

"More?" Her eyes grew wide and she backed up to the kitchen counter.

"Nothing to do with you and me, but I've found out what's been going on with your apartment and the rose and the payments from your bank account. Let's sit down."

I grabbed a bottle of wine—this was clearly not a celebratory moment—and two glasses and followed her to the kitchen table. We sat across from each other.

"It's taken me a while but it's beyond doubt that Mike Wilson has been snooping around your flat. He's the one skimming off the payments from the bank accounts, and he's the one who hid cameras at your place."

I couldn't imagine how she felt, having agreed to marry a man who turned out to be a criminal. But I was going to end up making her feel worse before she felt better.

"I actually don't think they've been there that long. He's been trying lots of different stuff."

"What does that mean?" she asked.

"I hacked into his computer and his email. He hid the withdrawals well, but once I was in his system, he'd barely covered his tracks. He's out of cash. His quest to find himself a rich wife in Monaco was fruitless, and from what I can make out, he thinks he let you and your family off too lightly."

"Too lightly?" She shook her head, incredulous.

"He's a con man, Parker. He doesn't think like the rest of us. Anyway, he's managed to fund his lifestyle with a series of small cons and getting payoffs from the families of women he's dated once they've checked him out and figured out what kind of man he is."

"Payoffs?"

"To make him go away and avoid unnecessary drama. He's dating high-profile women from wealthy families. They don't want the exposure. They don't want him anywhere near them, so they pay him off. It's the way he makes the money he needs to life the live of a wealthy man."

She frowned. "My dad would have had him checked out. How come he didn't find anything?"

"You two were engaged a long time ago. He was only at the start of his con-man, grifter—whatever you want to call it—career. He didn't have any kind of track record. After you, he got more sophisticated. I guess he figured out what he wanted and how to get it. Anyway, from what I can make out, he feels like you got away scot-free and that your father should have given him some money to go away, just like all the families of the other women he's been involved with since."

"So he decided to take it for himself? Direct from my bank account. And from Sunrise."

"Yes, he seems disorganized and a little erratic. He's been searching for an angle in respect to you for a long time."

"An angle? What does that mean?"

I didn't want to hurt her but she needed to know this guy was dangerous. "A way of extorting money from you or your family."

She frowned. "You're sure?"

"Completely. I can show you what I've found if you like. I just haven't worked out what his next move is. As soon as I do, you'll be the first person I tell."

"I . . ." Parker shook her head. "It's been a long day. I'm exhausted. I need some time to think. Some space."

"I know you're upset with me, Parker, but I wasn't trying to hurt you. I was in a difficult position."

She didn't react. "I'm going to sleep in the guest room tonight."

Disappointment crashed over me. I wanted to pin her down and make her understand that I hadn't meant to hurt her, but hopefully Parker was telling the truth when she said she just needed some space. I needed to respect that and give her what she was asking for.

"I'll take the guest room," I said.

She offered me a half-smile. "Thanks."

I swallowed and watched her leave. Realistically, I probably wouldn't make it to bed tonight anyway. Mike's trail was hot and I wouldn't rest until I figured out his next move.

I headed back to my study to be met with half a dozen notifications that I'd set up to alert me if there were any purchases on Mike's credit card or any emails sent from his accounts—he had three, and only one was encrypted.

I checked his credit card first. It was a charge from BA for a flight to London tomorrow morning. I shivered and my heart rate ramped up. London might be a city of eight million, but it was still too near for my liking. And why had he only just booked his ticket? What had changed so last minute?

Tonight was going to be a long one. I wasn't going to rest until I'd uncovered every last detail about Mike Wilson and his plans for my wife.

YES, I'd been up all night. Yes, I was tired. But that wasn't the reason why I was so completely and utterly furious.

It was just coming up to eight in the morning and I headed into the kitchen to find Parker eating her breakfast at the dining room table. She didn't look up as I came in.

She thought she had a right to be pissed off that I had told her father she was marrying to get access to her trust fund? She had some kind of nerve.

"Doing anything today?" I asked, wondering if she'd tell me what she had planned.

"Going to work," she said, still not meeting my eye.

"That all?" I asked.

She shrugged and took another spoonful of muesli.

"Not planning to tell me how you were meeting your ex-boyfriend for coffee this afternoon?"

Her spoon clanged against the bowl as she dropped it. "You're spying on me?"

"Yes I'm monitoring your emails. But if I hadn't, I'd have seen your reply to him in his emails. I'm also monitoring his credit cards, his—"

"You're monitoring my emails?"

Of course I was monitoring her emails. What did she expect? "I'm trying to keep you safe. How else was I supposed to figure out what was going on with the false transactions on your bank accounts?"

"It's one thing to keep an eye on my bank accounts, but my email? Without my permission? That's a step too far, even for you."

"Not like creeping off to meet your ex who walked out when he decided you weren't rich enough."

"I'm not creeping off anywhere, and I've not even decided whether or not I'm going to go."

"Why is it even a consideration? You should have come to me right away when you heard from him. I told you yesterday that he was the one taking the money and breaking into your flat. You didn't say anything. Why not?"

She stood and headed to the dishwasher. "I had other things on my mind. Just because I said I'd meet him doesn't mean I was going to. I hadn't decided. I still haven't."

She had to be kidding me. "What do you mean, you still haven't?"

"Well now I need to confront him about the cameras, the rose, and the payments."

"Jesus Christ, Parker. Why would you deliberately put yourself at risk like that?" I swallowed down my frustration. I really didn't want to tell her the next part, but she deserved to know the truth. And if it would keep her from meeting Mike, she needed to know.

"It's a public place. What harm can I come to? It's not like I'm going to be taken in by his charms again."

"You should know that he's planning to kidnap you. He's formulated an ambitious plan to . . . take you from your flat." I had to push down the urge to vomit at the thought.

"Take me?" Realization sheeted across her face. "Kidnap me?"

I nodded. "Hence the cameras. He could make sure you were alone and at your most vulnerable."

"Are you sure? Mike was shallow and selfish, but I can't believe he was capable—"

"He's gotten himself into debt. And he's been in contact with some people who—well, some dangerous people." If she asked, I'd tell her more, but she didn't need to know that after he'd gotten his money, he'd planned to sell her to a third party rather than release her. I squeezed my eyes shut, trying to block out the thought.

"We need to go to the police with what I have— although a lot of it I've obtained illegally. I also want to speak to your father."

"You've not done that already? I would have thought he'd have been your first call." She was still angry. "The last twenty-four hours has been . . . a lot. A lot of revelations. A lot of old memories. I need some time to take it all in. I think I might go to a hotel for a night."

My body turned to stone. I couldn't move. "Stay," I pleaded.

"I just need some time to process all this. I'll go to my parents'. They have security. I'll be safe there."

The churning in my gut that had been there since she'd walked through my front door yesterday evening, her face full of disappointment and anger, took over my entire body. "You'll be safe with me."

She shook her head. "I don't know who I can trust at the moment. I just want to— I want to go."

She was safe here. With me. She could trust me. But that didn't matter. She'd been prepared to put herself in danger in a way I couldn't comprehend and I would never be able to live with. It was better that she went back to her parents. If I hadn't seen the emails between them arranging the coffee, she may have been taken—kidnapped—and who knew what else. Every version of the future we might share could have disintegrated in an instant.

"What?" she asked.

What could I say? Her leaving was for the best. She'd be safe from Mike and I'd be safe from my world burning to the ground if anything ever happened to her. I'd spent my life not getting attached to women for this very reason. My feelings for Parker had crept up on me. Maybe the space she needed would give me room to extinguish them.

"Nothing," I replied. "You're happy for me to talk to the police and your father?"

"Yes," she said, disappointment in her tone.

"I'll get Sergei to drive you. He and his team are outside. You'll be safe with them."

This was better. Saying goodbye now would be easier, even if it was still sure to rip out my heart.

THIRTY-ONE

Parker

My limbs didn't move as quickly as they normally did, like I was stepping through syrup or wading through treacle. I opened my bedroom door and came face-to-face with Sutton.

We both hung up the phone. She'd dropped everything and come over, arriving before I'd finished telling her the whole sorry tale.

"Why didn't you tell me sooner about the money and the rose?" Sutton shuddered. "It's so creepy. You know I never liked that guy." She dropped her rucksack on the floor and enveloped me in a hug.

"My father will make sure he goes to prison. According to him, there's a clear plan. It's just about how they make it all happen because Tristan hacked into his computer, so technically, we shouldn't know any of this. Dad says it's just about moving pieces around a chess board. He's got him under surveillance and the security here is even tighter than normal. I know I'm safe and it's over . . . It's just been a lot."

She released me and plonked herself in the beanbag on the floor. I lay on my bed.

"I can't imagine. And what about Tristan? Have you come here because it's safer? Why isn't he here?"

Wasn't it obvious? "I told you my dad has known about the fake marriage and asked Tristan not to say anything?"

"Yeah, but you and Tristan hardly knew each other then. You were proposing to defraud your father of twenty-five million pounds."

I groaned and rolled onto my back. "Don't say it like that. It was always meant to be my money. And anyway, my dad knew about it all along."

"You can't hold that against Tristan. I won't allow it." She glanced around the room. "Do you have any snacks?"

"It's not just that. The whole stuff with Mike . . . Tristan was monitoring my emails and hadn't told me. My emails are like my diary. They're private and personal and him going through them like that? It's a huge betrayal.

"How am I supposed to trust anyone after everything that's happened? Mike was going to kidnap me so he could get my father to pay a ransom. This is a man I was supposed to marry. I'd known him nearly two years when we split up. I've known Tristan four months. It wasn't like we were really married."

"I hate to disagree with you, but you were really married. You *are* really married. And it's not like you haven't fucked his brains out. We need wine and snacks." She stood, grabbed her rucksack, and pulled out two mini bottles of red wine, a packet of almonds, and two KitKats. "If you eat the almonds in between bites of the chocolate, the calories in the KitKat don't count."

I sat up and she handed me a chocolate bar.

"Our marriage is just a formality. We never gave each

other any guarantees after ninety days and Tristan is a committed bachelor."

She handed me a bottle of wine and pulled her legs up under her chin. "Didn't seem like that at your wedding. I'd say he's turned over a new leaf."

"How do you know? It's not like I've had a camera on him the whole time. Besides, I don't have the greatest track record when it comes to picking men."

"You haven't been picking anyone since Mike. And I get it, it's difficult to trust anyone when you've been violated like that, but Tristan seemed to genuinely care about you."

I'd thought so too. "He's lied to me from the start. And he has no issue invading my privacy. I can't trust anyone."

"Come on," Sutton said. "You know that's not true. Your father was right when he said that Tristan was in an impossible position."

"I can get my head around that. Just. But there's been plenty of time since the beginning that he could have told me. When should his loyalty have shifted from my father to me?"

"He was probably just waiting . . ." She grimaced like she didn't have a good explanation for Tristan not telling me what my father knew.

"For what?"

"I don't know, a good time to say something? You need to talk to him about it. Ask him why he didn't mention it at some point."

"If he'd had a good reason, he would have told me. And I don't want to talk to him now I know he's been monitoring me. It feels weird—creepy—like I'm in a stalker special on Netflix."

"Maybe he just didn't see it as important. He was trying to protect you, I think. How have you left it with him?"

My stomach rolled once, then twice, then three times. "Tomorrow is ninety days. I get access to my trust fund the day after."

"Ninety days doesn't mean anything."

"Tristan agreed on ninety days and no more. He's a man of his word. As far as he's concerned, he's fulfilled his end of the bargain."

"But he hasn't said any of that. You need to talk to him. Figure stuff out with him. I'm sure you two can work through this."

"I've not spoken to him since I left."

"So call him. Or ask him to come over."

I picked up the A4 brown envelope from the coffee table that had been delivered earlier and handed it to her.

She took it from me, her eyes not leaving mine as she opened it. "Postnup? And *divorce* papers?"

"We had them all drawn up before getting married. We were both given copies. Never got round to signing the post-nup. I guess he decided he'd do both at the same time." I tapped on the back page where Tristan had signed the divorce papers.

"So, you're divorced now?"

"We have to wait a year. But I don't have to see him again."

"You think he's just trying to make life easier for you, or do you think he's sending you a message that he's out?"

I let out a bitter half-laugh. "I'm not sure we need to make a distinction. He's done."

"But maybe he just thinks you're done."

"I am." I took the papers from her and shoved them back into the envelope. We sat in silence for a few minutes.

"I'm sorry," Sutton said.

"It doesn't matter. Four months ago, I'd never even laid

eyes on the guy. This will pass." As I said it, my heart banged in my ribcage, shouting *Don't be so sure about that.* "I just wish . . . I feel like at the first opportunity to run, off he went. I was hurt—I *am* hurt by the fact that he knew my father knew our wedding was a ploy to get hold of my trust fund. But I wanted to get over it. I wanted him to say he was sorry and prove that since then things have changed. I wanted to know his loyalty was with me now. I wanted to get over it and then bam, the email monitoring? It puts him in a completely different light . . . I really liked him." My voice began to crack. I squeezed my eyes shut to stop the tears. "I thought he was different to who he turned out to be."

Sutton took my hand and pulled it into her lap. "This is awful. But I don't think he was just looking for a way out and he took the first exit he was offered. I don't know him that well, but he came across as a guy who just wanted to make you happy."

"You have another explanation for divorce papers?"

"What if he thought that's what you wanted? Maybe you should go round and see him? Can you use the excuse of going to collect your stuff?"

I sighed. "I don't want to see him. I don't want to be with a man who pretends to be one thing—honest and trust-worthy and focused on me and what will make me happy, like you said—when in fact he's monitoring me without telling me and reading my private messages. Mike wasn't the man I thought he was. Tristan wasn't the man I thought he was. I clearly can't be trusted to see what's right in front of me." I needed to go back to my life before Tristan. I'd been perfectly happy and I would be again. I hoped.

THIRTY-TWO

Tristan

The last thing I wanted to do was go for drinks with mates. But being at home just reminded me of Parker. I'd eaten nothing but Uber Eats for a week because I couldn't spend any time in the kitchen. I'd moved bedrooms to the top floor because I couldn't sleep in my bed without her. I was stretching out the time I spent in my office because what else would I do but work?

Not being with Parker was worse than expected. I was more miserable than I could have possibly imagined.

"Hey, Tristan," Brigette, the hostess at the Mayfair bar Beck had nominated today, greeted me with warm familiarity.

I managed a smile. Brigette was five ten, blonde, smile as wide as the Atlantic. She was also usually subject to my very best flirtation. We'd usually go back and forth—I'd tell her I'd like to take her out, show her the best date of her life. She would tell me there was nothing she'd like better but she wasn't allowed to date patrons. I would tell her that I was worth giving up her job for. She would tell me she'd have to have a ring first, etcetera.

But not tonight.

I didn't have it in me.

"Great to see you again, how have you been doing?" she asked.

"Good," I said. "Is Beck here yet?"

She stiffened at my reaction but I couldn't bring myself to care. "Right this way." She showed me to the table where Dexter and Beck were already seated.

"Holy shit, what happened?" Dexter asked. "You look like your cat died."

"Have you ordered drinks?" I asked.

"What do you want?" Beck asked.

"Anything alcoholic," I replied.

"I'll get it," Beck said. "Anyone object to champagne? I feel like we should celebrate the first baby of the group being born. That one is going to have to play referee between her parents her entire life."

"Sofia had the baby?" I asked.

"A little girl. They put a picture on the group chat," Beck said. "You didn't see it?"

I'd turned my phone off because I'd been obsessively checking to see if Parker had called or messaged. It was sending me half mad. "I must have missed it. A girl. Right. That's nice."

"Mate, you're not very convincing," Dexter said. "Anyone would think I told you they just bought a sofa."

"I'm genuinely happy for them," I said.

"Then tell your face," Dexter said. "What's got into you? I've never seen you like this."

"I'm fine," I lied. "I just have a lot going on at work

and . . . you know, I'm not sure this thing with Parker is going to work out."

"Did I just hear that right?" Beck said, coming back with champagne. "Parker is amazing and great for you. What's the problem?"

"It's nothing to do with her specifically." She specifically was amazing; Beck was right. "I just don't think I'm made to be with someone in the long term. I've always said that."

Beck and Dexter both stayed silent. I looked up in time to see them exchange a glance.

"What?" I asked.

"I was just thinking we need Andrew," Dexter said.

Beck cleared his throat. "Or Gabriel at least."

"All of us probably need to be here," Dexter added.

"I don't need an intervention. I'm different from you lot. I never saw myself with anyone."

"I know," Beck said. "What's brought this mood on?"

I thought back to the divorce papers I'd sent her yesterday. She needed space. She'd had a lot to take in. I hadn't kept her safe. I understood it.

I explained to Beck and Dexter what happened when Parker found out Arthur had known about our ruse all along. And then how she'd completely overreacted about the email monitoring.

"But you barely knew her then. You owed your loyalty to Arthur."

"Agreed. But at the same time, I could have told her after things developed between us, even though Arthur had asked me not to. She would have been angry at me either way, but I think the right thing to do would have been to encourage her to speak to her father before now." I regretted that. It was a testament to her character that she went to tell her father the full story before she got her hands on her trust. I should have encouraged that at least.

"You should have asked her before you started monitoring her emails," Beck said. "That's kinda not okay."

"She knew I was trying to get to the bottom of what was going on with the money transfers and the break-ins. I told her I put cameras in her house. And she knew I was monitoring her bank accounts. Of course I was monitoring her email."

Beck sighed. "I don't think she would have necessarily assumed you were monitoring her emails. It's normal for *you* to hack into someone's private messages but not normal for most normal people."

Maybe I should have told her. I really hadn't thought it was a big deal. I'd assumed she'd known.

"Okay, so you had a falling out," Dexter said. "Isn't it fixable?"

I went on to tell them about her ex and the would-be kidnapping attempt. "It's completely understandable that she'd want her space after finding out something like that," I said.

"Is it?" Beck asked. "What am I missing?"

"She's been under a tremendous amount of stress—her life was potentially in jeopardy. The last thing she needs is me."

"What are you talking about?" Dexter asked. "She needs you now more than ever."

"She asked for space. I'm not going to argue with her. It's completely understandable that our relationship wouldn't weather this storm. Her ex was a nasty piece of work."

"I've never seen you with a woman the way you were

with Parker. Don't your feelings for her make you want to fight for her?" Dexter said.

I let out a laugh. "My feelings about her are precisely why I don't want to fight."

"I'm not following you," Beck said.

"Maybe we could get over this, but I don't know if she could ever trust me again. But say we do, and then what? We build our lives together and then something hits us that we *can't* recover from. Where does that leave us?"

"So you're saying leave now because it won't hurt as much?" Dexter said.

I shrugged. There was nothing to add. Dexter had boiled it down to its core.

"No," Beck said. "If she's the kind of woman you'd never recover from losing—that's the one you have to chase. *That's* the woman you have to fight for."

"Why?" It made no sense to me. Better I protect us both from getting our hearts ripped out and our lives destroyed at a later date.

"Well first of all, because what you're feeling right now —that snarling dog of regret that howls at you every night— isn't going to go away."

Dexter started nodding as if he knew what the hell Beck was talking about.

"That regret will burrow deep—so deep eventually you'll come to realize that *not* fighting for her was the worst mistake of your life. But worse than that, you'll never be all the man you could be if you don't have her by your side. If she's the right woman, she'll challenge you in a way that makes you better. She'll love you in a way that makes you stronger. Just being with her will make you more of the person you were always meant to be."

I felt trapped, paralyzed with fear as a juggernaut of truth came at me at a hundred miles an hour. What Beck was saying made sense. Parker made me better. I knew I was happier, stronger, *more* with her by my side. "But I'm not in control of everything. If she doesn't want me, I can't change that. If she dies, I can't change that. If she wants a divorce when we've got kids and a life together . . . that will break me."

I clenched my jaw, trying to hold back a lifetime's worth of hurt. Being with Parker was even more terrifying than being without her. What if she put herself in danger again and got hurt? What if she left me? I'd rebuilt my life after my family was torn apart. I wasn't sure I could do it a second time.

Dexter slung his arm around my shoulder. "That's why you need her. Because you'll be broken without her. There's always a risk that somewhere down the line, something will change and tear you apart. Grief. Death. Whatever it is. But to avoid joy, to avoid *life* to keep yourself safe, isn't living."

Beck nodded solemnly. "You can't avoid life, mate. You can't purposefully avoid falling in love with the woman you're meant to be with. It's not right. I think your parents would tell you the same thing."

I never talked about my sister with my parents. I never spoke about their divorce or the way my childhood had been overshadowed by illness, death, and divorce. What was the point? I'd learned my lesson—that I never wanted to feel like that again. I'd always thought that the easiest way to make that happen was not to care too much about anyone. Now with Parker gone, I was beginning to feel like I'd already let things go too far.

THIRTY-THREE

Parker

As we sat around the boardroom table talking about the next six months' strategy for Sunrise, I had to constantly pull my attention back to the room. My mind kept wandering back to Tristan, to the way he'd told me he'd lie to me again if he had to do things all over again, the way he held my hand as he told me about Mike, the divorce papers sitting on my bedside table at home.

"I think another auction would be a great idea," someone said. "The last one raised a lot of money.

"That's because Parker had her husband bid," another person answered.

I forced a smile, glancing at my ring finger on my left hand. I still wore the rings he'd given me. I wasn't sure when I was supposed to take them off. When I moved out? When I signed the divorce papers? When I got over him?

"We can't do another auction before the next gala, which isn't until next year," I said. "We should keep it as a special event."

"Do you think we can convince Tristan to put himself up next year?" Ana said.

I bristled at the question. He was still my husband and would be for a while yet. We couldn't file the divorce papers for months. But I wasn't naïve. Even if he wasn't put up for auction, Tristan would be dating soon enough.

"I'm not sure he'll be amenable," I said, trying to keep my tone as soft as possible.

"That's a shame," Ana replied. "I'd have bid."

I checked the time on my phone. "I'm going to have to excuse myself. I have a meeting with a potential donor."

I stood and exited the boardroom. I needed distraction, not discussion about Tristan. I turned into the reception area and saw someone waiting. Maybe my meeting was early.

"Parker, Mr. Fisher is here for you."

I turned, and the elderly man in the grey suit in reception stood.

"Parker Frazer?"

I smiled and stepped forward to shake his hand. "Mr. Fisher."

"It's a pleasure to finally meet you."

"And you. Let's go through to a meeting room." I guided us down the corridor, invited him to sit, and set about pouring us some coffee.

"I must ask," Mr. Fisher said. "I couldn't help notice the spelling of your surname. Any relation to Arthur Frazer?"

"Yes," I said. "Arthur is my dad."

"He's a good man. Rare that you get someone who's so successful who doesn't have any enemies. You can always count on him to do the right thing." Mr. Fisher chuckled to himself. "I know it's not a fashionable thing to say, but I honestly believe that it was because he married young and stayed married that he managed to keep balance in his life. He kept his priorities straight. We all need to remember that first and foremost we are someone's son, daughter, husband, wife, mother, father."

"I agree. It's important to remember who we are to the people we love first and foremost."

Did Tristan think of me as his wife in anything but name? Did he love me like I was beginning to realize I loved him?

"Exactly," he said as sadness swept over his face. "My granddaughter means everything to me. She's suffering, but we're lucky that we can pay for the best possible medical care. I want to give something to your charity so that other families get the same opportunities we have." He blinked back tears.

I clasped a hand over his. "I'm so sorry. It's a terrible time."

He nodded and I took away my hand as he regained his composure. "I keep telling my son that he must hold his wife and children close. And he tries. But it's so much pressure on him and on them as a family."

I nodded, wanting to listen to his pain, hoping it would lessen if he had someone to talk to. "I worry about my grandson too. He's not having the childhood he should. Everyone is so focused on illness and hospitals. It's just awful."

I thought back to how Tristan must have felt as a helpless child when his sister was getting treatment and then died. He must have felt powerless. And then when his parents split, his world fell apart.

The urge to drop everything and run to him was almost overwhelming. I wanted him to feel better. I knew he carried that pain with him still.

"I just hope they push through together as a family. As a unit. They're stronger together."

Mr. Fisher kept talking but I couldn't hear a word he was saying. All I could think about was Tristan, and how his family unit had disintegrated when he needed them most. He must live in fear of people abandoning him when he needed them the most. Had I been guilty of that? Tristan should have told me about my dad knowing about our arrangement, and he shouldn't have been monitoring my emails without my permission, but did that mean he wasn't the man I thought he was?

Did it mean I couldn't trust him?

THIRTY-FOUR

Parker

I'd spent last night on speakerphone to Sutton while I sat in my cow-print pajamas and a face mask, snacking on choco-late-covered raisins just like I'd done on Friday nights for years. Sutton was definitely of the view I needed to give Tristan a second chance. If we'd just been facing the issue of him not telling me what my father knew about us, I might be able to get past it. I understood he was in a difficult posi-tion and was being loyal to my father. Monitoring my emails without me knowing was proving more difficult for me to get over. I didn't know how to reconcile what he'd done with the trust I thought we'd built. Now, I was facing Saturday night at my parents' place, just like so many lonely weekends in my past. In many ways life had gone back to what it was before Tristan. Except it hadn't. Because I couldn't stop thinking about him and wondering if things would have been different if we'd have met under easier circumstances.

I padded downstairs as the clock struck quarter past seven.

My mother glanced at me. I'd reached for the mascara before I'd come down, wanting to distract from my blotchy face. She grinned. "Are you expecting anyone?" she asked. My mother was firmly on Team Tristan. She'd tried to send me back to his place the day I arrived.

"Nope. I'm wearing mascara for me. I told you, Tristan and I agreed on ninety days." It's not that we weren't ever together. We had been. At some point what was pretend had become real and then had faded to nothing.

Mum made a tutting sound and told me I was ridiculous. "He was a lovely boy. I hoped things would last between the two of you."

"He was a thirty-four-year-old man, Mum."

"Men are always boys at heart. You'd do well to remember that."

I did my best not to roll my eyes. Luckily, Dad came out in a butcher's apron and interrupted our to-and-fro. "Can you help us into the dining room with some of these plates?" If only the thousands of people who worked for my dad could see him now, in an apron, being told by my mum he was still a boy at heart.

I took the stack of plates Dad pointed out with his spatula and ferried them into the dining room. "Mum," I called as I followed her back into the kitchen.

She turned. "Yes, my love."

"I just wanted to tell you how much I love you."

She gave me a look that I hadn't seen since I was a teenager—a mixture of worry and suspicion.

I scooped my arm around her waist. "I'm not on drugs, Mum. Don't worry. I just don't tell you enough."

"I love you too, Parker."

Dad came through carrying a board with a half leg of lamb. "Mind out, you two. Come on, sit down or everything's going to get cold."

We took our usual seats around the dining room table and Dad carved up the lamb joint.

"Is there any reason we're having roast dinner on Saturday night?" I asked.

My father shot me a look. "It's your favorite, isn't it?"

I was so lucky to have him as my dad.

"Arthur, I'm going to be making lamb pasanda from now until Christmas. Can you shop for three rather than thirty-three next time?"

My heart shifted slightly, as if it didn't quite fit correctly. I'd felt the same twinges ever since Tristan had left.

"I wasn't sure how many people were coming," Dad said. "I thought Parker and Tristan might have made up now all this Mike thing is sorted out."

"Sorted out?" I asked.

"Didn't Tristan tell you?" Dad asked. "He was arrested and charged with attempted kidnapping. He's been denied bail and is on remand pending trial."

A mixture of relief and horror coursed through me. "Charged already?"

"I guess they had a lot of evidence," Dad said. "No doubt thanks to Tristan."

"Wow, that's a relief, right?" I glanced at Mum.

"Absolutely. We can all sleep a little easier." She patted my hand and poured me a glass of wine.

"You think Tristan helped the police?" He said he was going to speak to them but after the divorce papers he'd sent me, I had no reason to assume he was still helping.

Dad shot me a familiar look that said *you know the answer to that question.*

Of course Tristan had helped the police. That was the kind of man he was.

"Did I ever tell you that when I first started working at the bank, they put me in a role where I had no clue what I was meant to be doing?" Dad said. "I was straight out of university—a graduate trainee. All of a sudden I had a responsibility that, deep down inside, I knew was beyond me. I was completely out of my depth."

My father rarely talked about work at home—he seemed completely content to leave his work life in the office while my mother and he planned trips, argued about politics, and tried to decide what to do with the abandoned vegetable patch in the garden.

"No one would believe that now you're responsible for everyone's paychecks."

"Quite," he said, passing me a bowl of broccoli and carrots. "I was dropped in at the deep end and at the time I wasn't quite sure if I was going to sink or swim, but I ended up catching my breath and making it to shore."

My mother patted my father on the arm. "Like an Olympic gold medalist."

"The first day I came home from work, I remember thinking I wasn't going to go back. I couldn't even find my way to the loo. There was no hope I was going to manage all the spreadsheets I'd been given, let alone make sense of the meetings that had been put in my diary. I came home, poured myself a glass of whisky, and wrote out my resignation letter."

My mother laughed. "You silly goose."

"It felt overwhelming," my father continued. "I was supposed to have all these answers, to know what I was doing. I didn't see any alternative other than to quit. Otherwise, I risked everyone finding out I was incapable."

I couldn't imagine my father ever feeling like he wasn't the king of everything he did. He even made a pretty mean roast dinner. "You didn't hand the letter in though, did you?"

He shook his head. "Nope. I drank my whisky and decided that the next day, I was going to see how it went when I *pretended* to know what I was doing. I went in there with the confidence of an employee who'd been working there five years. If I didn't know something, I asked. If I needed help, I said so—because if I'd been there five years and didn't know something, I'd ask. Basically, I faked it. I faked experience and confidence. It worked. It didn't take long until one night I got home, I poured out my whisky, and I realized I had a really good day. I wasn't pretending anymore. I actually knew what I was doing."

My stomach flipped over. He'd faked it until he made it.

"And now of course I realize that every graduate trainee who ever starts a job feels overwhelmed. They don't know what they're doing. They don't even know where to pee. So each year, with each new intake, I tell them the story of what I did on my second day on the job." He took a sip of his wine. "Just because something feels overwhelming doesn't mean you should just resign and walk away. Sometimes it's worth sticking around, asking for help. You never know, sooner than you think, the whole thing turns real."

My mother dropped her knife and fork and it clattered onto her plate. "Like you and Tristan! It started off as a fake marriage but it seems to me like it turned real."

I gave my mother a half-hearted laugh.

"Your father's head of the bank now," my mother said, "because he stuck around and faked it until he made it. You need to stick with it with Tristan. Look where you could end up."

My father winked at me. "Just in case you didn't figure out my point."

I had hoped something real had come out of what had started off fake between Tristan and me. But if it had been real, he wouldn't have given up at the first hurdle. We'd have gotten through the obstacles. If we were down and out after just a few months of marriage, then we couldn't have a future.

"Relationships aren't like work," I said. I wished it was as easy as they were both making out. "And when you've lost trust in someone, what's left?"

"You mean relationships *are* work," my mother corrected me. "I get it, you're annoyed at Tristan. I understand he breached your trust, but you're a smart woman, Parker. Tristan isn't Mike."

"How do I know? I didn't think Mike would turn out to be a criminal."

"You know because you're different. You've met Tristan's friends and family. You know who he is through the eyes of the people who love him as well as your own. How often did you meet Mike's family?" She knew the answer to that was never. He'd always said his parents lived in Hong Kong, and although he'd been to visit them a couple of times while we were together, I could never join him because of my work. "But it's not even that. You know because you're not a twenty-two-year-old who doesn't know any better. What Mike did was awful. He's a terrible person. But being with him gave you life experience—valuable life experience. It honed your gut instinct. You've seen what's bad so you can now recognize what's good."

I shrugged. It wasn't like this was all my decision. "He's

hardly breaking down the door, trying to win me back."

"Have you reached out to him?" she asked.

"No, but . . ."

"So you read a book that told you that he should be the one to reach out?" she asked. "Or maybe there's a law somewhere I don't know about." She raised her eyebrows in that you-know-I'm-right way. "Don't let your pride get in the way of your happiness. Your father and I decided when we first got married that however successful he got, however many people bowed and scraped to him at the bank, as soon as he walked through the front door, he wasn't a CEO, he was a husband and father. We knew we wanted to stay married. You need to figure out if you do too, Parker."

That's why my father had just always been "dad" to me. It was why I found it so difficult that people always treated me differently because of who my father was. But that had been a conscious decision by both of them. And I was thankful for it.

Mum was right. Only pride had stopped me from picking up the phone to Tristan. I could invite him over to talk rationally about how I felt, and he could explain to me what was going through his head and why he hadn't been in contact. We could pretend we were functioning adults and have a conversation. What we had was worth that at least, wasn't it?

"You're the best mum and dad I could ever wish for," I said. "And Dad, you make fantastic roast lamb."

"I did the mint sauce," my mum added. "Which I think makes the whole dish."

"Wouldn't be roast lamb without mint sauce," my dad said and leaned over to give my mum a kiss.

I might be an adult, but my parents still had a lot to teach me.

THIRTY-FIVE

Parker

Despite being resolved to call Tristan, it took me twenty-four hours before I summoned the courage to send him a message asking him if he wanted to go to lunch. I hit send and threw my phone on the sofa like it was on fire. Immediately it started to ring. I grabbed it and Tristan's name was flashing on the screen.

My heart squeezed in excitement but I wasn't prepared to speak to him. Maybe he was calling to tell me no—to say he wanted to break all ties forever.

If I didn't answer, I'd never know. I swiped up.

"Hello," I answered.

"Hey," he said. "I thought I'd call."

"I see that."

"Thanks for the message," he said.

"Thanks for calling," I replied. This was awkward and weird and I wanted to race back to sitting opposite him at his dining room table, sharing a bottle of wine.

He took in a breath and all I could imagine was him saying no to me.

"Look," I blurted out. "You don't have to say yes if you don't want to. I just thought—"

"I can't do lunch," he said, cutting me off.

I knew it. He was calling to try to let me down gently.

"But I could bring a takeaway over to your place if that works for you. Your dad said you'd moved back there now Wilson has been arrested. Tonight even."

"Tonight?" Even though it was only six, I was already in my jammies.

"You probably have plans tonight already. We could do—"

"Tonight is good."

He sighed with what sounded like relief. "Good."

"Good," I replied.

"An hour?"

"Perfect."

We hung up and I clutched the phone to my chest. An hour wasn't long. The sooner the better. The only problem was, I hadn't quite figured out one last piece of the puzzle. But I had to carpe the diem. I wasn't going to turn down a date with my husband.

THIRTY-SIX

Tristan

Dates never made me sweaty. I'd never had even the slightest hint of nerves when I'd taken a woman out before, but walking up to Parker's building, takeaway in one hand and everything else I needed in the other, the beads of sweat gathered at my hairline like they were teenage girls waiting for a Justin Bieber concert.

I let myself in using my Amazon key fob and took the stairs up to Parker's flat two at a time. I'd had my phone in my hand when I'd received her message earlier. I'd been trying to work out whether I should message her, call her, or just drop by. When my phone buzzed with her message, I took it as a sign and dialed her number. No time like the present. I'd been without her for far too long. It was time to make this right. I had no idea why she'd invited me to lunch or what she'd planned to say to me, but it was a chink of daylight in the dark, and I wasn't willing to waste it.

When she opened the door, I swept my gaze down her body. It was so good to see her. Being this close to her felt like home, like the last thirty-four years had lasted just a flash and the few months with Parker had taken up most of my life. She was home. She was where I belonged. "No cow pajamas?"

She grinned up at me. "I changed."

"You look beautiful." She wore the red blouse from our first date and matching lipstick. She was perfect. Just like she always was. It didn't matter what she wore.

"So do you," she replied.

I glanced down at myself. I just had on jeans and a t-shirt. Just like I almost always did.

"Come in," she said, holding the door open. "What kind of food did you bring?"

"Mexican. Is that okay?"

"More than. I have some wine—"

"You do the wine and I'll set out the food and bring it through." I didn't want her to see me prepare what I had planned.

She shrugged, took a bottle of wine from the fridge, together with two wine glasses, and headed back into the living room. There was a small dining table pushed up against the far wall.

I set all the Mexican food out on a tray with some dishes and even remembered the serving spoons. Then I pulled out a bowl, tore open the packet of chocolate-covered raisins, and poured them in.

I grabbed the tray and met Parker at the table.

"I chose red. I hope that's okay," she said. Normally she wouldn't ask, because she didn't need to. I didn't care about the color wine we drank. I just cared that I was here. With her.

"Great."

We took our seats and began sharing out the food

between us. Food was really the last thing on my mind. We were here together. That's all that mattered.

"Thanks for coming," she said.

"I'm glad to be here. I was about to call you when you messaged."

"You were?" She seemed genuinely surprised, as if she couldn't fathom what I might have to say to her. I hoped that wasn't a bad sign. I didn't care. I was here, determined to allay any concerns or fears she might have about taking me back.

"I was. I miss you." My heart began to thunder in my chest. I put down my cutlery and just looked at her. "I missed you a lot."

She nodded and put her cutlery down too. The food had just been a device to get us to this moment. What mattered were our words. Our feelings.

"I know I hurt you," I said. "I know you don't like that I kept things from you. And I know you're upset because I said I wouldn't do anything differently in respect of your dad. And I know I should have told you about monitoring your emails." I wanted her to understand that I had been listening, even though we didn't agree on what I'd done. "I just went into automatic mode and did whatever I needed to do to catch that little fucker, but I'm sorry."

She nodded.

"It won't happen again. I didn't deliberately not tell you that I was monitoring your emails. I just got caught up and it's so second nature to me that—it didn't occur to me that you wouldn't know I was monitoring your emails."

"I accept your apology."

My heart inched higher in my chest.

She kept nodding. "And I understand you were doing the right thing by my dad when you kept his secret. You owed no loyalty to me but yes, I wish you'd have told me sooner."

"I'm sorry," I said again.

"I accept your apology. And I'm sorry I just left and didn't stay to have a conversation like the one we're having right now."

"Maybe we both needed a little time to come to our senses."

"Maybe," she said. "But I need you to know that I'm in this. I'm not going to jump ship at the first opportunity or even the last. I need you to know that I'm here. Committed to you. I'm not going to walk away." She took a breath. "I love you."

It was like someone had rammed a tree trunk into my chest—searing pain followed by the relief of sucking in a breath full of oxygen.

I thought I could protect myself from caring about someone. I'd had my life turned upside down by grief and I didn't want it to happen again.

It was already too late.

Sitting here, it was obvious that the damage was done. If I lost Parker now, my entire world would fall apart.

"I love you too." It was a relief to say those words, words representing feelings I'd been running from for far too long. "I thought I could avoid having another person in my life who could turn my world upside down if I lost them. But . . . I don't want to avoid it any longer. It was pointless to try."

She nodded. "I get it. It makes sense."

How was she accepting all this so quickly?

"I'm sorry I hurt you, Parker. I want to do everything I can to make it right."

She sighed and picked up her fork. "Mexican food helps. But where are the cream puffs?"

"If I get you cream puffs, I'm forgiven?"

"Cream puffs or no cream puffs, you're still forgiven. We love each other. We're married—"

Shit, I'd forgotten I'd signed those bloody papers. I stood. "Did you sign those papers? Where are they?"

"Relax, I never signed them. Anyway, we couldn't submit them until our first anniversary."

"You never signed them?" I asked. "You didn't give up on us?"

"I guess not. I never took off my rings." She lifted her hand to show me.

I pulled her to her feet and swept my thumbs over her cheekbones. "I'll never give up on us."

"Sounds like a promise."

It sounded like marriage.

I pressed my lips to hers and her hands pushed into my hair as our tongues met. She was everything I could have ever hoped for—sweet and sexy, kind but feisty.

I pulled back and took a breath. "There's one more thing I need to say."

She looked confused by my change of pace.

"Stay there," I said, squeezing her shoulders and heading back into the kitchen. I opened the fridge door and pulled out the box of cream puffs I'd brought with me. I put one on a plate, took a breath, and headed back into the living room.

She tilted her head as she saw the plate. "You brought cream puffs?"

"How could I forget, Cream Puff?"

I set the plate down on the table "It's not a diamond and we're not in the Seychelles or a fancy restaurant. There are no fireworks or—" I was babbling. I needed to get on with it. "The fact is, I love you. And if I promise to keep you in cream puffs for the rest of your life, will you be my wife? For real this time."

"For real?" she asked as if she hadn't heard me right.

I dropped down on one knee, so she was in no doubt. "Will you marry me?"

She flung her arms around my neck. "Like this, you're the perfect height."

"Is that a yes?"

"Yes, that's a yes. There's just one thing."

My heart inched higher in my chest. I didn't want her to have a single doubt. "What?"

"What do I need to do for you that will make you see that I'm with you for good? Through good times and in bad. Whatever happens, I won't ever lose sight of that, Tristan. How can I make you see that I guarantee me for you?"

I stood and brought her with me. She wrapped her legs around my waist as we kissed.

"You did already," I replied. "You picked up the phone and asked me to lunch. It's what I needed. Thank you for that."

"Anything for you," she replied.

This was exactly where I was meant to be. With Parker. I didn't need anything else.

"You didn't need to propose again," she said.

"I get the feeling there's going to be a lot of negotiation during our marriage. And I'm here for it. But you need to understand one thing that's not negotiable: I'm going to give you more than you need."

Her cheeks reddened to the shade of her lips. "Being with you, I already feel like the luckiest woman ever. I don't need anything more." Her palms skated up my back. It felt so good to have her in my arms. For good this time.

Warmth gathered in my chest. So many seeming coincidences had conspired to bring us to this moment, and I was grateful for each one of them. I had accepted Arthur's invitation before knowing what the charity was. I had stepped out to take a call. Parker had run into me like a freight train —physically and metaphorically. Every time fate could have torn us apart, it brought us closer together. With Parker, I was stronger; together, we were unbreakable. No matter what life threw at us, I had a feeling that would never change.

EPILOGUE

Ten Days Later

Parker

I laughed to myself as I went into the bedroom from where Tristan had just called me. He was lying down and his feet were dangling over the edge of my bed. He was too tall for his own good.

"We need to have a conversation," he said.

"About how ridiculously tall you are?" I replied.

He rolled over, propped his head up on this hand, and patted the bed in front of him. "About logistics."

I'd been expecting him to say this. We'd been squeezed into my Maida Vale flat for the last ten days and it was just too small for the both of us.

I slid onto the bed next to him. "You're right. We should move back to your place." I don't know why I hadn't said something sooner. I just knew that when I moved out of this place, I'd never move back. I supposed I'd been saying goodbye these last ten days.

"I'm not so sure," he replied.

"You want to stay here?"

"No. But at the same time, I don't want you just to move into my place. I think we should get something that neither of us have lived in before."

He was impossibly thoughtful. "That's a nice idea. Where were you thinking?"

"I'm not sure I have a preference," he replied. "Let's start thinking about it. But in the meantime, can we go back to Notting Hill so I can get a good night's sleep?"

"I think that sounds like a good idea."

"And another thing, Cream Puff . . ." He grinned as he spoke, delighted at the nickname he'd coined for me. I wouldn't ever tell him, but I thought it was cute that he thought back to the first time we ever met every time he used it.

"Another thing? What more can you possibly want from me?" I flopped my arm over my forehead like a fainting maiden in an historical romance.

He reached into his back pocket and pulled out a check.

"Who uses checks anymore?" I asked.

"Me. I can't make electronic transfers from this account."

"What's it for?"

He pushed the check into my hand, but before I had a chance to see who it was made out to, he said, "It's a joint decision, but I thought we should give ten percent of our net income to your charity."

I reached out to stroke his cheek. "That's so nice."

I glanced at the check and then looked more carefully.

"You can't be serious. You're giving Sunrise . . . five hundred thousand pounds?"

"No," he replied. "*We're* giving Sunrise ten percent of my net income. I figured your salary was a little lost in the rounding."

I sat bolt upright. "You're telling me you earned—wait, that's an insane amount of money."

"What?" he asked. "You thought I was poor?"

"No, but this is a lot of money."

"Right, which is why I'm discussing it with you." He sat up and pulled me onto his lap. "I don't want to do anything you don't think is right, so if you'd prefer to split it among a few good causes or—"

I turned in his lap and pressed my lips to his. "How did you get to be such a kind and generous man?"

"I'm inspired by you," he said without missing a beat. "You've made me reevaluate almost everything in my life. Including what I do with my money. Although not on the interior design front. Your taste is . . . awful." He glanced over at the rabbit lamp on my bedside table.

I prodded him in the stomach. "It's eclectic."

"I can't do eclectic." His hand shot into his hair the way he did when he was anxious about something.

"Hey," I said, my finger rubbing over his eyebrow. "If it bothers you that much, you can design the entire place, wherever we end up."

He exhaled and his shoulders dropped. "That would make me feel so much better."

"I'm not accepting that I have bad taste. Just that you're more particular."

"Whatever you need to tell yourself." He grinned at me. "So I have your solemn promise that you won't get involved in any design of our new house and you won't buy anything for the house without my express agreement?"

"Wow, you mean business," I replied.

"Honestly, I love you, Parker, but being in your flat stresses me the bloody hell out. It's all too much."

I laughed and lifted my right hand. "If that's important to you, then I solemnly swear not to get involved in any interior design discussions, and I shall make no home purchases ever at all for as long as we both shall live." Nothing was more valuable to me than making Tristan happy.

"You can have one room where you can go wild. Apart from that, it's what I say all the way."

I nodded resolutely. "Yes sir."

He growled and pushed me to my back. He'd just climbed over me when the doorbell went.

"That's Sutton."

"I was about to ravage you," he replied.

"Ravaging can wait. She hears about her hospital placement today." I scampered off the bed and went to open the front door.

Sutton looked like she'd just been slapped in the face with a frying pan. I could almost see the cartoon halo of stars circling over her head.

"What is it?" I pulled her inside. "Tristan, we're going to need tequila," I called. "Come and sit down."

"I got into the Royal Free." She collapsed onto the sofa.

I was confused. It sounded like good news. "Wasn't that your top choice?" I sat down next to her and patted her on the back.

"Absolutely," she said. "But I didn't expect them to pick me. I'm an older student and everyone wants to be on their program. It must be some kind of mistake."

Tristan came through carrying a tray of shot glasses and

a bottle of tequila I wasn't sure I'd seen before. "I'd like to say I'd leave you two to it, but given we live in a two-room shoebox, there's nothing you can say that I can't hear."

"Of course it's not a mistake," I said, ignoring Tristan. "Tell her," I said, glaring at him.

"What's not a mistake?"

"Well, you just disproved your own theory." I rolled my eyes. "Sutton got the job she wanted at the Royal Free Hospital and thinks they must have made a mistake."

"Of course they didn't," Tristan said, pulling up one of the dining chairs—it was between that and the floor in terms of seating options.

"But I'm older than most of the candidates."

"Not by much," I said, trying to be reassuring.

"That would likely go in your favor," Tristan said. "More life experience and maturity."

"And your exam results were epic," I added.

She grabbed my hand. "Don't forget about me, will you? These next few years are going to be intense. And now you have this husband." She nodded toward Tristan like he was a lamp I'd just acquired. "And he has a thousand friends with wives and girlfriends. You're not going to be able to fit me in."

"Of course I am." I squeezed her hand. "This is exciting. It's the job you dreamed about. Yes, you're going to be working hard, but we'll just be around the corner—we're moving. You'll be able to pop round and have dinner when you've finished a shift."

She looked up at me. "You're moving to Hampstead?"

Tristan was shooting me devil stares as he poured out shots of tequila.

"We have to find a place still, but why not?" What wasn't there to love about Hampstead? I was sure we could find a place there. "And I'm going to task Tristan with finding a new friend he can hook you up with."

She groaned. "I don't need a boyfriend. I just need to be good at my job and not get sacked on the first day." She needed my dad's pep talk ASAP and a hefty amount of distraction.

Tristan handed Sutton a shot glass of tequila and then gave one to me.

"I'm not going to be able to drink tequila again. Not after I start at The Royal Free. I have to be . . . like a grown-up. I'm going to be a doctor."

"Better get as much in as possible now, then," Tristan said, tipping back his shot. I watched his Adam's apple bob up and down as he swallowed and held back from pinning him to the floor and licking his neck from collarbone to chin.

I clinked my glass to Sutton's. "This is amazing news, Sutton."

"We're all growing up and moving on," she said.

"Where does Hartford work?" I asked Tristan. "Isn't that The Royal Free?"

Tristan shrugged. "No idea. You want me to text her?"

I shook my head. "Whatever happens, we're always going to be the best of friends."

She sighed. "I'm never going to have a man like Tristan to come home to. Taking this job is basically receiving my single-for-life certificate."

"I thought I had one of those," Tristan said. "Beware. They have a tendency to disintegrate when you're not watching."

Sutton laughed. "Never going to happen. I need to throw myself into the job. It's okay. I'm choosing that. I love the fact that I'll get to be a doctor. There's just a sacrifice.

You know?" She sucked in a breath. "Until then, one more tequila won't hurt."

Tristan poured out second shots for us all and I caught his eye, trying to convey how much I loved that he was sitting here, celebrating and consoling my BFF. I knew that whatever we were doing, there was nowhere he'd rather be than with me. There was no better feeling.

June later that year

Tristan

Just a couple of years ago, the idea that there'd ever be a day when I'd witness Joshua say "I do" was ludicrous. The idea that my wife would be by my side was a step past insanity. But here we were, and I'd never been happier.

"I swear Hollie is glowing. Even if she hadn't told us she was pregnant, it would be totally obvious," Parker said as Hollie and Dexter walked toward us.

Hollie and Dexter had dropped their news a couple of weeks ago. They wanted to be sure it didn't take away from Joshua and Hartford's ceremony. I didn't want to tell Parker, but I wasn't sure Hollie looked much different to how she normally did.

"I don't know why they were worried about overshadowing this though." Parker swept her arm across the green lawns.

"Joshua's wedding was never going to be low key," I said. Of course he'd chosen Cliveden House to get married. Nothing but grandeur and opulence for Joshua. And if Claridge's wasn't going to accommodate him and his bride, then he wouldn't wait for him.

"Shall we get married again?" I asked.

Parker shook her head. "I only intend on getting married once, thank you very much."

I chuckled. "A vow renewal then? Some kind of celebration where we're both in it forever."

"Isn't that every day?" Parker said. "It won't make me love you anymore than I already do, because that's impossible."

I circled my arm around her waist, dipped her, and kissed her dramatically before standing her upright.

"You two are just adorable," Hollie said as she came toward us, hand on stomach, Dexter by her side.

"Joshua and Hartford look happy," I said, not wanting to discuss our adorableness any more. Not that we weren't adorable.

"Everyone does," Gabriel said as he and Autumn joined our group.

I waved at Stella across the lawn. She tugged on Beck's sleeve and they headed toward us.

"God, I bet they have great sex," Autumn said, nodding toward Andrew and Sofia as they came down the steps to our group.

"You don't think we have great sex?" Gabriel said, slightly affronted.

"Wow, did I say that out loud?"

Gabriel widened his eyes.

"Duh, of course we do." Autumn lifted herself up on her toes and kissed Gabriel's jaw, then squeezed his bottom. "The best ever. You have moves that would win—"

I cleared my throat. I didn't want images of Gabriel and Autumn in my head that I was never going to be able to get rid of.

"What's everyone talking about?" Sofia asked as she and Andrew joined the group.

"We were just saying that the group of committed bachelors are committed husbands or fiancés now," Parker said, saving the day. "And I need a favor from you. My best friend thinks she's going to be single the rest of her life because she's just starting as a junior doctor. We need to put our heads together and find her a man. Even if it's for a bit of fun."

Parker hadn't been joking when she'd told Sutton we'd move to Hampstead. We'd started house hunting exclusively in a mile radius of the hospital Sutton was going to be working at come September. If it made Parker happy, I didn't mind where we lived as long as she didn't decorate it and we had an Alaskan king bed. Sutton was important to her. Which meant she was important to me. "We'll find her someone," I said.

"I bet Hartford can set her up with a single doctor," Autumn said.

"Anyone want to take bets on how long it will take for Joshua and Hartford to get pregnant?"

"Do they want children?" Parker asked. Parker and I agreed that the time wasn't right for us at the moment. I wanted to be with Parker forever, and I wanted a family. At some point. But I needed some time for just the two of us first. Parker felt the same. When the time came, she'd make the best mother I could imagine. But right now, I was happy to focus on being a great husband. That's what she deserved. She was the best wife a man could ask for.

"Joshua's far too vain to let his genes go to waste," Andrew said.

Parker laughed beside me. She was still getting used to Andrew's idea of social chit-chat. She was still getting used to all my friends, but she understood how important they all were to me, so they were important to her.

Our group of six had been boys when we'd met. Now we were men with wives and fiancées, and soon we'd be six families who'd navigate this world together, through the ups and downs, the good times and bad. With the loves of our lives at our sides, all six of us were stronger and better than we'd ever been. With Parker by my side for the rest of my life, I knew the future could only be bright.

WANT to read Sutton's story? Read **Dr. Off Limits**.

Never agree to a blind. I caught an incurable fever for a doctor who is strictly OFF LIMITS!

You'll see more of Tristan and Parker as well.

Have you read

Mr. Mayfair - Stella & Beck

Mr. Knightsbridge - Dexter & Hollie

Mr. Smithfield - Gabriel & Autumn

Mr. Park Lane - Joshua & Hartford

Mr. Bloomsbury - Andrew & Sófia

Mr. Notting Hill - Tristan & Parker

IF YOU LIKE fake marriage romances, try **Duke of Manhattan**

BOOKS BY LOUISE BAY

All books are stand alone

The Doctors Series

Dr. Off Limits

Dr. Perfect

The Mister Series

Mr. Mayfair

Mr. Knightsbridge

Mr. Smithfield

Mr. Park Lane

Mr. Bloomsbury

Mr. Notting Hill

The Christmas Collection

14 Days of Christmas

The Player Series

International Player

Private Player

Dr. Off Limits

Standalones

Hollywood Scandal

Love Unexpected

Hopeful

The Empire State Series

The Gentleman Series

The Ruthless Gentleman

The Wrong Gentleman

The Royals Series

King of Wall Street

Park Avenue Prince

Duke of Manhattan

The British Knight

The Earl of London

The Nights Series

Indigo Nights

Promised Nights

Parisian Nights

Faithful

What kind of books do you like?

Friends to lovers

Mr. Mayfair

Promised Nights

International Player

Fake relationship (marriage of convenience)

Duke of Manhattan

Mr. Mayfair

Mr. Notting Hill

Enemies to Lovers

King of Wall Street

The British Knight

The Earl of London

Hollywood Scandal

Parisian Nights

14 Days of Christmas

Mr. Bloomsbury

Office Romance / Workplace romance

Mr. Knightsbridge

King of Wall Street

The British Knight

The Ruthless Gentleman

Mr. Bloomsbury

Second Chance

International Player

Hopeful

Best Friend's Brother

Promised Nights

Vacation/Holiday Romance

The Empire State Series

Indigo Nights

The Ruthless Gentleman

The Wrong Gentleman

Love Unexpected

14 Days of Christmas

Holiday/Christmas Romance

14 Days of Christmas

This Christmas

British Hero

Promised Nights (British heroine)

Indigo Nights (American heroine)

Hopeful (British heroine)

Duke of Manhattan (American heroine)

The British Knight (American heroine)

The Earl of London (British heroine)

The Wrong Gentleman (American heroine)

The Ruthless Gentleman (American heroine)

International Player (British heroine)

Mr. Mayfair (British heroine)

Mr. Knightsbridge (American heroine)

Mr. Smithfield (American heroine)

Private Player (British heroine)

Mr. Bloomsbury (American heroine)

14 Days of Christmas (British heroine)

Mr. Notting Hill (British heroine)

Single Dad

King of Wall Street

Mr. Smithfield

Sign up to the Louise Bay mailing list www.louisebay/newsletter

Read more at www.louisebay.com

Made in the USA
Monee, IL
12 June 2022

97929532R00163